Defying the Crown

C.G. Macington

ISBN-13: 978-1-7389180-4-1

Library of Congress Control Number: 2018675309
Printed in Canada

Table of Contents

Act 1	7
Chapter 1	9
Chapter 2	17
Chapter 3	31
Chapter 4	43
Chapter 5	51
Chapter 6	59
Chapter 7	67
Act II	75
Chapter 8	77
Chapter 9	89
Chapter 10	95
Chapter 11	101
Chapter 12	109
Chapter 13	115
Chapter 14	121
Chapter 15	131
Chapter 16	141
Chapter 17	151
Chapter 18	161
Chapter 19	173
Chapter 20	177
Act III	183
Chapter 21	185
Chapter 22	193
Chapter 23	201
Chapter 24	209
Chapter 25	219
Chapter 26	223
Chapter 27	229
Chapter 28	239
Chapter 29	251
Chapter 30	259

Act 1

C.G. Macington

8

Chapter 1

Daniel

"Daniel are you still with me?" my therapist Michael asks, glancing at me from across his notebook.

My eyes jerk up to meet his, realizing that he's caught me drifting away again. I've been staring at the abstract painting on the wall behind him, losing myself in the swirls of color and my thoughts.

"Yes, sorry. I'm listening."

"I don't think you were," he says with a frown. "If you aren't going to take these sessions seriously, why are you even bothering to come here?"

I hesitate, scrambling to find an answer that will appease him. "It's not that I don't care. I just sometimes zone out and get lost in my head."

He pauses for a moment, considering my words. "And what gets you lost in there?"

His question is simple, but the answer isn't. I could tell him about the constant loop of failures playing in my mind. I could tell him about the loneliness that clings to me like a second skin. I could tell him about the voice that whispers I'm not good enough, that I'm unlovable, that I'm a burden. But instead, I hold that back because I don't think I want to give a voice to those feelings. That would make them real, and then I would have to deal with them.

"Sorry, I was just thinking about work, and my boss. She has been on my case lately, and it has been stressing me out a bit."

It's not a lie, really. Cassandra has been riding me hard ever since I came back from my medical leave last year. She's always on my back, nitpicking every little thing I do. I can feel my mind starting to spiral just thinking about her, about the leave, about why I needed it in the first place. I yank myself back from that dark path before I go too far down it.

"Well, all in all, I would say that's a normal thing to be worried about," Michael says, his calmly reassuring English accent grounding me. "You don't need to stress yourself out over these things, I'm sure you're excellent at your job."

I smile back hollowly, going along with him and nodding my head. I know I'm not excellent at my job. I'm barely holding on, just going through the motions. But I don't tell him that.

"Have you given any thought to what we discussed our last session? I think that you could benefit from being able to discuss your feelings with someone other than me," he says, changing the subject.

"Yeah, I have been thinking about it. I don't know that I feel comfortable talking to strangers online about my life, and what happened." Talking about what happened last year makes me feel timid and small, and you can hear it in my voice.

Michael sighs, leaning forward with a kind expression. "Daniel, we've been seeing each other for over a year now. In that time, I've seen you make great strides. Yet, you're stuck on this until you've fully processed it. You can't move on until you let yourself feel everything your mind wants you to feel. Maybe this website can do that for you; what's the harm in trying?"

"I'll think about it," I reply noncommittally.

"Please do," he says, glancing at the clock. "Ah, well would you look at that, I think our time is up for today." Michael rises from his seat and leads me to the door of his small office. "Try to work on some of the exercises we discussed, and I will see you the same time next week. Alright?"

"Definitely, see you next time."

Stepping out into the rain and heading towards the nearest subway station, I glance around the busy streets of New York City. People are huddled under umbrellas, rushing to get out of the downpour. I left mine at home, so I'm soaked within minutes. The rain is cold, but it feels almost refreshing, like it's washing away the heaviness of the therapy session.

Descending into the subway station, I wait for the train to arrive at the platform. The sign says it will be here in 3 minutes, but I know better than to trust that. Finally, after what feels like forever, the tired train pulls up and I grab a seat before it's taken. My mind already drifts off, even as I vaguely hear the garbled announcement of the train's destination over the ancient crackling speakers.

As much as I hate to say it, Michael's not wrong. I feel like I'm stuck in a rut, and every time I think about what I did I spiral and get locked up in those emotions. I haven't processed it, more just avoided it as much as possible. Apart from my job, I don't have a lot of people in my life. Growing up as a foster kid, bouncing from home to home didn't do me any favors when it came to having a family to turn to for support.

The only people I really have are my best friend Jayda and her long-term boyfriend Caleb. Coincidentally, they are also my roommates in our cramped 2-bedroom apartment. Life isn't cheap in New York, but we've made the best of it and made it affordable by splitting the rent three ways. They have both been there for me over the years, ever since we met each other at the coffee shop job I had after I aged out of the system.

I'm distracted from my thoughts as I hear the announcement for my stop and quickly get up and move toward the door. The train stops and a rush of people flood out of it, carrying me along with them. I weave through the crowd, finding my way out of the station and into the lobby and creaky elevator of my shabby apartment building.

The old brick building is as run down as it can be without being condemned by the city, and it probably has more rats living in it than people on any given day. But, when the only other option is being homeless, it's still better than that.

Slotting the key into my apartment's door and opening it, I'm assaulted by the sound of angry punk music blasting from the kitchen. The kitchen looks like a bomb has gone off, which means that Jayda is baking. She's in her usual goth outfit, looking as fierce as ever, while also being covered head to toe in flour. She sees me and smiles.

"Daniel, you're home!" she cries gleefully. "Come help me make cookies, Caleb refuses to be my assistant."

"It's not that I refuse to be your assistant, it's just that I have more self-preservation skills than you, and don't want to inhale all the flour into my lungs. If Daniel is smart, he will do the same," Caleb pipes up from the nearby couch. He greets me with a nod, before turning back to the book he has in his hands.

Where Jayda looks like she just came from a punk concert, Caleb is the opposite. If you were to look up hipster in the dictionary, I'm sure you'd find a picture of him as the definition. He's tall and slim, with a small goatee, black plastic-rimmed glasses, and an ever-present beanie on his head. They make an odd couple, but somehow it just works for them.

"I'd be very careful what you say, or there won't be any cookies for you," Jayda says ominously, before turning back to me with bright eyes. "Please Daniel!"

I cave, tossing my wet jacket off to the side and joining her in the kitchen. Jayda is a force of nature, and there really is no opposition to her when she wants something.

She hums to herself happily, measuring the ingredients as I obediently follow her directions and mix them together. As we bake together, she chats about her day and all the little things in her life that she wants to share. Contrary to her appearance, Jayda is probably the sweetest and most bubbly person you could ever meet. She's also crazy protective of those she loves, which luckily enough includes me.

"So, how did your therapist session go?" she asks, glancing up at me innocently.

"It went like I thought it would; like it always does. He asks me questions; I do my best to avoid answering them." I say with a sigh, eyes resolutely staring down at the mixing bowl and the whisk in my hand.

"Oh honey, you need to be open to the process. I know after last year, and what Alex did, you don't want to relive it, but you need to go through it."

Alex. Just hearing his name makes me feel rage and despair all at the same time. He was supposed to be the one, the guy that was going to be my happily forever after. We built a life together, and then all in one swift moment it all came crashing down like a house of cards.

"I don't really want to talk about him," I say, hastily trying to change the subject.

"Well too bad, we're going to," she insists. "You need to move on from that asshole; I get he broke your heart, but you can't let him hold this influence over your life forever Daniel. He's already hurt you enough."

In my mind, I know she's right, but my heart still won't accept it. How do you get over finding the love of your life in your bed with another man?

"Why don't you try that website your therapist told you about? Maybe you can find someone who gets what you've been through. With Alex and…after that," she says softly.

"Yeah maybe, I dunno. It just feels weird."

"Seriously Daniel, you need to try to be happy again. You know we are both here for you, but we want our little ray of sunshine back! You can't keep living like this."

"You know what, I think I'm feeling pretty tired from today. I'm going to head to bed early." I say, hastily tossing the whisk back and stepping away towards my room.

"Daniel, please. We just want to help you be happy again; just let us in."

"I'm fine, don't worry about me," I say, rushing behind the bedroom door and closing it firmly then dropping to my bed.

I curl into a ball, holding myself tight. Part of me wants to sob, knowing that they're right. I'm not happy and I haven't been in a long time. Another part of me is angry at myself for being weak and showing them that I couldn't take care of myself.

There is also that quiet voice inside my head telling me that I'm not worth it, and why do I keep trying when it would be so much easier to just give up. That voice comes and goes, and when I let it control my actions bad things happen. Last year was horrible, and the voice was fully in charge then.

I sit up, forcing myself to stop dwelling on it and ignore the voice. I grab my laptop and bring up the website they all want me to sign up for, www. mindsupport.com. The homepage has flashy graphics and talks about being there to support one another with mental health, so basically the same corny lines that the therapist throws out each session. At this point, I already know this site is a waste of time. I might as well just sign up so I can tell them all I did it and get them off my back.

I make an account with the username mindovermatter and start navigating the site. There's a forum where people post their stories, and there's the typical tragic stories like "help me, I'm so stressed, I have exams, I'm broke, I don't know what to do". None of these people know what it's actually like to have issues and not know where to turn or what to do. They don't know the real feeling of helplessness and impotence when you feel trapped.

I bring up the create a post tool and write up a little about me blurb and my story. I might as well put something on here, otherwise Michael might call my bluff about signing up. Quickly writing it up I hit send, then slap my laptop shut.

I can feel the siren call of my bed and after today I need the sleep. Maybe tomorrow will be better.

New Post by Mindovermatter:
19Sep2024 21:42
Hi,

I don't even really know what to say here, so I guess I'll just start by telling you about myself and my story. I'm an American and live in New York City. I'm twenty-four years old, a guy, gay, and latino. I wouldn't say I'm hot stuff, but I also don't think I'm bad looking either. I'm about 5'10", 160 pounds, and very little to no muscles to show for those 160 pounds. I also suffer with depression, and because of this my therapist suggested I come here.

I grew up in the foster system, and being a gay kid in the foster system didn't do me any favors. Most families didn't want me, and I was bullied at every school I went to. I bounced from foster home to foster home until I aged out of the system, and then didn't have a home. Luckily, I met some friends who helped me find a place, a minimum wage job, and took care of me. For the first time in my life, I felt appreciated and worth something.

With their support, I was able to get a better job. I started taking care of myself, doing the things I liked doing, and eventually I even thought I found love. I met this guy named Alex, and I thought he was perfect. He was quiet and calm, yet passionate and ferocious all at the same time. He had this way of building you up and making you feel like you were the most important thing in his life. He made me feel like I was special and loved and, at least for a while, I felt like I was worth something and that life was worth living.

That's when things came crashing down, and I realized that I'd been living a lie. I came home after a year of us dating to find Alex in my bed with another guy. Some random he found off Grindr apparently, not that I really wanted to know that. He broke my heart and then left me. I discovered after the fact that he had been seeing guys behind my back for the entirety of our relationship. I guess I was his running joke, and he laughed about it with his friends. At least, that's what one of his friends drunkenly texted me after he left.

I went from feeling like I was the center of his life and valued, to realizing that I was nothing more than a booty call and a joke. Everything that made me feel valued and like life was worth living was taken away from me, and I spiraled into a deep depression.

Suffice it to say that this didn't go anywhere good, and I became a little too familiar with a sharp knife. After that I spent 6 weeks being looked after by doctors in white lab coats, before being deemed healthy enough to return to the real world.

And that leads us back to here, with me posting on this site. Now you know my story!

Chapter 2

Harald

I sit silently, observing the conversation between my father and Prime Minister Carl Hansen. The man's voice is grating as he drones on about economic turbulence and recessions, his nervous energy palpable. I can see the sheen of sweat on his brow, the way his fingers fidget with the papers in front of him. It's a stark contrast to my father's stern, unmoving figure.

"Your Majesty, as you can see from these projections, the country is set to go into a recession if we do not act decisively to address this economic turbulence in the markets," Hansen says, adjusting his round-framed glasses as he looks toward my father, King Magnus.

I glance up at my father, his weathered face a mask of indifference. Even with his stoic demeanor, I can tell he's as disinterested in this conversation as I am. These meetings with the Prime Minister are little more than a formality, a routine that seems pointless given our role as figureheads in this constitutional monarchy. Yet, here we are, listening to Hansen prattle on about issues he should be handling himself.

"Carl, you know as well as I do that I cannot provide you guidance on how to resolve this matter," my father says, his voice laced with a hint of exasperation.

"Your Majesty, I understand your position, yet I felt I should still speak with you about this," Hansen replies, his gaze flicking nervously between my father and me.

Hansen is a short man, his suit straining against his frame, the thinning hair on his head doing little to conceal the sweat beading on his scalp. He was elected as the best of the worst options, and it shows. He's indecisive, his mannerisms reflecting his uncertainty. It's a stark contrast to my father's resolute demeanor, his clear stances, and sparing words.

"I have every expectation that you and your government will handle this crisis with ease. You have my utmost confidence," my father says, signaling the end of the discussion. "Now if you don't mind, my son and I need to depart. We have a prior engagement at a charitable event and it wouldn't be polite to be late."

As we stand, Hansen quickly shakes my father's hand, then turns to me. I rush to my feet, extending my hand. His handshake is as weak as his leadership, his palm damp with nervous perspiration. I can't help but grimace, pulling my hand away as quickly as politely possible.

"I strongly suspect that man will not be Prime Minister for much longer," my father says, turning toward me as we walk through the marble-lined halls of Amalienborg Palace, his footsteps echoing authoritatively with each step.

"He does seem to be lacking, not that there is anything we can do about it," I agree, carefully measuring my words. Part of being modern royalty is having the lesson beaten into you that you cannot interfere with politics or have an opinion, but at the same time it's not hard to see the man is not suited for the role. Hansen's nervous energy and constant need for guidance make that painfully obvious.

"Hmm, no we cannot. Regardless, we have other matters to attend to where we can affect change. Have you prepared your speech for tonight's fundraiser?" His stern gaze fixes on me, searching for any sign of weakness or unpreparedness.

I nod, keeping my face carefully neutral. It's often better to say the bare minimum around my father, or it gives him ammunition to use against you later. I've learned this lesson the hard way over the years.

"Good, see to it that you impress them. You're my heir, and you need to make a suitable impression on them." My father is all business as usual, and doesn't mince his words. His tone carries that familiar undercurrent of disappointment that I've grown accustomed to.

Having given his orders, he walks away leaving me alone momentarily, his perfectly polished shoes clicking against the floor. That's quite typical for him, it's always all about the family business and personal relationships come second. My father has always treated myself and my sister like we were his employees, more than his children. Nordic men are also not known to be the most emotional at the best of times, stoic and all that. At least, that's what he told me growing up every time I showed my emotions in public and received a scolding for it. The memory of those harsh reprimands still makes me wince.

The family business really is just showing up to charitable fundraisers, saying a few nice words, then sitting there while random strangers fawn over you. My father has done it all his life, and now I am expected to do the same, another link in the chain of royal obligation.

"Are you alright, your Royal Highness?" my private secretary, Erik, asks briefly looking up from his desk as I enter my residence area of the palace. His concerned expression tells me he's noticed my troubled mood.

"I'm fine, thank you. How much time do we have before this horrible event tonight?"

"By horrible event, I assume you are referring to the fundraiser to save the Black-Browed Albatross?" Erik's pen taps against his notebook as he speaks.

"Yes, that one. What other event could I possibly be referring to?"

"Well I can never be quite sure, your flair for the dramatic makes it difficult to anticipate what you've signed up for today," Erik replied, his usual tone snarky as ever. "The event is in an hour. We should probably get you ready for it; wouldn't want the Prince to be late as the guest of honor. What ever would your father think?"

Erik has been my private secretary for as long as I can remember, even growing up as a child he was a fixture in the palace as his father served my father and we were childhood friends. He was officially assigned to me when I was sixteen years old and began making public appearances, and since then he has been the only person I can rely on and turn to for guidance. He knows me better than anyone, and he knows all the skeletons in my closet as well. Sometimes I wonder if he knows me better than I know myself.

Erik quickly provides the formal attire I'll be wearing for the evening - a perfectly tailored black suit with all the appropriate medals and ribbons - and excuses himself while I get changed. Once I've made myself present-able, and Erik has checked me over and made his necessary corrections to my appearance with practiced efficiency, I emerge and head out from the palace into my private vehicle with my driver, Sven, waiting.

"Your Royal Highness, always a pleasure. How are we doing today?" Sven asks, jovial as always, his familiar smile visible in the rear-view mirror.

"I'm being carted off to yet another event where I have to pretend to be happy and interested in a cause for which I know nothing about. There I'll have to deal with the random well-wishers who want to be seen with the Crown Prince, who will promptly turn around after greeting me and gossip about me. So great, just peachy you could say." I sink into the leather seat, already exhausted.

"So it's just another Friday then?" Sven says, cackling from the driver's seat, his laughter filling the car's interior.

I sigh to myself, rubbing my temples to relieve the headache I can feel building behind my eyes. I can already tell it's going to be a long night, filled with fake smiles and even faker conversations.

* * *

I politely laugh along as the elderly woman regales me with her tale about wine, pretending to be amused by her not-so-subtle bragging about being able to afford thousand-dollar bottles. She's the widow of some oil magnate, and the charity organizers clearly invited her hoping she'll write a substantial cheque. She's just one of many similar guests; looking around the room, I can count the number of non-billionaires on one hand and still have fingers left over.

Desperate for an escape, I excuse myself from her monologue about vintage wines, catching Erik's eye across the crowded ballroom and subtly gesturing for him to rescue me.

"How much longer do we need to stay before it's considered polite to leave?" I whisper to him when he arrives at my side.

"Not enjoying yourself, I take it?" he asks, though he knows the answer.

I fix him with a look that I hope conveys exactly how much I'm not enjoying myself.

He sighs, resignation clear in his expression. "You need to stay until after you've made your speech, then we can quietly make our way out of here."

"This speech had better come soon," I grumble under my breath, tugging at my too-tight collar.

"It would appear you're in luck then," Erik replies, his eyes focused on the stage.

I turn to see the event host has taken her place behind the microphone, and the elegant chatter of the room dies down as she begins to speak.

"Ladies and Gentleman, I would like to thank you all for attending this year's gala event." The audience offers polite applause before falling silent again. "As you are all aware, we are here tonight to bring light to the endangered status of the Black-Browed Albatross, and to raise funds to aid in protecting them. I have the distinct pleasure to introduce tonight's guest of honor, his Royal Highness Crown Prince Harald."

She turns toward me with an expectant smile, gesturing for me to join her. I plaster on my best royal smile - the one I've practiced countless times in mirrors - and make my way to the stage, shaking her hand and murmuring thanks before taking my position at the microphone.

This is always the worst part of these events. Despite years of practice and countless hours of etiquette training beaten into me since childhood, public speaking still makes my palms sweat and my heart race.

"Thank you for your warm welcome tonight," I begin, my voice steady despite my nerves. "On behalf of my father, King Magnus, and the rest of the Royal Family, I would like to emphasize how important this event is to us. The preservation of Denmark's native species is always a priority, and one we truly believe is vital for our nation."

The audience applauds, and I continue with the carefully crafted speech the palace writers prepared. I've memorized it so well that I go into autopilot, my mind wandering even as my mouth forms the words. It's not until I'm wrapping up that I hear what I'm actually saying, and my blood runs cold.

"With your continuing support tonight, we can help preserve the arctic seals native environment for generations to come. Thank you." I step back from the podium into deafening silence, before scattered, uncertain applause begins.

The host looks like she's been slapped, but quickly recovers her composure as she returns to the microphone. "Thank you again your Royal Highness, Prince Harald, for that wonderful speech in support of the

Black-Browed Albatross," she emphasizes, trying to salvage the situation.

The audience laughs, and I can already feel the headlines forming. My father is going to be livid - he despises any hint of embarrassment to the Royal Family, and I've just provided plenty of fodder for the tabloids. I'll be lucky if he doesn't lock me in the palace for a month after this disaster.

Erik materializes at my side as I leave the stage, efficiently whisking me toward the exit as I mutter hasty goodbyes.

"That...could have gone better," he says diplomatically, his face twisted in sympathy.

That's putting it mildly. It's just one more piece of evidence proving what I've always known: I'm a disappointment as both a son and an heir. Father will make sure I don't forget this particular failure anytime soon.

* * *

Denmark National Tribune
September 20, 2024
By Dane Andersen

Crown Prince Gaffe: Prince Harald doesn't know the difference between a bird and a seal!

Yesterday his Royal Highness Crown Prince Harald attended a charitable fundraiser in Copenhagen to support the protection of the endangered Black-Browed Albatross. While expressing his family's strong support for their protection, the Prince failed to recall which animal he was trying to protect and instead referred to Arctic Seals. After making this embarrassing error, he quickly fled the event.

The Palace issued an official statement, claiming that the Prince felt unwell during the event and made a regrettable error. They insist that he misspoke, and that the Royal Family is very passionate in the preservation of the Black-Browed Albatross.

This public gaffe highlights yet another stumble for the Royal Family as King Magnus attempts to solidify his legacy within the nation. Prince Harald has often been described as sickly, and has a checkered history with the public since his mother's death and his assumption of a public role at the age of 12. Rumors of the Prince's mental health issues have abounded over the years, and it seems that this event proves that these issues may not be in the past.

Attendees of the event stated that the Prince seemed disengaged and uninterested in the fundraiser. More than one guest overheard him speaking to his secretary, asking when they would be able to leave.

Sigrid Frederiksen, chair of the anti-monarchist league, had this to say. "This is yet another clear example of why this outdated institution needs to be abolished. Denmark does not need a monarchy, nor do we need an unelected Prince who doesn't know the difference between a bird and a mammal. The people of Denmark deserve better!"

Karl Larsen, head of the Danish Monarchist Society disagrees. "The Royal Family contributes greatly to the Danish society and culture. We should not be discussing throwing away our heritage over a simple error made by Prince Harald. People make mistakes, and our Royals are simply people too."

Regardless of the controversy and debate, it's clear that all may not be well in the halls of Amalienborg. Only time will tell if the Crown Prince is up to the task of leading the country as King Magnus ages and his health deteriorates.

For the Palace's official statement, turn to page 10…

For the Palace's official statement, turn to page 10…

* * *

I sit there as my father roars at me, his face livid with veins bulging in his neck. "Do you understand what you've done?"

I can feel myself shrinking under his glare, his anger making me feel like I'm a little boy all over again, that same scared child who could never measure up.

"Yes," I reply meekly, my voice barely above a whisper.

"No, I don't believe you do. If you did, then you wouldn't be sitting here acting like nothing had happened!"

"How else am I supposed to act? I can't help that I misspoke, and I can't go back and change it," I say, trying to keep my voice steady despite the tremor I feel building inside. "I know that I've put us in a bad light, but it will pass. The media will find some other spectacle to report on in a day or two, they always do!"

"No Harald, what you've done is shame the Crown by your actions. We have a standard to uphold, and we must be flawless! Any improper actions or allegations of incompetence threatens not just your reputation, but the reputation of the Royal Family as a whole. Royalty is divine, not mundane, and how you acted was worse than mundane," my father lectures, sneering at me with that familiar look of disappointment that I've grown far too accustomed to seeing.

My throat feels tight as I force out the words, "I'm sorry. It won't happen again."

"You're right, it won't," he says, his voice suddenly eerily calm and calculated in a way that sends chills down my spine. "If it does, I think it might be time I revisit the line of succession. Perhaps your cousin Oskar would be a more worthy successor than you to take the throne? At least we don't have to worry about allegations of his mental competence. He would have the strength and constitution to take over the throne, both things you seem to be lacking."

I freeze at his threat to disinherit me, my blood running cold. He's never gone this far before, nor has he ever been this cruel to me. He's always shown himself to be an uncaring father, especially after my mother died, but I have never seen this side of him. The calculated cruelty in his eyes makes my stomach turn.

"Father, I don't know how they got wind of my issues. I didn't tell anyone, and you made certain that the doctors and hospitals kept their silence." I can hear my inner panic start to come out in my voice as I say this, my words tumbling out faster than I can control them.

"It doesn't matter how or why, all that matters is that you stop this nonsense immediately. I've had enough of this for today; I'll leave you to reflect on your actions and the harm you've caused this family."

He storms out of the room, the heavy door slamming behind him with a finality that makes me flinch. I'm left alone with my younger sister, Ella, who looks at me like a bomb has just gone off. It's silent for a moment as we both try to process what just happened, the tension in the air thick enough to cut with a knife.

"I can't believe he just said that." Ella says, breaking the cold silence first, her voice tight with anger.

"That's our father, he always wins the parent of the year award." I reply, trying to hold my feelings in as I feel myself going teary-eyed, though I can't quite keep the bitterness from my voice.

"Our father is an asshole" Ella cries, jumping up to come and hug me as she sees me begin to lose it. "He's always been an ignorant ass, and tonight just proves it. Don't let him get to you!"

"I try not to, but then things like this happen. I'm not perfect, and I don't think I will ever be able to live up to his unrealistic expectations." My voice cracks on the last word, and I hate how weak I sound.

"You don't need to live up to his expectations! He needs to live up to ours, he just hasn't realized it yet. You are going to be okay, I promise" she says soothingly, her arms tightening around me.

Ella is like a carbon copy of our mother in most ways. She inherited her calm and warm demeanour, and her blond hair and blue eyes. She also inherited her fire, making her 5'3" of pure energy and spite that you wouldn't want to meet in a dark alley. I think it actually pains my father to see her; the resemblance to my mother is uncanny at times. She always seems to be able to see what you're thinking and how you're feeling before you even know. Even though I'm older than her by two years, it feels like she spends more time taking care of me than I do her.

"Thanks Ella. I feel bad for bothering you with this stuff; you've got your own things to deal with as well." I run a hand through my hair, a nervous habit I've never been able to break.

"Don't worry about me, I have things well in hand" she replies, easily dismissing my guilt. "I'll always be here for you. You've also got the other means of coping the doctors suggested the last time you went in."

I shudder at the mention of the doctors. I'd had a meltdown in public and lost my shit; thankfully Erik had been there to quickly smuggle me away before anyone noticed. That had ended up with me spending three weeks in a hospital talking to psychologists and therapists, all of whom felt obligated to give me advice and tell me that this was normal. Maybe it's normal for regular people, but not for any of my father's children. The memory of those sterile white walls and sympathetic faces still haunts me.

Of all the doctors and medical professionals I saw in the hospitals, only one of the therapists I spoke to actually seemed to want to help me. Now I see Ingrid regularly, and she has helped me keep a lid on some of my more volatile emotions. She's one of the few people who sees me as Harald the person, not Harald the Crown Prince.

"Maybe I'll reach out to Ingrid and move up our next session." I say, already feeling the need to talk through everything that just happened.

"Yes, I think you should. Why don't you try reaching out to her now?

I'm sure she'll take your call, it's not too late. I'll give you some space; let me know if you need anything!"

Ella leaves the room, and I pull up the contact list on my smartphone. My finger hovers over Ingrid's name for a moment before I hit it and wait for the call to connect, trying to steady my breathing as the phone rings.

"Hello, is that you Harald?"

"Hi yes it's me. Do you have a few minutes to talk? I really need someone to talk to right now."

"Yes of course. I thought I might be hearing from you after seeing today's newspaper headlines. I've been keeping an eye on things."

"I'm not sure how I should feel about you expecting me to call" I reply anxiously, fidgeting with the edge of my sleeve.

"I wouldn't worry about that, I just saw it and assumed that things would get quite heated at home after what you told me about your father. I know how these situations tend to escalate."

"You're not wrong. He threatened to disinherit me tonight." I can hear Ingrid gasp in shock, and she's quiet for a moment. The silence feels heavy between us.

"I'm sorry he said that. How are you feeling? Really feeling?"

"Honestly, I'm halfway between a having a panic attack or just taking a long sad bath where I ponder how my life got this messed up. Maybe both at the same time."

"That's fair, though I wouldn't say your life is messed up. You just have people in your life who put an immense amount of pressure on you. It only seems reasonable that you would struggle with it, anyone in your position would. This isn't a normal situation for anyone to handle."

"Not my father" I reply bitterly, my free hand clenching into a fist.

"I don't believe that for a second. He might not show his struggles, but I'm sure he does have them. Have you talked about this with anyone else apart from me? It might help to get their perspective on what happened. Sometimes fresh eyes can see things differently."

"Yeah, Ella was there when he said it. She called him, and I quote, an "asshole." Her exact words." Ingrid laughs, the sound warm and genuine.

"Your sister certainly has a way with words, and I'm glad you have her to support you. Have you managed to find anyone else you can talk to? You need a support system that doesn't just include your sister, your secretary, and your therapist. It's important to have different perspectives."

"No, you know how it is. Everyone knows I'm the Prince, and I can't trust anything

they say to me. For all I know, they are just sucking up to me to turn around and sell my stories to the highest bidder. It happened before when I was in school, and father had to intervene."

"Well, what if you found a place where you could be anonymous and just talk to other people with similar struggles? There are websites and forums where you can anonymously talk to people with problems like yourself. Places where no one would know who you are."

"I don' t think I can just go on there and post 'Hi I'm the Crown Prince of Denmark and I'm depressed and sad and my father hates me'" I reply sarcastically, rolling my eyes even though she can't see me.

"I'm going to choose to ignore your sarcasm just now. You know what I mean. This could be good for you."

I sigh, recognizing the firm tone in Ingrid's voice. That's the tone where she shows she has a hard side, and isn't all soft and squishy. She's not going to back down until I give in and let her tell me what she's thinking. I've heard this tone enough times to know what's coming.

"There's a site I heard about from one of my colleagues. I'm going to forward it to you; try it and see what happens. No pressure, just give it a chance."

"Okay, I'll take a look at it. Thanks for listening Ingrid. Really."

"Always. Now go get some sleep, it's getting late. And Harald? Try to be kind to yourself."

The phone line disconnects, and I hear my phone chime with an incoming message.

I scoff at the message. Ingrid is predictably consistent, and from past experience she isn't going to drop it until I do this. I grab my laptop, quickly bringing up the website, and create an account. I pick the username DeprimeretPrins, smiling to myself at my own little joke; it means depressed prince. The chance of anyone knowing what that means outside of Denmark is slim to none. Besides, sometimes the best place to hide is in plain sight.

The forum is full of posts with lots of stories of people struggling. It seems like everyone on here introduces themselves in the same thread with their backstory, so I might as well do the same. I quickly write up a post, being careful not to expose who I am and remain vague enough. It's actually kind of cathartic to write this all down, rather than bottling it up and waiting for it to explode. My fingers hover over the keyboard for a moment before I begin typing.

New Post by DeprimeretPrins:
20Sep2024 22:35
Hi,

It looks like everyone introduces themselves on here, so I guess I'll do that too. I'm 26 years old, male, and I live in Denmark. I'm 6 feet tall, blond hair, blue eyes, just your typical Nordic guy blessed with good genes, I suppose. Though sometimes these "blessings" feel more like a curse, constantly being noticed when all I want is to fade into the background. I'm also gay and in the closet, my father is deeply homophobic and me being gay would never be accepted.

For most of my life I've struggled with depression and anxiety. I'm forced to cope with the demands that my family places on me, and this causes those issues to flare up. My mother died when I was young, and after that my father became even more closed off and cold than he already was with us. He has high expectations for me especially, and I consistently fail to meet them. He thinks of me as an embarrassment, and at times I can't help but feel embarrassed of myself too. The constant criticism wears you down, like waves against a cliff, until you start to crumble.

My family is well off, so I don't work, but I do spend a lot of time engaged in charitable events. I feel useless more often than not, and I don't feel like anything I am doing in my life has worth or value. At the same time, I also feel powerless because my family expects me to do this and I don't have a choice in it. Every day feels like going through the motions, smiling when expected, speaking when prompted, like some wind-up toy performing for others' entertainment.

A few months ago I fell into a deep depression, which was the result of the pressure of my father's expectations becoming too much. I was at a charitable event and basically lost it and had a meltdown. After that I spent three weeks in a hospital being poked and prodded by doctors, before they finally released me back to my gilded cage. The whole experience was humiliating, but at least it forced everyone to acknowledge that something wasn't right.

The only good thing to come from my time in the hospital was one of the therapists, who is actually the person that suggested I come here. Hopefully this site will help me find and connect with others! Sometimes just knowing you're not alone can make all the difference.

I submit the post and go to scroll away from the page when one of the messages catches my eye. It's from a user with the name MindoverMatter, and his story grabs my attention. Reading through it, I can tell he's had a hard life and it almost makes me feel like I already know him. His stay in the hospital sounds a lot like mine, minus the knife. There's something raw and honest about his words that resonates with me deeply. I post a comment, trying to be witty, before closing my laptop. I'm sure that won't go anywhere, but at least I did respond to someone. Maybe reaching out, even in this small way, is a step in the right direction.

C.G. Macington

Chapter 3

Daniel

"**M**s. Sanders, I understand what you are saying. However, what I'm telling you is that this medication is not currently covered under Schedule H of your employer's benefit plan" I say, mentally banging my head against the wall in exasperation. I can hear phones ringing around the large cubicle filled office and my coworkers all repeating word for word the same line as me. The fluorescent lights above flicker slightly, giving me a headache that's becoming all too familiar.

To clarify, I work for a large medical insurance company named Insuricarica processing health claims. By processing, what I mean to say is finding creative ways to deny claims whenever possible to increase the profit margins for our corporate overlords. Yay capitalism. Sometimes I wonder if there's a special circle of hell reserved for insurance companies, right next to people who talk during movies.

"I've never been treated so badly before! I'm going to be speaking to my attorney!" The line goes dead as she hangs up on me. I resist the urge to bang my head on my desk, knowing it would only draw unwanted attention from my colleagues.

As if my life wasn't already sad enough, I do this job Monday to Friday from nine to five. It's depressing and soul sucking, but in this economy I don't really have many choices. You take what you can get when you can get it. The alternative is no job, no money, and no crappy apartment in a rundown building in a bad part of town. And trust me, I've seen enough of being without those things to last a lifetime.

I look at the clock, and see that it's finally noon. Half my day in this penal colony has passed, and I'm now eligible for my legally mandated unpaid lunch break. Sending a quick message to my team, I quickly sign out and head to the sad corporate lunchroom. The walls are plastered in inspirational posters and corporate slogans, basically all the things someone higher up thought would motivate us peasants. My personal favorite is "TEAMWORK MAKES THE DREAM WORK" written in Comic Sans, because nothing says professional quite like that font choice.

I grab my sad brown paper bag lunch from the break room fridge, dodging Karen from Accounts Payable who always wants to tell me about her latest MLM scheme. The tables are mostly full of my fellow corporate drones, all of us wearing the same defeated expressions and business casual attire that somehow makes everyone look equally miserable. I spot an empty corner table - my usual spot where I can scroll through my phone in peace while picking at whatever leftovers I managed to throw together this morning.

The fluorescent lights buzz overhead, casting that sickly artificial glow that makes everyone look like they're one deadline away from a nervous breakdown. Another poster catches my eye - "SUCCESS IS A JOURNEY, NOT A DESTINATION" - which feels like a cruel joke when you're stuck processing denied claims all day. At least they didn't write that one in Comic Sans. Small mercies, I guess.

I pull out my slightly squished sandwich and try not to think about how I have another four hours of mind-numbing spreadsheets ahead of me. Sometimes I wonder if this is what social workers mean when they talk about "stable employment" - death by a thousand paper cuts in an office where the highlight of my day is when the coffee machine actually works.

Sandy from Human Resources glares at me from the table across the room. She's hated me ever since I forgot her Secret Santa present last year; I'm almost eighty percent certain she's the reason my bonus was lower this year. That woman can hold a grudge like nobody's business, and considering she's the one who processes our year-end reviews, I probably should have tried harder with that gift.

"How are you Sandy?" I ask, trying to be polite. My mother - or what I remember of her before she gave me up - always said kill them with kindness. Though in Insuricarica's break room, that strategy seems about as effective as using a water gun against a forest fire.

"We don't need to talk; neither of us want this conversation" She replies bluntly, standing up to pack her lunch bag and going to leave the room. The way she aggressively zips up her designer lunch bag makes me wonder if she's imagining it's my neck.

"Always a pleasure." I mutter under my breath, watching her storm out like I'd personally offended her entire family tree.

My phone chimes and I glance at it to see a notification pop up for a new message on the support website Michael forced me to sign up for. Another one of his "healthy coping mechanisms" that he insists will help me process everything that happened with Alex.

I click into it and can see multiple replies, mostly from bots, advertising Sexy Single Latinas in my area or Incredible Crypto Investing Opportunities - Guaranteed Returns. Clearly they don't know their target market if they're commenting on my post. I'm both gay and broke. Like, eating-ramen-for-dinner-three-nights-a-week broke. I stop at the last comment though, and it makes me unexpectedly laugh.

From DeprimeretPrins
20Sep2024 22:45
So I read your post and feel like you and I have a lot in common. I do have one extremely pressing question though, which I think needs an answer immediately if we are to be internet stranger friends. How was the Jell-O in the hospital, and did they have pudding?

Out of my entire post, the most important thing this guy picked out was that I was in the hospital, and therefore that had to mean that I had eaten either Jell-O or pudding. I'm not sure whether to be shocked or amused. His dry sense of humor is almost disarming, and makes me smile. It's refreshing compared to the usual pity-filled responses I get when people find out about my hospital stay. I quickly bring up the comment bar, my fingers hovering over the keyboard for just a moment before I dive in with my own brand of sass.

From: MindOverMatter
21Sep2024 12:10

So out of all the things I wrote, you decided the Jell-O was the most important aspect of the post? This either implies poor decision making and prioritization skills or a complete obsession with Jello-O. Which do you think it is?

Also, yes there was Jello-O. I ate it all. They "ran out" of Jell-O during my stay; I'm sure they were lying. It was a Jello-O conspiracy. Pudding is the devil; no one likes it. The texture alone is enough to make me question humanity's decisions as a species. IF we are to be judged on our creations, then pudding would indicate that we should not be the dominant species on this planet.

Sincerely,

Your Internet Stranger Friend

PS: Sexy Single Latinas can go away now, it's not happening ladies. Wrong tree, wrong bark, wrong everything.

As my lunch break finishes up, I start heading back to my desk only to find the path blocked by Cassandra. She's 5'2" and at least 200 pounds, though I suspect that's a conservative estimate. Her receding hairline is accentuated by the thick jowls that quiver as she walks, reminding me of a bowl of particularly active Jell-O. At the same time, she acts and talks like she's Dolores Umbridge from the Harry Potter series, which is fitting since they both share that same fake sweetness that makes my teeth hurt.

"Daniel sweetie, would you come see me in my office? We need to have a chat." She says, voice sickeningly sweet with a southern accent that's as authentic as the designer bag knockoff she carries.

"Sure Cassandra" I say, following her into her cramped office and taking the seat across from her. The desk and walls of her office are plastered in random photos of her extended family and her dogs; it feels like she has tried to make her office into her home. The overwhelming smell of vanilla air freshener makes me want to gag.

"Thank you for coming to see me. I just wanted to go over your performance recently. I pulled several recordings of your calls, and looked at your KPIs and I have to say that I am disappointed."

Her face doesn't look disappointed. In fact, she looks like she just won the lottery, hit the jackpot, and found a golden ticket to Willy Wonka's factory all at once.

"I'm sorry to hear that. I thought my performance was perfectly acceptable." I reply neutrally, channeling every ounce of customer service voice I can muster.

"Well honey, things change. Your claim denial rate might have been enough to scrape by a year ago, but with new targets from management you're under performing badly. We expect a denial rate of at least fifty percent, and you're barely cracking twenty eight percent. You need to do better, or you might not have a job here if things continue like they are."

That little not so subtle threat lingers in the air between us like a bad smell, and I take a second to control my facial expression. I'm not going to give her the satisfaction of seeing how she has upset me, though my stomach is doing somersaults worthy of an Olympic gymnast.

"I see, well I suppose I will need to think about this and how I can do better. Was there anything else you wanted to discuss?"

Cassandra's smile drops from her face, the facade of sweet southern hospitality gone faster than free donuts in the break room.

"No darling, you can get back to work now."

I nod and leave her office, numbly navigating back to my cubicle and flopping down onto my firm worn out office chair. The ancient cushion squeaks in protest, probably plotting its own resignation.

"You cool bro?" Piper asks, his head popping up over the cubicle divider like a particularly concerned meerkat. Piper is my next door work neighbour, and is probably the only person in the office that I actually get along with. With surfer vibes and long tangled blond hair he looks completely out of place in the office, but he has been here for longer than I have and somehow hits top performer targets every month while making it look effortless.

"Yeah I'm fine," I say absentmindedly, shuffling papers around my desk just to look busy.

"Really, cause you don't look fine," he says, raising an eyebrow. "What did the Dollar General Barbie have to say that has you so upset? You look like someone just killed your houseplant."

"Oh just the usual doom, gloom, and torture. Basically threatening to fire me if I don't increase my rejection rate. Apparently they want us to reject fifty percent of our claims now," I reply, trying to act nonchalant as I'm feeling a rising feeling of panic inside. My hands are shaking slightly as I continue to reorganize the same stack of papers.

"Fuck, she is the Wicked Witch of the West isn't she? Can you imagine paying what our clients pay for the shitty health coverage we provide then half of them getting told that their claims are denied for some bullshit reason every time they try to use it?" His usual easy-going expression morphs into one of genuine disgust.

I snort, trying to hold back my laughter at his indignant response. My anxiety eases slightly at his righteous anger on behalf of our clients. "Funny enough I can, our health insurance goes through us as well remember? They reject all my claims almost every go around. Last time I tried to get my prescription filled, it took three appeals."

"Ah, I almost forgot. Well fuck her and fuck them. If she fires you, maybe that's a sign there are better things out there for you then! Either way, this place isn't the final destination for you or me," Piper replies decisively, before ducking back down behind his cubicle wall, leaving me with that small nugget of hope to cling to.

"Thanks Piper, I guess we'll see what happens," I reply softly, finally letting my hands rest on my keyboard.

* * *

I collapse onto my bed face-first, still in my work clothes. The memory of Cassandra's smug face haunts me like a particularly annoying ghost. My phone buzzes - probably Jayda asking about dinner plans - but I can't bring myself to check it yet.

Instead, I roll over and grab my laptop from the nightstand. The forum loads up instantly. My fingers hover over the keyboard before I start typing:

"Today was absolute garbage. My boss threatened to fire me because I'm not heartless enough to deny people's insurance claims. Sometimes I wonder if there's any point trying to be a decent person in a world that rewards being awful."

I hit post before I can overthink it. Usually these kinds of rants disappear into the void, but within minutes a notification pops up. It's DePrimeretPrins - or whatever his real name is.

"I understand completely. Currently dreading a meeting where I have to sit through hours of people talking AT me rather than WITH me. They all expect me to just nod and agree, even when their ideas are terrible. Sometimes being 'professional' feels like slowly dying inside."

I sit up, surprised at the quick response. My fingers fly across the keyboard:

"At least you're important enough to be in meetings. I'm just a cubicle drone who's apparently not evil enough for corporate America. Though your meeting sounds

mind-numbingly boring. What's it about?"

His reply comes faster this time:

"Trade policies and economic forecasts. Riveting stuff. I'd rather watch paint dry. And trust me, being 'important' just means more people watching you fail. At least in your cubicle you can roll your eyes without making headlines."

I laugh despite myself. There's something weirdly comforting about commiserating with a stranger who seems just as trapped as I am, even if we're trapped in completely different ways.

My fingers hover over the keyboard as I consider my reply. I want to match his wit and snark, but in my own charming way of course.

"At least your day can't be worse than mine - unless you're stuck in a meeting with Satan's middle manager too? My boss told my team today that all of our reports need to be color-coded by 'emotional resonance.' Whatever that means...maybe I need to get my chakras aligned to understand it?"

I hit send with a smirk, feeling pretty pleased with myself. Take that, anonymous stranger on the internet. Your turn.

His response pops up a few minutes later:

"This might be too forward, but would you want to continue this conversation over text instead? I'm enjoying our banter but I feel that this might be better done in private. No worries if not, I know swapping numbers with internet strangers isn't exactly recommended."

I pause, my thumb hovering over the screen. He's right, giving out my number to some random guy online is probably a terrible idea. Then again, terrible ideas are kind of my specialty.

I think of the long empty evening stretching out before me, another microwave dinner with Jayda and Caleb lost in their couple bubble. What's the worst that could happen? If he turns out to be a creep, I can always block him.

"Eh, you seem relatively sane. For now. Here's my number - don't make me regret this!"

I type out my cell and hit send before I can second guess myself. My phone buzzes almost immediately.

Unknown Number: Let the regret begin! :) I'm Harald by the way.

I save the contact, chewing my lip as I debate my next move. *"I'm Daniel. So...come here often?"*

A knock at my door interrupts my texting and I hastily click send.

"Come in," I call out, not looking up from my screen.

Jayda bursts in, her platform boots thudding against the floor. "I heard about the Cassandra situation. That absolute witch." She plops down next to me, the bed creaking under our combined weight. "Want to hear my foolproof plan to dispose of her body?"

"Do tell. Also how did you hear about it; I didn't tell anyone about it yet?" I close my laptop, already feeling lighter.

"Easy; Piper texted me about it. He's actually a nice guy, despite the fact he thinks he has a chance with me and refuses to give up. Anyway, back to the Cassandra situation. So first, we drug her morning coffee with anti-freeze - it's sweet, she'll never notice. Then we wrap her body in copious amounts of chicken wire before dumping her in the Hudson where the fish and sharks will rapidly consume her leaving no evidence of the crime." Jayda's eyes gleam. "The wire ensures the body sinks and stays down when it, you know, bloats. More than it already is, that is. "

"Someone's been watching too much Criminal Minds." I nudge her shoulder.

"Please, this is pure Forensic Files knowledge." She holds up a paper bag that smells like heaven. "But before we commit the perfect murder, I brought dinner. Your favorite from that Thai place on 9th."

"You're an angel." I peek inside the bag. "Pad see ew?"

"Extra spicy, just how you like it." She pulls out containers and plastic forks. "Though I still think we should consider my murder plan. I also know how to dissolve a body in lye."

We sprawl across my bed, sharing noodles and plotting increasingly ridiculous ways to off Cassandra. By the time we're scraping the bottom of the containers, my sides hurt from laughing at Jayda's detailed scheme involving three chickens, a rubber duck, and somehow making it look like a tragic shuffleboard accident.

"Feel better?" She asks, gathering up our empty containers.

"Much." I lean against her shoulder. "Thanks for always knowing exactly what I need."

Jayda bumps my shoulder with hers. "Hey. We're a team, remember? You, me, and Caleb against the world. Whatever happens, we've got your back."

I smile, feeling a rush of affection for my best friend. "I know. I don't know what I'd do without you guys."

As if summoned, Caleb appears in the doorway, a bottle of vodka in hand and a mischievous grin on his face. "You know what this calls for? Dancing and bad decisions."

Jayda's eyes light up. "Hell yes. We're going out tonight." She turns to me, her expression brooking no argument. "And don't even think about saying no. You need this."

I groan, burying my face in a pillow. "Guys, I appreciate the thought, but I'm exhausted. It's been the day from hell."

Caleb waves the vodka bottle. "Which is exactly why you need to blow off some steam. Come on, when was the last time we all went out together?"

I rack my brain, realizing it's been months. Between my soul-sucking job and Jayda's erratic coffee shop shifts, our schedules rarely align for more than quick meals or movie nights on the couch.

Jayda pokes my side. "See? You can't even remember. That means it's been too long." She hops off the bed, pulling me with her. "Now come on, let's get you out of those work clothes and into something that screams 'I'm young, I'm hot, and I'm ready to make questionable decisions with a sexy young finance bro.'"

Caleb nods sagely. "Amen to that. I'll call an Uber."

I let Jayda drag me to my closet, too tired to put up much of a fight. She rummages through my clothes, tossing aside anything she deems unworthy.

"Nope, nope, definitely not, oh hello-" She holds up a pair of black skinny jeans I forgot I owned. "These are perfect. Pair them with that transparent net shirt where you can see your nipples and your doc martens and you'll be irresistible to all the boys."

"Yes ma'am." I give her a mock salute before stripping off my slacks and button-down. As I shimmy into the jeans, I have to admit they do make my ass look fantastic. Maybe this isn't such a bad idea after all.

* * *

Twenty minutes later, we pile into the Uber, Jayda in her signature goth getup and Caleb in his usual hipster attire. The vodka gets passed around as we head towards the club, the burn in my throat a welcome distraction from the day's events.

By the time we reach the club, I'm buzzing pleasantly, the stress of work and Cassandra's threats feeling far away. Jayda grabs my hand, grinning wildly.

"Ready to dance your ass off and forget about the corporate world for a night?"

I grin back, letting her pull me towards the pulsing music. "Absolutely."

We push our way through the writhing bodies, the beat pulsing through my bones. Sweat glistens on skin as the crowd moves as one to the thumping bass. Jayda and Caleb dance close, lost in each other's eyes, while I let the music take over, my body moving of its own accord.

After a few songs, I gesture towards the bar, mouthing "drink" to Jayda. She nods, still wrapped up in Caleb. I weave my way off the dance floor, the press of bodies giving way to cool air as I approach the bar.

"Whiskey sour," I call to the bartender over the din. As I wait, I feel a presence beside me. Glancing over, I'm met with the sight of a handsome older man, salt and pepper hair artfully tousled, suit jacket straining against broad shoulders.

"Hey there," he purrs, eyes raking over my body appreciatively. "Can I buy you that drink?"

I swallow hard, suddenly feeling out of my depth. It's been so long since I've flirted with anyone, let alone a gorgeous man like this.

"S-sure," I stammer out, internally cringing at how lame I sound.

He smiles, signaling the bartender. "Two whiskey sours." His eyes find mine again. "I'm Liam."

"Daniel," I manage, taking a large gulp of my drink as soon as it's placed in front of me.

Liam chuckles, leaning in close. His expensive cologne fills my nostrils. "Nervous?"

I laugh shakily. "Is it that obvious?"

"It's endearing," he murmurs, tucking a stray hair behind my ear. His face is inches from mine now, his intentions clear.

Panic rises in my throat as memories of Alex flash through my mind. I jerk back, nearly toppling off my barstool.

"I-I'm sorry," I choke out, shame heating my cheeks. "I can't do this. It's too soon and I'm not ready for this..."

Liam straightens, disappointment flickering across his chiseled features before being replaced by a polite yet cool mask. "No worries. Your loss though, we would have had a lot of fun." He winks, knocking back his drink before melting into the crowd.

I stare into my glass, the amber liquid blurring as tears prick at my eyes. What the fuck was that and why did I chicken out? Will I ever be ready to move on?

The tough looking bartender catches my eye as I blink back tears, her brow furrowed in concern. She leans over, her voice raised to be heard over the music.

"Hey, you okay? Don't let that guy get to you. He's a regular here and trust me, you dodged a bullet. Pretty sure you'd catch something nasty from him." She winks conspiratorially.

A surprised laugh escapes me and I feel some of the tightness in my chest ease. "Thanks for the warning. Guess I should be more careful who I let buy me drinks, huh?"

She grins. "Stick with me, kid. I'll steer you right."

I raise my glass in a toast. "To dodging bullets and not catching STDs!"

We clink glasses and I down the rest of my whiskey sour, the alcohol burning away the last of my embarrassment. Setting the empty glass on the bar, I flash her a grateful smile before turning to head back to the dance floor.

Jayda spots me and waves me over, her face flushed and glowing. "There you are! We were about to send out a search party!"

I force a laugh, letting her pull me into the crush of bodies. "Just needed a drink to keep up with you two."

Caleb slings an arm around my shoulders, pulling me close. "Stick with us, we'll keep you young!"

I let the music take over again, my body finding the rhythm. But even as I lose myself in the beat, I can't help but feel a pang of emptiness as I watch Jayda and Caleb dance, wrapped up in their own little world. The love they have for each other is so tangible I can almost reach out and touch it.

I close my eyes, trying to push away the ache inside me. Maybe one day I'll have that again. But for now, I'll dance until I can't feel anything at all.

42

Chapter 4

Harald

I slouch in my chair, watching Carl Hansen's latest attempt at wrangling the coalition partners into a budget agreement dissolve into chaos. The Prime Minister's round glasses fogged up as he mopped his forehead with a handkerchief for the fifth time in ten minutes.

"Perhaps if we redirected funds from the infrastructure portfolio..." Carl's voice trailed off as his Finance Minister Larsen cut him off with a sharp wave.

"We've been over this already. The bridges need repair now, not in five years and it cannot be put off any further."

I fought the urge to massage my temples. Father should have been here, guiding them, but he'd delegated this to me as "practice." More like punishment for the fundraiser disaster.

My phone buzzed in my pocket. I snuck a glance while the Energy Minister Petersen launched into another tirade about wind farm subsidies. Daniel had responded to my comment.

"At least your day can't be worse than mine - unless you're stuck in a meeting with Satan's middle manager too? My boss just told my team that all of our reports need to be color-coded by 'emotional resonance.' Whatever that means...maybe I need to get my chakras aligned to understand it?"

A laugh escaped before I could stop it. Heads swiveled toward me, Carl's nervous energy temporarily redirected as he blinked rapidly in my direction.

"Your Highness? Did you have something to add?"

Heat crept up my neck. "No, my apologies. Please continue."

As they resumed arguing, I typed quickly: *"This might be too forward, but would you want to continue this conversation over text instead? I'm enjoying our banter and I feel that this might be better done in private. No worries if not, I know swapping numbers with internet strangers isn't exactly recommended."*

My heart pounded as I hit send. This felt different, more real somehow. I'd never reached out directly to someone from the forum before. What if he said no? What if he said yes? What if he somehow figured out who I really was?

The reply came a minute later, which felt like an eternity: *"Eh, you seem relatively sane. For now. Here's my number - don't make me regret this!"*

I stare at Daniel's contact information on my phone screen, a small smile tugging at the corners of my mouth. Our brief exchanges had been the highlight of an otherwise dismal week. His witty comebacks and self-deprecating humor were a breath of fresh air in the stuffy world of royal protocol and political maneuvering.

As the budget meeting droned on around me, my mind wandered to our previous interactions. The way he'd commiserated about his boss's ridiculous demands, the clever quips about the absurdities of adult life. For the first time in longer than I could remember, I felt a genuine connection with someone who knew nothing about my title or family name.

It was refreshing, exhilarating even, to be seen as just another person navigating the ups and downs of existence. With Daniel, I wasn't the Crown Prince or the face of a nation - I was simply a fellow human being trying to make sense of it all.

My thumb hovered over his contact, a sudden impulse to reach out directly nearly overwhelming me. What would I even say? "Hey, it's me, the guy from the forum who also happens to be next in line for the Danish throne"?

I shook my head, a wry chuckle escaping under my breath. No, I couldn't risk revealing my true identity, not yet at least. But maybe, just maybe, there was potential for something more with Daniel. A friendship, a confidant, someone who understood the weight of expectation and the struggle to find one's place in the world.

I settle for a simple message instead, deciding my real first name isn't a risk to share: *"Let the regret begin! :) I'm Harald by the way."*

A response comes in quickly and I have to stifle another laugh at his message: *"I'm Daniel. So...come here often?"*

As the Energy Minister's voice rose in another impassioned plea, I slipped my phone back into my pocket, the ghost of a smile still playing on my lips. For now, I would savor the connection we'd forged, the brief moments of levity in an otherwise heavy existence. And perhaps, with time and trust, it could grow into something even more meaningful.

* * *

Erik

I shifted in my seat, unable to keep my eyes off Harald during the budget meeting. The afternoon sun caught his profile, highlighting the sharp line of his jaw and the way his brow furrowed in concentration. Even in moments of tedium, he carried himself with an innate grace that came from years of royal training.

The Prime Minister droned on about fiscal responsibilities while I pretended to take notes. My pen traced meaningless patterns across the page as my thoughts wandered to forbidden territory. The slight curl of Harald's hair at his neck. The way his hands moved when he spoke. The rare, genuine smile that transformed his entire face.

My chest ached with the familiar weight of these feelings I'd carried for years, ever since we were just friends and teenagers. They were as much a part of me now as breathing, and just as automatic. I'd learned to live with them, to pack them away in a corner of my heart where they couldn't interfere with my duties.

A sudden snort of laughter broke through the monotony of the meeting. Harald's phone lay face-down on the table, but I caught the ghost of a smile playing across his lips. Something had caught him off guard – something that brought a spark of joy to his eyes I hadn't seen in months.

The coalition partners exchanged irritated glances at the interruption, but I couldn't tear my gaze away from Harald's face. Color rose in his cheeks as he composed himself and apologized, yet that light remained.

Whatever message he'd received had pierced through his carefully maintained facade.

I knew his secret, carried it like a precious stone in my pocket. The weight of it grew heavier each time I watched him force himself into the mold his father demanded. But this moment – this unguarded flash of genuine happiness – made me wonder what had finally managed to crack through his walls.

The meeting dragged on, but Harald's fingers kept straying to his phone, typing what looked like a longer message. His eyes held a warmth I hadn't seen since before his last anxiety attack, and despite the bittersweet ache in my chest, I found myself hoping that whatever – or whoever – had caused this change might help him find his way back to himself.

The meeting finally adjourned, and I watched as Harald practically leapt from his chair, his long strides carrying him out of the room before anyone else had even gathered their papers. I took my time, nodding politely to the coalition partners and the Prime Minister as they filed out. My mind was still back in that moment, replaying the way Harald's face had lit up at whatever message he'd received.

I made my way back to the office given to representatives of the Crown in the government buildings, my steps measured and unhurried. I knew I'd find him there, probably already engrossed in his phone. The thought made my heart clench in a familiar way, a mixture of fondness and resignation.

As I pushed open the door, I caught a glimpse of Harald's profile, his head bent over his phone as he typed furiously. The intensity of his focus was almost palpable, and I had to take a steadying breath before I could trust my voice.

"Anything interesting?" I asked, aiming for casual as I settled into my own chair across from him.

Harald's head snapped up, and for a moment, I saw a flicker of guilt in his eyes before he schooled his features into a neutral expression. "Just catching up on some messages," he said, his tone carefully even.

I nodded, pretending to shuffle through the papers on my desk. "Of course." The words tasted bitter on my tongue, but I swallowed them down. It wasn't my place to pry, no matter how much I longed to be the one he confided in.

As the afternoon wore on, I found my gaze drawn to him again and again. The way his fingers danced across the screen of his phone, the slight curve of his lips as he read something that pleased him. Each stolen glance was a tiny knife in my heart, a reminder of the feelings I could never voice.

I loved him. I had loved him for years, through every triumph and every struggle. But I knew, with a certainty that settled like lead in my stomach, that my love would always be unrequited. Harald was destined for greatness, for a life that had no room for a loyal secretary with a foolish heart.

So I sat, and I watched, and I ached. And I promised myself, as I had a thousand times before, that I would be content with this. With being by his side, even if I could never truly be with him. It was enough, I told myself. It had to be enough.

* * *

Harald

The comforting aroma of Ella's homemade Frikadeller meatballs wafted through the dining room as I entered, the warmth of the candlelight softening the room's grand edges. Ella bustled about, her blonde hair swishing as she set out steaming plates.

"There you are, big brother," she teased, her blue eyes sparkling. "I was beginning to think you'd gotten lost on your way from your royal chambers."

I laughed despite myself, shaking my head. "Very funny, Ells. You know I'd never miss your cooking, even if affairs of state tried to get in the way."

She grinned, pulling out a chair for me with an exaggerated flourish. "Well then, Your Highness, please take a seat. Dinner is served."

I settled into the proffered chair, breathing in the comforting scent of the meatballs and potatoes. It smelled like home, like the rare happy memories of childhood when Mother would cook this same meal.

Ella took the seat across from me, passing the basket of bread. "So, how go the trials and tribulations of princedom today? Slay any dragons? Rescue any damsels?"

"Ha, I wish." I tore off a hunk of bread, staring at it. "No, just the usual - disappointing Father, as per usual."

Her smile faded and she reached across to squeeze my hand. "Harald, you could never be a disappointment. Father just doesn't see all that you are."

I swallowed hard against the lump in my throat. "I don't know, Ells. Sometimes I wonder if he's right about me. If I'm really cut out for this whole heir apparent thing."

"Well I have no doubt." Her voice was fierce, eyes flashing. "You, big brother, are going to make an incredible king one day. Never forget that."

I shook my head, pushing the meatballs around my plate. "It's not just about being king, Ella. It's about being me. The real me."

She tilted her head, studying me with those perceptive blue eyes that always seemed to see right through me. "What do you mean, Harald?"

I took a shaky breath, my heart hammering against my ribs. "I'm gay, Ells. And Father...he'll never accept that. I can never be who I truly am, not with the throne hanging over my head."

To my surprise, Ella just smiled softly, not a hint of shock or judgement on her face. "Oh, Harald. I know. I've always known."

My jaw dropped. "You...you have? But how?"

She laughed lightly. "Call it sisterly intuition. Also you don't do a good job of deleting your web browsing history. And for the record, I love you all the more for it. It's a part of what makes you, you."

Tears pricked at the corners of my eyes and I blinked them back. "But Father-"

"Father's opinions on the matter don't concern me," she cut in, her voice unwavering. "Or anyone else for that matter. The people would love you for your truth, Harald. They'd respect you all the more for living authentically."

I let out a shuddering breath, feeling like a weight had lifted from my chest. "You really think so?"

"I know so." She squeezed my hand again, her smile radiant. "The world is changing, big brother. And when you're ready, I'll be right there beside you, cheering you on as you show everyone the incredible man I've always known you to be."

I fidgeted with my napkin, feeling embarrassed at my reaction to her unequivocal support. Her unconditional love felt amazing, and yet I still wondered if it would be enough if the truth was exposed about me.

Deciding to change the subject to something lighter, I took a deep breath. "So in other news, I...I made a friend. Online."

Her eyebrows shot up in surprise. "Really? That's wonderful! Tell me more."

I couldn't help but smile at her enthusiasm. "We met on a forum Ingrid suggested. We've been talking a lot, about everything really. Mostly about life, and personal stuff..."

Ella leaned forward, her interest piqued. "Personal stuff? Like what?"

I shrugged, feeling a bit self-conscious. "Just...struggles, I guess. Things I don't really talk about with anyone else."

Her expression softened. "Harald, that's huge. I'm so glad you've found someone you can open up to."

But then her brow furrowed slightly. "Just...be careful, okay? Remember who you are. I don't want you getting hurt or taken advantage of."

I nodded, understanding her concern. "I know, Ells. I'm being cautious. I haven't told them who I really am."

She tilted her head. "What do you mean? Who do they think they're speaking to?"

I swallowed hard. "They don't know I'm...you know, a prince. I just told them that I come from a wealthy family and don't work, apart from being involved in the family's charitable ventures."

Ella reached across the table to squeeze my hand. "Harald, you don't have to hide who you are. If this person is a true friend, they'll accept you, all of you."

I withdrew my hand, my head moving side to side. "Things are more complicated than that, Ella. I'm different from everyone else. I'll never measure up - not in Father's eyes, not as heir to the crown. Here, in this one space where my identity is unknown, I don't have to stress about people cozying up to me just because of my social status and royal background. I will just be myself to him, and if that isn't good enough then I guess that's just a sign for what's to come down the road."

My voice cracked on the last word and I blinked back the sudden sting of tears. Ella's face crumpled with sympathy.

"Oh, Harald. Don't you see how incredible you are? You have such a good heart, such strength. Anyone would be lucky to know the real you."

I wanted to believe her, I did. But the doubts lingered, the fear of judgment and rejection.

"I don't know, Ells. It's just...it's easier this way. To keep that part of myself hidden."

She sighed, but her eyes were full of understanding. "I get it, I do. But promise me you'll think about it, okay? About being yourself, fully and un-apologetically. Because the world deserves to know the amazing man and big brother I see in front of me."

Her words wrapped around me like a warm hug, soothing the frayed edges of my nerves. I felt a small smile tug at the corners of my mouth. "Thanks, sis. I don't know what I'd do without you."

Ella grinned, a mischievous glint in her eye. "Probably wallow in self-doubt and never leave your room."

I laughed, the sound surprising me. "Probably."

She leaned forward, her expression turning playful. "So, this new friend of yours. Is he cute?"

I felt my cheeks flush, and I ducked my head. "I don't know. We haven't exchanged pictures or anything."

Ella waggled her eyebrows. "Well, maybe you should ask for one. You know, for research purposes."

I rolled my eyes, but I couldn't help the smile that spread across my face. "You're impossible."

She shrugged, unrepentant. "Just looking out for my big brother's love life."

I shook my head, but the warmth of her support, her unwavering love, settled into my bones. For the first time in a long time, I felt a flicker of hope in my chest. Maybe, just maybe, I could do this. I could be myself, even if it was just with one person for now.

And with Ella by my side, cheering me on, anything felt possible.

Chapter 5

Daniel

The morning light pierced through my eyelids like a dagger, my head throbbing with every breath. I rolled over and fumbled for my phone on the nightstand, squinting at the screen. My eyes widened as I saw multiple messages from Harald.

"Good morning, Daniel. I hope you slept well."

I couldn't help but smile despite the pounding in my head and the nausea roiling in my stomach from last night's overindulgence. We had only been chatting for a few days, but somehow Harald's thoughtful messages never failed to lift my spirits and bring a grin to my face, even in the depths of a wicked hangover. There was just something about him that drew me in and made me feel special.

I typed back, *"Morning, Harald. Or is it evening there? I'm a bit worse for wear after last night. Jayda and Caleb dragged me out to the club."*

"Yes, it's late in the evening for me. Oh? Do tell. I'm intrigued," he replied almost immediately.

I chuckled, my fingers flying across the screen. *"Well, you definitely don't know this but I love to dance. The music was pumping, the drinks were flowing... it was a great night. Even if I am paying for it this morning."*

A few moments later, my phone buzzed with his response. But this time, it wasn't just a text. Harald had sent a picture. My breath caught in my throat as I opened it.

There he was, smiling at the camera, his blond hair tousled and his blue eyes sparkling with mischief. He was incredibly handsome, with chiseled features and a jawline that could cut glass. I felt my heart skip a beat.

"Your turn," he wrote. *"I showed you mine, now you show me yours."*

I hesitated, glancing at my reflection in the mirror. I looked like death warmed over, my hair sticking up at odd angles and dark circles under my eyes. But something about Harald made me want to take a chance.

I snapped a quick selfie, grimacing at the camera, and hit send before I could second guess myself. *"Don't judge,"* I wrote. *"I warned you I was hungover."*

My hair was a disheveled mess and there were dark circles under my eyes from the late night out with Jayda and Caleb. But hey, this was me - Daniel Ramirez in all my unfiltered glory.

My phone buzzed again almost immediately. I opened the message, expecting a witty retort or playful jab at my disheveled appearance. Instead, what I saw made my heart skip a beat.

"If that's you hungover, then you have nothing to worry about. You look great, Daniel."

I felt a blush creep up my cheeks as I read his words. Before I could even process the compliment, another message came through. It was a selfie of Harald, his face contorted into an exaggerated grimace, his blond hair sticking up at odd angles.

I burst out laughing, the sound echoing through my bedroom. He looked ridiculous, but somehow still managed to be devastatingly handsome. It was clear he was trying to make me feel better about my own less-than-stellar appearance.

"There, now we're even," he wrote. *"Two equally terrible selfies, misery loves company."*

I grinned, my fingers already typing out a response. *"Misery loves company, right? Although I have to say, you wear it well. I look like I got hit by a truck, but you still manage to look like a Calvin Klein underwear model."*

I hit send before I could second guess myself, my heart racing in my chest. Was I flirting with him? I wasn't sure, but something about our easy banter felt natural, like we had known each other for years instead of just a few days.

"A model, huh?" he replied. *"I'll have to add that to my resume in addition to 'bil-*

lionaire philanthropist and mental nutcase'. It has a nice ring to it, don't you think?"

I snorted, shaking my head at his ridiculous joke. *"Oh definitely,"* I typed back. *"I'm sure your family's business ventures and charitable pursuits won't be affected by this terrible selfie. Don't worry, I'll keep it nice and safe so no one else sees it but me."*

His response popped up a few seconds later - a selfie of him in some ornate gilded room, eyes crossed and cheeks puffed out. The text below read: *"You're one to talk, Bedhead! Some of us have to attend fancy meetings, I'll have you know. No rest for the wicked (or the wealthy)."*

We continued to message back and forth, trading quips and jokes like old friends. For a moment, I forgot about my pounding headache and the fact that I had to be at work in a few hours. All that mattered was the easy rapport we had fallen into, the way his messages made me feel like I could be myself without fear of judgment.

* * *

I settled into my cubicle, logging into my computer and preparing for another day of soul-crushing work. But as I started sorting through the endless stack of claims, my phone buzzed with a new message from Harald.

Harald had sent a message hoping my morning was going well. He'd attached a selfie showing him lounging in his bed, wearing what looked like fancy pajamas.

I smiled at his message, noting again how attractive he was. I typed back, snapping a quick selfie of me rolling my eyes. **"Thanks, I'm just getting started but I'm pretty sure the day is going to be terrible as always. The hangover doesn't help either."**

We continued to text throughout the morning, trading jokes and commiserating about our respective workdays. I shared anecdotes about my personal experiences, as well as the issues that weighed on my mind. I opened up about my background growing up in the foster care system, while he confided in me about his family and the mortifying mistake he had committed at a recent charitable event. Every time my phone buzzed with a new message, I felt a little thrill of excitement, eager to see what Harald had to say.

I glanced at the time on my computer. It was already almost noon here in New York, which meant it had to be the middle of the night in Copenhagen. I frowned, typing out a message to Harald.

"Hey, isn't it super late where you are? What are you still doing up texting me?"

His response came a few moments later. *"Ah, you know how it is. Insomnia is a cruel mistress. Plus, I have to admit, I'm enjoying our conversation far too much to stop now."*

I couldn't help but grin at that. It was flattering to think that Harald found me interesting enough to stay up late chatting with. And if I was being honest, I was really enjoying our back-and-forth too.

"Well, I'm happy to keep you company if you can't sleep," I typed back. *"Though you really should try to get some rest. Beauty sleep and all that, you know."*

"Are you saying I need beauty sleep? I'm wounded," Harald replied, adding a crying face emoji for good measure.

I laughed out loud at that, quickly stifling it when I caught Piper glancing over at me curiously.

"Nah, you're pretty enough as is," I wrote, feeling a little surge of boldness. *"I just don't want you to be a sleep-deprived zombie on my account."*

"I appreciate your concern," Harald messaged back. *"But I'd much rather talk to you than stare at my ceiling all night. Besides, this is the most fun I've had in ages."*

I couldn't stop smiling as I read his words. It was crazy to think that I'd only started talking to Harald a short time ago. But already, I felt like we had this amazing connection, like he just got me in a way most people didn't.

"Okay, you twisted my arm," I replied, still grinning. *"What do you want to talk about?"*

"Why anything and everything of course. Can you tell me when your hateful relationship began with pudding?"

* * *

Around lunchtime, Cassandra stormed into my cubicle, her face twisted into a scowl. "Daniel, I need those reports on my desk by the end of the day," she snapped, her voice dripping with disdain. "And try to make them actually readable this time, will you?"

I bit back a retort, forcing a smile onto my face. "Of course, Cassandra. I'll get right on that."

As soon as she was out of earshot, I grabbed my phone and snapped a selfie, my face contorted into an exaggerated grimace. *"Help, I'm being held hostage by a tyrant,"* I wrote, sending the picture to Harald.

His response came a few seconds later - a selfie of him making a sympathetic face, his hand held up in a mock salute. *"Stay strong, soldier. You'll make it through this battle."*

I grinned, feeling some of the tension drain out of my shoulders. Somehow, knowing that Harald was there, even just through a phone screen, made everything seem a little more bearable.

As the day wore on, we continued to exchange messages and selfies, each one more ridiculous than the last. Harald sent a picture of him pretending to be asleep in a meeting, while I responded with a shot of me buried under a mountain of paperwork.

By the time 5 o'clock rolled around, I was actually in a pretty good mood, despite the stress of the day. As I packed up my things to head home, my phone buzzed one last time.

"Until tomorrow, Daniel," Harald had written, attaching a selfie of himself tucked in between luxurious sheets and a soft comforter smiling gently at the camera. *"Thanks for making today suck a little less."*

* * *

I collapse onto my couch after a long, exhausting day at work, feeling completely drained from dealing with Cassandra's incessant demands and the utterly soul-crushing nature of my mind-numbing job. My body sinks into the cushions as I let out a deep sigh, the weight of the day slowly lifting from my shoulders. Just as I'm about to close my eyes and try to relax, allowing myself a brief moment of peace, my phone suddenly buzzes with an incoming message. Glancing at the screen, I see it's from Harald, and a small smile tugs at the corners of my lips despite my weariness.

"Daniel, I'm freaking out. I have this gala event tomorrow and I don't think I can do it. What if I make a mistake again and embarrass myself and my family?" Harald's text reads, the words practically vibrating with his anxiety even through the screen. My heart clenches in sympathy, remembering how he described the last event and the mistake he'd made. I want nothing more than to wrap my arms around him and tell him it'll be okay, that he's stronger than he realizes. I quickly type back a response, hoping my words can provide some measure of comfort and support, even from an ocean away.

"Hey silly, take a deep breath. You've got this, Harald. I know it's scary, but you're going to be great. "

Harald's response comes a few moments later. *"I just keep thinking about the last event. I completely blanked on my speech and said the wrong thing. Everyone was staring at me, judging me. I felt like such a failure. The press will probably have a field day with this too, they always do. I can already imagine the headlines..."*

That sensation hits close to home for me. I've definitely been through times when I disappointed both others and myself. Though I'll admit, dealing with reporters isn't something I've ever faced.

"I get it, trust me. But that was one mistake. It doesn't define you. You're smart, sexy, capable, and you care about these causes. That's what people will see when you speak from the heart."

We continue messaging back and forth, with Harald listing off his various anxieties about the event. From worrying about tripping on stage to forgetting his lines, he seems to have thought of every possible worst-case scenario.

But with each fear he shares, I counter with a reassurance. I remind him of his strengths, his compassion, and his ability to connect with people. I tell him that even if he stumbles, what matters most is that he's trying his best to make a difference in the world.

As our conversation winds down, Harald seems to have calmed down a bit. *"Thank you, Daniel. I don't know what I'd do without you. Talking to you always seems to make me feel better."*

I smile at my phone, feeling a warmth spread through my chest. *"Anytime, Harald. Now go get some rest. You've got a big day ahead of you, and I know you're going to crush it."*

My phone chimes one more time, and my cheeks flush as I read Harald's latest message. *"So on another note, you think I'm sexy, huh?"*

I stare at my phone, my mouth suddenly dry as I try to formulate a response. Did I really call him sexy in my pep talk? I scroll back up through our conversation and sure enough, there it is in black and white. *"You're smart, sexy, capable..."*

I groan, burying my face in my hands. I can't believe I let that slip out. It's not that I don't find Harald attractive - quite the opposite actually. But we've never really flirted like this before. Our conversations have always been strictly in the friend zone.

My mind races as I try to figure out how to respond. Do I play it off as a joke? Pretend it was a typo? Or do I lean into it and flirt back?

After a few moments of internal debate and sheer panic, I decide to go with a lighthearted approach. *"Ha ha, very funny,"* I type back. *"I think someone needs to go to bed before they get too cocky. Wouldn't want that ego of yours getting any bigger."*

I hit send before I can second guess myself, my heart pounding in my chest. I'm not used to this kind of playful banter with Harald, but I have to admit, it's kind of thrilling. I don't think I've felt my heart beat this fast since I was with Alex, and that realization both excites and terrifies me. After everything that happened with my ex, I swore I wouldn't let myself get caught up in these butterflies-in-the-stomach feelings again. Yet here I am, grinning at my phone screen like a lovesick teenager.

A few seconds later, his response pops up on my screen. *"Oh, I'm definitely cocky now. But you're right, I should probably get some beauty sleep. Gotta look my best for all of the adoring public tomorrow. Night, Daniel. And thanks again for everything."*

I can't help but grin at his message, shaking my head in amusement. *"Goodnight, you dork. Sweet dreams,"* I reply, adding a kissy face emoji for good measure.

My heart does a little flip as I hit send, and I can't help but wonder if maybe I'm being too forward. But something about Harald just makes me want to let my guard down, even though every rational part of my brain is screaming at me to be careful. I set my phone on my nightstand, still smiling like an idiot in the darkness of my bedroom. Who would have thought a simple slip of the tongue could lead to such a fun, flirty exchange?

I close my eyes, replaying our conversation in my head. For the first time in a long time, I feel a flutter of excitement in my chest - a hint of possibility that maybe, just maybe, there could be something more than friendship between Harald and me.

But for now, I push those thoughts aside, content to bask in the warm glow of our playful banter. Tomorrow is a new day, and who knows what it might bring?

Chapter 6

Harald

I groaned as I forced myself out of bed, my body protesting the lack of sleep from staying up late talking to Daniel. But even through the haze of exhaustion, I couldn't stop the smile that crept onto my face as I thought about our conversation. Despite my royal obligations and the mountain of meetings ahead of me today, those precious hours we spent messaging back and forth felt worth every moment of fatigue. There was something refreshing about how easily he spoke to me, completely unaware of my title or responsibilities - just two people connecting in the quiet hours of the night.

I stumbled into the kitchen where Ella was already making breakfast, the aroma of fresh coffee and pastries filling the air. She looked up at me with a knowing smirk, her blue eyes twinkling with that sisterly intuition that always made me feel like she could read my mind. The spatula in her hand paused mid-flip as she took in my disheveled appearance and the dark circles under my eyes.

"Well, well, well. Look what the cat dragged in. Late night?"

I rolled my eyes but couldn't hide my grin. "Maybe."

"Mmhmm. And would this have anything to do with a certain someone named Daniel?" She waggled her eyebrows at me suggestively.

I felt my cheeks heat up. "We were just talking, Ells. Getting to know each other better."

She placed a plate of eggs and toast in front of me. "I'm just teasing, Harry. I'm happy for you, really. It's good to see you coming out of your shell and making a connection with someone. I don't think I've seen you make a connection with someone like this in a long time, at least not since you were in school. Even then I'm not so sure, since they knew who you were and that influenced how they acted toward you."

I took a bite of toast, considering her words. She was right - it did feel good to be opening up to Daniel, even if it was just through texts and silly selfies at the moment.

"Thanks, sis. I don't know where this thing with Daniel will go, but...I like talking to him. He makes me laugh and forget about all the pressure and expectations for a little while."

Ella reached over and squeezed my hand. "That's wonderful, Harry. You deserve to have someone like that in your life. Just promise me you'll be careful, okay? I don't want to see you get hurt."

I met her concerned gaze and nodded. "I promise. We're taking things slow, just getting to know each other. But I have a good feeling about him, Ells. A really good feeling."

She smiled at that, and we ate our breakfast in companionable silence, my thoughts drifting to Daniel and the undeniable connection growing between us.

A soft knock at the door drew my attention away from my reveries and I glanced up to see Erik entering the room, a thick portfolio tucked gracefully under his arm. He nodded respectfully to Ella before turning to me with a small smile.

I fidgeted nervously seeing the thick portfolio tucked under his arm. Erik quickly spreads out the portfolio's documents on the table before us.

"Your Highnesses, I apologize for the intrusion, but I have some information about an upcoming event that requires your attention."

My stomach churned at the mention of another social event. Memories of the disastrous fundraiser flooded my mind, and I could feel my palms growing clammy.

"Of course, Erik. What's the event?"" Ella interjected, noticing my growing unease.

Erik continued, oblivious to my rising anxiety. "It's the annual charitable gala, ma'am. It's scheduled for tomorrow, and the royal family's attendance is expected, as always."

Ella nodded, her expression serene. I feel myself beginning to lose control, and Ella reaches over quickly with a gentle expression and grasps my arm lovingly.

"Harry, it's okay. We'll get through this together, just like we always do."

I gulped, struggling to find the words and managing only a faint murmur. "I... I don't know if I can do this, Ells. Not after what happened last time."

"You can, and you will. We'll prepare, we'll practice, and we'll make sure everything goes smoothly. I'll be right there with you, every step of the way."

I manage a nod, and Erik quickly launches into the minutiae of the event - the guest list, the menu, the entertainment. But his words faded into a distant buzz as my mind raced with worst-case scenarios. What if I said the wrong thing again? What if I embarrassed myself in front of all those important people?

My chest tightened, and I could feel my breathing growing shallow. I clenched my fists under the table, trying to ground myself. But the more Erik talked, the more overwhelming it all seemed.

Ella glanced over at me, her brow furrowing with concern. She reached out and gave my hand a gentle squeeze, anchoring me back to the present.

"It sounds like a lovely event, Erik," she said smoothly. "I'm sure Harald and I will do our best to represent the family well."

I nodded mutely, grateful for her intervention. But even as Erik moved on to other topics, I couldn't shake the sense of dread that had settled in the pit of my stomach. Another high-profile event, another opportunity for me to embarrass myself and my family. How was I ever going to survive this?

* * *

Erik

I couldn't avoid noticing the fatigue etched onto Harald's face as I stepped into the room where he and Ella were quietly having their morning meal. He moved sluggishly, his eyes half-open, and he poked at his food without much enthusiasm, barely taking a bite. A pang of worry struck me - Harald had been through so much lately, and it pained me to witness him struggling like this, day after day. I wished there was more I could do to ease his burdens.

As I discreetly observed him, trying not to stare too obviously, I couldn't help but ponder what had him so drained and exhausted. Could it be the stress of the most recent gaffe eating away at him? Or perhaps it was something else entirely, some other worry or problem that he hadn't confided in me about?

A thought abruptly crossed my mind then - could it be that Harald had been up late into the night, conversing with someone? Chatting or texting with a friend, or perhaps something more? The idea sent a twinge of... something unpleasant through me. Jealousy, perhaps? No, that couldn't be accurate. I cared for Harald deeply, and I wanted nothing more than for him to be happy and content, even if his affections and attentions lay elsewhere, with someone else. Still, the notion of him connecting with someone, opening up to them, even if only through a screen, gave me a tiny glimmer of hope amidst my selfish feelings.

Harald had been so consumed lately by his duties, his anxiety, and the weight of his father's expectations constantly bearing down on him. Maybe this new person, whoever they were, was providing him a much-needed outlet - someone he could truly be himself with, without fear of judgment or disappointment. The very thought of Harald finding that kind of solace and comfort warmed my heart, even as I felt the cold tinge of jealousy cut through me. I knew I needed to set aside my own unrequited feelings, and simply be glad that he had found a small slice of happiness, in whatever form it took. Harald deserved that and so much more, even if I could never be the one to give it to him.

I cleared my throat softly, hating to interrupt the siblings' quiet morning together, but knowing I had important news to deliver. "Your Highnesses, I apologize for the intrusion, but I have some information about an upcoming event that requires your attention."

Ella looked up at me with a warm smile, always the picture of grace and poise. "Of course, Erik. What's the event?"

I glanced down at my tablet, double-checking the details. "It's the annual charitable gala, ma'am. It's scheduled for tomorrow, and the royal family's attendance is expected, as always."

As I spoke, I couldn't help but notice Harald's reaction out of the corner of my eye. His already pale face seemed to drain of all remaining color, and his eyes widened with what I could only describe as sheer panic. My heart clenched at the sight, knowing all too well the reasons behind his distress.

Ella, ever the observant and protective sister, immediately reached out and placed a comforting hand on Harald's arm. "Harry, it's okay. We'll get through this together, just like we always do."

Harald swallowed hard, his voice barely above a whisper as he responded. "I... I don't know if I can do this, Ells. Not after what happened last time."

I felt a surge of sympathy for him, recalling the disastrous events of the previous fundraiser all too vividly. The embarrassment, the humiliation, the way his father had berated him afterwards... it was no wonder he was hesitant to put himself in that position again.

Ella's grip on his arm tightened, her voice firm but gentle. "You can, and you will. We'll prepare, we'll practice, and we'll make sure everything goes smoothly. I'll be right there with you, every step of the way."

"It sounds like a lovely event, Erik," Ella said smoothly. "I'm sure Harald and I will do our best to represent the family well."

As I watched the siblings interact, I couldn't help but marvel at the strength of their bond. Ella truly was Harald's rock, his unwavering support system, and I knew that with her by his side, he could face anything. Even so, I silently vowed to do everything in my power to make this gala a success, to shield Harald from any further pain or embarrassment. He deserved nothing less.

* * *

I took a deep breath, straightening my tie in the mirror one last time before heading out to the waiting car with Ella. My stomach churned with anxiety as we rode to the gala, my mind replaying the mortifying mistake from the last event on loop. Ella reached over and squeezed my hand.

"You've got this, Harry. We practiced your speech a dozen times. It's going to be great."

I gave her a tight smile, wishing I had even a fraction of her confidence. "Thanks Ells. I just hope I don't freeze up and forget everything again."

We arrived at the gala to a barrage of flashing cameras. I plastered on my public smile, waving to the press as we made our way inside. Father was already there, speaking with the event organizers. He glanced our way, his expression stern as always. I felt myself shrinking under his critical gaze.

The gala was in full swing, a glittering throng of wealthy donors and influential figures. Servers wove through the crowd with trays of champagne and hors d'oeuvres. I accepted a glass, hoping it would calm my nerves. Ella and I made the rounds, smiling and making polite conversation.

I felt my phone buzz in my pocket and stole a glance at the screen. It was a message from Daniel, reminding me not to worry and just be myself. Despite everything, I felt myself smiling. His words of encouragement from earlier echoed in my mind. I took a fortifying sip of champagne, drawing strength from the knowledge that someone out there believed in me, even if they didn't know the real me.

All too soon, it was time for the speeches. My mouth went dry as I stepped up to the podium, hundreds of expectant faces turned my way. I caught Ella's eye in the crowd and she gave me an encouraging nod. I cleared my throat.

"Good evening, distinguished guests," I began, my voice sounding far more confident than I felt. "It is my great honor to be here tonight in support of the World Wildlife Fund's vital conservation efforts."

I spoke about the importance of protecting endangered species and preserving fragile ecosystems. As I reached the middle of my prepared remarks, I suddenly felt my mind go blank. The words on the teleprompter blurred before my eyes. Panic rose in my throat, that familiar tightness that had plagued me since childhood. My fingers gripped the podium's edge until my knuckles turned white, and I could feel a bead of sweat rolling down my temple. These moments were what my father always warned me about - a Crown Prince should never show weakness, never falter. The weight of centuries of royal composure pressed down on my shoulders as I struggled to maintain my facade.

My eyes darted around the room, searching for something, anything to ground me. That's when I caught sight of my father in the crowd, his brow furrowed in disapproval. The King of Denmark could always sense when I was on the verge of losing control, and the weight of his judgment only intensified the panic rising within me.

I saw Ella next to him, her eyes narrowed as she glared daggers at our father. She knew how his constant criticism affected me, how it chipped away at my already fragile self-esteem. Ella caught my gaze and mouthed, "You can do it," her expression softening with encouragement.

Then I remembered Daniel's message from the night before, the words lighting up my phone screen at 3am when my anxiety had kept me tossing and turning. *"You're going to crush it,"* he had said. *"You're smart, sexy, capable and you care."* Even now, the memory of his earnest encouragement made my chest feel warm, gave me something solid to hold onto. Daniel didn't know he was texting a prince - he just saw me, just Harald, and somehow that made his words mean even more.

I took a deep breath, Daniel's encouragement lending me strength, his words echoing in my mind like a protective shield against my rising anxiety. I abandoned my scripted speech and began to speak extemporaneously, trusting in my genuine passion for conservation rather than the carefully vetted words scrolling across the teleprompter. My hands trembled slightly on the podium, but my voice remained steady as years of royal training kicked in.

"When I was a child, my mother instilled in me a deep love and respect for the natural world," I said, my voice growing stronger. "She taught me that it is our sacred duty to be stewards of this planet and all the creatures who share it with us. Though she is no longer with us, her passion lives on in me."

I spoke about my personal connection to conservation, sharing anecdotes from my childhood adventures exploring the forests and fjords of Denmark. The audience leaned in, engaged by my authenticity.

"We have a choice," I said, coming to my conclusion. "We can be passive observers as species disappear and habitats crumble. Or we can be champions for change, using our voices and our resources to make a difference. I choose the latter. I hope you will join me."

As I stepped back from the podium to enthusiastic applause, I caught Ella's eye. She was beaming with pride, tears glistening on her cheeks. Even my father looked pleasantly surprised.

I felt a rush of elation, hardly able to believe I had managed to pull it off. I messaged Daniel a quick update, letting him know that the speech went well.

Daniel quickly responds: *"Knew you could do it! So proud of you. Celebrate tonight, you deserve it!"*

I grinned, feeling lighter than I had in ages. For the first time in a long time, I felt a flicker of hope. Maybe I could do this after all. Maybe I could be the leader my country needed, while still being true to myself.

Chapter 7

Daniel

I slowly blinked my eyes open, the morning light filtering through the blinds and casting a soft glow across my bedroom. Rolling over, I reached for my phone on the nightstand, my heart skipping a beat when I saw a message from Harald. A smile tugged at the corners of my mouth as I read his words wishing me a goodnight, feeling a warmth spread through my chest.

It feels like our connection is going stronger day by day, evolving from casual banter to something deeper, more meaningful. I find myself eagerly anticipating his messages, savoring each moment of our conversations. There is an undeniable spark between us, a chemistry that transcends the distance and the screens that separates us.

But as I lay there, staring at the ceiling, a mix of excitement and apprehension swirled within me. What did this budding relationship mean for us? Could it be more than just a virtual friendship? I couldn't help but let my mind wander, imagining what it would be like to meet Harald in person, to see if the connection we shared online would translate to real life.

I thought back to my ex, Alex, and how different he was from Harald. Where Alex had been selfish and dishonest, Harald was kind and genuine. He listened to me, supported me, and made me feel valued in a way I hadn't experienced before. I found myself wishing that Harald was here with me, that I could look into his eyes and see if the spark between us was real.

My mind drifted back to the flirty messages Harald and I had exchanged, the way his words made my heart race and my cheeks flush. I couldn't help but imagine what it would be like to be in a relationship with him, to feel desired and cherished again.

I thought about the way Harald always seemed to know just what to say to make me smile, how he could turn even the most mundane topics into engaging conversations. I pictured us staying up late into the night, sharing our hopes and dreams, our fears and vulnerabilities. In my mind's eye, I could see us laughing together, our eyes sparkling with mischief and affection.

I imagined what it would be like to wake up next to him, to feel his arms around me, his breath warm against my skin. I wondered if his touch would ignite a fire within me, if his kisses would leave me breathless and aching for more. The mere thought of it sent a shiver down my spine, a longing so intense it almost took my breath away.

But even as I allowed myself to indulge in these fantasies, a part of me hesitated. After everything I had been through with Alex, the betrayal and the heartbreak, could I really open myself up to that kind of vulnerability again? Could I trust Harald not to hurt me the way Alex had? My heart had been shattered once before when I ventured down this path, and I doubted it possessed the resilience to endure such agony a second time.

And yet, there was something about Harald that made me want to take that leap of faith. The way he made me feel seen and understood, the way he brought light into my life just by being himself. I couldn't help but wonder if maybe, just maybe, he could be the one to heal my battered heart.

Rolling out of bed, I padded over to the window and gazed out at the bustling city below. My heart raced as I allowed myself to dream, to hope that maybe, just maybe, Harald could be the one I'd been searching for all along. But a part of me hesitated, afraid to let myself fall too hard, too fast. I knew I needed to be cautious, to protect my heart from another devastating blow.

* * *

Jayda pounded on my bedroom door, her voice muffled but insistent. "Daniel, get your lazy ass out of bed! It's farmer's market day and you promised to come with us!"

I groaned, burying my face in my pillow. "Five more minutes," I mumbled, my voice rough with sleep.

"Oh no you don't," Jayda said, barging into my room without invitation. She yanked the covers off me, ignoring my yelp of protest. "Up and at 'em, sunshine. Caleb's already waiting in the living room."

I sat up, rubbing my eyes and glaring at her. "You're a menace, you know that?"

Jayda grinned, completely unrepentant. "You love me anyway. Now hurry up and get dressed, I want to get there before all the good stuff is gone."

Twenty minutes later, I found myself trailing behind Jayda and Caleb as we navigated the crowded aisles of the farmer's market. The air was thick with the scent of fresh produce and the chatter of eager shoppers.

I couldn't help but chuckle as I watched Caleb blend seamlessly into the crowd of hipsters, his beanie and thick-rimmed glasses making him look right at home. He stopped at a stall selling artisanal cheeses, engaging the vendor in an animated discussion about the merits of aged gouda versus brie.

Jayda, on the other hand, stood out like a sore thumb in her all-black ensemble and combat boots. She eyed the organic kale with suspicion, as if it might leap out and attack her at any moment. The morning sun glinted off her silver nose ring as she wrinkled her face at the leafy greens, making me smile at how out of place she looked among the yoga moms and health food enthusiasts. Even the vendor seemed unsure how to approach her, probably wondering if she'd wandered in by mistake from some underground punk concert.

"Remind me again why we're here?" she grumbled, crossing her arms over her chest.

"Because it's good for us to eat healthy sometimes," Caleb said, handing her a reusable tote bag. "And because Daniel promised to make us his famous veggie stir-fry for dinner tonight."

I grinned, grabbing a bunch of carrots from a nearby stall. "That's right, and I need the freshest ingredients to make it perfect."

Jayda rolled her eyes, but I could see the hint of a smile tugging at the corners of her mouth. "Fine, but if you try to sneak any of that kale into my portion, I'll never forgive you. Don't forget I know where you sleep."

We continued to make our way through the market, Caleb excitedly pointing out new finds while Jayda trailed behind, looking like she'd rather be anywhere else. But despite her grumbling, I knew she was secretly enjoying herself. After all, there was nothing quite like spending a Saturday morning with your best friends, even if it meant enduring a little bit of healthy eating along the way.

After finishing up at the farmer's market, Jayda suggested we grab some lunch at a nearby ramen place. The idea of a steaming bowl of noodles and rich broth sounded perfect, so Caleb and I readily agreed.

We settled into a cozy booth, the savory aroma of simmering pork and miso filling the air. As we waited for our orders, I couldn't resist pulling out my phone to reread the messages Harald had sent me the day before. A smile crept onto my face as I scrolled through our conversation, chuckling at his witty remarks and feeling a warmth spread through my chest at his words of encouragement.

"Okay, spill," Jayda said, her eyes narrowing as she leaned across the table. "What's got you grinning like a lovesick puppy?"

I felt my cheeks heat up, caught off guard by her directness. "What? Nothing, I'm just reading something funny," I stammered, quickly locking my phone screen and sliding it face-down onto the table. But I knew Jayda wouldn't buy that excuse - she could read me like a book and had an uncanny ability to sense when I was hiding something, especially when it came to matters of the heart.

Jayda raised an eyebrow, clearly not buying my excuse. "Mhmm, sure. You've been attached to that phone all morning, and I haven't seen you smile this much since before..." She trailed off, her expression softening. "Since before Alex."

I winced at the mention of my ex, the familiar pang of hurt and betrayal twisting in my gut. But as I looked back down at my phone, at the messages from Harald, I realized the pain wasn't as sharp as it used to be. Something had shifted, and I knew it had everything to do with the unexpected...whatever you want to call it I'd found online.

"It's nothing serious," I said, trying to downplay the significance of my connection with Harald. "I've just been talking to someone I met on that mental health forum. He's really easy to talk to, and he makes me laugh."

Jayda's eyes lit up with interest, that familiar mischievous glint I'd come to know so well over the years. She leaned closer, her dark painted nails drumming against the surface of the tabletop. "Oh really? And does this mystery man have a name?" I could already tell from her expression that I wasn't going to hear the end of this anytime soon.

I hesitated, feeling strangely protective of my budding relationship with Harald. But as I looked at Jayda and Caleb, at the genuine curiosity and concern in their eyes, I knew I could trust them with this new part of my life. After all, they'd been there through everything with Alex, through my darkest moments, and never once judged me. If anyone deserved to know about this unexpected bright spot in my life, it was them. Still, I found myself unconsciously fiddling with my phone case, trying to find the right words to explain something I barely understood myself.

"His name is Harald," I said, a small smile tugging at my lips. "He's from Denmark, and he's been going through some stuff too. We just kind of clicked, you know?" I felt my cheeks warm as I thought about our conversations, how easily we'd connected over our shared struggles. "It's different from what I had with Alex - there's no pressure, no games. Harald actually listens when I talk, and he understands what it's like to deal with... with the darker stuff. Plus, he's got this ridiculous sense of humor that makes me laugh every time I message him."

Jayda reached across the table, squeezing my hand with that gentle reassurance that always made me feel safe. "I'm happy for you, Daniel. You deserve to have someone who makes you smile like that." Her dark-painted lips curved into a knowing grin, and I could tell she meant every word. After everything that happened with Alex, seeing her so supportive of my new connection with Harald made my heart feel lighter than it had in months.

Caleb cleared his throat loudly, interrupting my thoughts. "Okay, as touching as this moment is, can we please eat already? I'm starving over here!"

Jayda rolled her eyes, but I could see the smile she was trying to hide beneath her dark lipstick. "Way to ruin the moment, babe. But you're right, we should dig in before the noodles get all soggy." She reached for her chopsticks, giving Caleb that look of playful exasperation I'd seen a thousand times before. It was the same look she always got when he said exactly what we were all thinking, just with zero filter. I had to admit though, the smell of our lunch was making my stomach growl too.

I laughed, feeling the tension drain from my shoulders. "Alright, alright, let's eat. I didn't brave that farmer's market just to let this ramen go to waste." The memory of pushing through the crowded stalls and haggling with that grumpy vendor over the fresh noodles was still fresh in my mind. At least the epic quest for authentic ingredients had been worth it - my legendary veggie stir-fry was going to be amazing.

As we slurped our noodles and sipped the savory broth, the conversation flowed easily between us. Caleb regaled us with stories from his latest hipster adventures, while Jayda snarked about the pretentious art show she'd been dragged to by her coworkers. I found myself chiming in with my own tales of annoying customers and office drama, feeling lighter than I had in weeks.

"Oh man, remember that time Daniel accidentally cc'ed the entire office on that email about his boss's bad breath?" Caleb snickered, nearly choking on a piece of pork belly.

"How could I forget?" Jayda cackled, her eyes sparkling with mirth. "I thought he was going to have an aneurysm when he realized he had accidentally copied the entire office!"

I groaned, burying my face in my hands as the embarrassing memory resurfaced. "Don't remind me! I thought I was going to get fired on the spot when I realized what I'd done. My heart nearly stopped and I could feel the blood draining from my face. Thank god for HR and their 'three strikes' policy or else I would have been out on my ass faster than you can say 'unemployed'. Now that I think of it, that whole mortifying incident might be the source of Cassandra's seething hatred for me. She's never quite looked at me the same since then, her beady eyes always narrowed in displeasure whenever they land on me."

We dissolved into laughter, the sound echoing off the walls of the small restaurant. As I looked at my friends, their faces flushed with joy and ramen steam, I felt a surge of gratitude wash over me. No matter what life threw at me - cheating exes, soul-crushing jobs, or mental health struggles - I knew I could always count on Jayda and Caleb to have my back.

And now, with Harald's unexpected presence in my life, I couldn't help but feel a flicker of hope for the future. Maybe, just maybe, I was finally ready to start healing and let myself be open to the possibility of something new.

But for now, I was content to sit here with my best friends, slurping noodles and trading jokes like we didn't have a care in the world. And in that moment, with the savory scent of ramen in the air and laughter on my lips, I knew that no matter what happened next, I was exactly where I needed to be.

C.G. Macington

74

Act II

Chapter 8

Harald

I stretch out on the plush sofa in my private sitting room, a contented smile playing at my lips as I think back on last night's gala. For once, I didn't make a fool of myself or bring shame upon my family. Quite the opposite, actually. My speech went off without a hitch, the words flowing from a place of genuine passion rather than a carefully crafted script. The audience seemed to respond to my authenticity, their applause and kind words afterward filling me with a newfound sense of confidence.

As I relive the moment, Daniel's words of encouragement echo in my mind. It's almost as if he was there with me, his steadfast belief in my abilities like a comforting presence by my side. My heart swells with gratitude for this man who, in such a short time, has become an invaluable source of support and understanding.

But it's more than just gratitude I feel. With each passing day, each shared message and inside joke, I find myself falling deeper and deeper for Daniel. The realization both thrills and terrifies me. As the Crown Prince, my life has always been one of duty and restraint, but Daniel makes me want to throw caution to the wind and follow my heart.

My soul yearns to be in Daniel's presence, to witness the radiant beauty of his smile and have my heart sing at the melodious sound of his laughter without the cold, impersonal barrier of a phone screen separating us. Though I've never had the pleasure of hearing Daniel's voice in person, I imagine it would envelop my senses - deep and comforting, yet tinged with an alluring sultriness that sends shivers down my spine. I fantasize about reaching out to caress his skin, to have my fingertips dance across the smooth warmth of his body and feel the comforting strength of his arms enfolding me in a loving embrace. It's an all-consuming desire, a desperate longing, unlike anything I've experienced before. Thoughts of him pervade my mind from the moment I wake until I drift off to sleep at night, my dreams haunted by tantalizing visions of what it would be like to finally be together.

And yet, a part of me hesitates. What if Daniel doesn't feel the same way? What if the connection we've forged online doesn't translate to the real world? The thought of losing him, of jeopardizing our friendship, fills me with an icy dread.

But as I gaze out the window at the sprawling gardens below, I can't help but imagine Daniel by my side, his hand in mine as we explore the winding paths together. The image fills me with a longing so intense it steals my breath. I know it's a risk, but it's one I'm willing to take. For a chance at true happiness, at love, I'd face a thousand uncertainties.

A sharp knock at the door startles me from my Daniel-infused reverie. I scramble to sit up straight, hastily smoothing down my rumpled shirt as Ella strides into the room. She takes one look at my flustered state and snorts, a knowing smirk playing at her lips.

"Hey sis," I stammer, trying to regain my composure. "How are you doi-"

"Cut the crap, Harry," Ella interrupts, plopping down beside me on the sofa with a dramatic sigh. She fixes me with one of her patented piercing stares, the kind that makes me feel like she can see right through to my soul. One perfectly sculpted eyebrow arches up in amusement as her lips curl into a knowing smirk. "You've got that dopey, lovesick puppy dog look on your face again. The one that screams 'I'm a fool in love'. Don't even try to deny it - I can read you like an open book, brother dear. So spill it. Don't tell me you've gone and fallen completely head over heels for this Daniel guy already."

I feel the heat rising in my cheeks, a telltale blush giving away my secret like a neon sign flashing above my head. I open my mouth to deny it, to brush off her accusation with a casual laugh and wave of my hand, but the words stick in my throat, refusing to cooperate. There's no point in lying to Ella - she's always been able to see right through me as if I'm made of the clearest glass. My sister has an uncanny ability to read me like an open book, every emotion laid bare on the pages for her keen eyes to absorb.

"I...I think I have," I admit softly, my gaze dropping to my lap as I fidget with the edge of my sleeve, a nervous habit I've never managed to break. "I know it's crazy, we've never even met in person, we haven't even talked on the phone, but I can't help how I feel. He just...he gets me, Ells. In a way no one else ever has." My voice grows stronger as I continue, finding comfort in finally voicing these feelings that have been building up inside me with no release. "When I message with Daniel, I don't feel like the Crown Prince or father's disappointment - I'm just Harald. Just me. And somehow, that seems to be enough for him."

Ella's expression softens, her teasing smirk melting into a gentle smile that reminds me so much of our mother it makes my chest ache. She reaches out to take my hand, giving it a reassuring squeeze that some-how manages to anchor me in the moment, just like she's done since we were children. The familiar warmth of her touch helps steady my racing thoughts.

"Oh, Harry," she sighs, her voice laced with affection. "I've been watch-ing you this past week, seeing the way your face lights up every time your phone buzzes. I've never seen you like this before, so...happy. So alive."

I glance up at her, surprised by the earnestness in her tone. Ella's always been my fiercest protector, the one person I could count on to have my back no matter what. But to hear her so openly supportive of my feelings for Daniel, it means more than I can express. My throat tightens with emotion as I remember all the times she's stood between me and Father's disapproval, how she's held me through panic attacks and sleepless nights. Even now, she's looking at me with that same unwavering love that's been my lifeline since Mother died, and I find myself wondering how I got lucky enough to have a sister like her.

"You really think so?" I ask, hating the note of vulnerability in my voice.

"I know so," Ella replies firmly, giving my hand another squeeze. "And if this Daniel is even half as amazing as you make him out to be, then he'd be a fool not to fall for you too."

I let out a shaky laugh, feeling a weight lift from my shoulders at Ella's words. She always knows just what to say to ease my fears and bolster my confidence.

"Thanks, sis," I murmur, pulling her into a tight hug. "I don't know what I'd do without you."

"Probably pine away in your room like a lovesick puppy," Ella teases, her voice muffled against my shoulder. "But lucky for you, you've got me to keep you in line. God knows you'd just sit there overthinking everything until your brain short-circuits." She pulls back and gives me that knowing look she's perfected over the years - the one that says she can see right through my anxious thoughts. "And we both know how well that usually turns out for you, big brother."

I let out a laugh, shaking my head at Ella's playful jab. She's right, of course. Left to my own devices, I'd probably work myself into a panic attack trying to figure out the perfect way to tell Daniel how I feel. But with Ella's support, I feel a newfound sense of determination. I take a deep breath, trying to steady my racing heart as I meet her gaze.

"I want to meet him, Ells," I confess, my voice barely above a whisper. "In person. I want to see his smile, hear his laugh, hold his hand...I want it all. But I'm terrified. What if he doesn't feel the same way? What if I ruin everything by asking?" The words tumble out in a rush, my deepest fears laid bare.

Ella's expression softens, her eyes filled with understanding. "Oh, Harry," she sighs, reaching out to brush a stray lock of hair from my forehead. "I know it's scary, putting yourself out there like that. But you can't let fear hold you back from something that could be truly amazing."

I nod, swallowing hard against the lump in my throat. "I know, I know. But how do I even bring it up? I can't exactly just blurt out 'Hey, I know we've never met, but I'm kind of in love with you, want to grab coffee sometime?'" I let out a humorless laugh, running a hand through my hair in frustration.

Ella purses her lips, considering for a moment before her face lights up with an idea. "Why don't you start with a phone call?" she suggests, her tone gentle but encouraging. "You said you've never actually talked on the phone before, right? So maybe that's a good first step. See how it feels to actually hear his voice, have a real conversation. And if it goes well, then you can bring up the idea of meeting in person."

I mull over her words, feeling a flicker of hope spark in my chest. A phone call. It's not as daunting as jumping straight to a face-to-face meeting, but it's still a step forward. A chance to deepen our connection beyond the confines of a screen.

"That's...actually a really good idea," I admit, a small smile tugging at the corners of my mouth. "I think I could handle a phone call."

Ella grins, giving my shoulder a playful shove before standing up to leave the room. "Of course it's a good idea, I came up with it," she teases, her eyes sparkling with mischief. "But seriously, Harry, you've got this. Just be yourself, and let things unfold naturally."

With Ella's departure, a whirlwind of emotions consumes me. Speaking to Daniel on the phone simultaneously thrills and terrifies me. Our effortless online rapport has become second nature, but the notion of hearing his voice sends my pulse skyrocketing.

Imagining myself tongue-tied and flustered fills me with dread. Concerns plague me that our virtual connection won't survive the transition to a live discussion. Insecurities and uncertainties swarm my brain, the what-ifs relentless in their assault.

Yet Ella's comforting reassurances echo in my mind, her steadfast confidence in me a beacon. I know she's correct - I can't allow anxiety to impede me, not with such a precious opportunity at stake. Inhaling deeply to compose myself, I summon Daniel's info on my phone.

My heart pounds in my chest as I stare at Daniel's contact on my phone screen, my thumb hovering over the call button. Ella's words echo in my mind, urging me to take this leap of faith. Before I can second-guess myself, I hit the button and bring the phone to my ear, my breath catching in my throat as it starts to ring.

One ring. Two. Three. With each unanswered tone, my anxiety builds, a knot forming in the pit of my stomach. Maybe this was a mistake. Maybe he's busy, or asleep, or just doesn't want to talk to me. I'm about to hang up, ready to chalk it up as a failed attempt, when suddenly...

"Hello?" Daniel's voice fills my ear, warm and slightly breathless, as if he'd rushed to answer the call.

For a moment, I'm speechless, my mind going blank at the sound of his voice. It's different than I imagined, deeper and richer, with a slight rasp that sends shivers down my spine. I clear my throat, trying to find my words.

"H-hey, Daniel," I manage, cringing at the way my voice cracks nervously. *"It's Harald. I hope I'm not catching you at a bad time?"*

There's a pause, and for a heart-stopping second, I'm sure he's going to say yes, to politely brush me off and end the call. My fingers tighten around the phone, and I can hear my own rapid heartbeat drumming in my ears. But then I hear the smile in his voice as he replies, *"No, not at all! I'm actually really glad you called. It's great to finally hear your voice."* The warmth in his tone makes my chest feel light, and I release a breath I didn't even realize I was holding. It's such a relief after what feels like an eternity of texting to finally hear that genuine enthusiasm, even if my royal status still hangs between us like an invisible wall.

Relief washes over me, a giddy smile spreading across my face as Daniel's warm voice fills my ear. My heart flutters in my chest like a caged bird finally set free. *"Yeah, I've been wanting to call for a while now,"* I admit, feeling a blush heat my cheeks as I pace nervously across my private study. *"I just wasn't sure if...I mean, I didn't want to overstep or anything."* The words tumble out before I can stop them, and I silently curse my royal upbringing that makes me second-guess even the simplest interactions.

Daniel lets out a soft laugh, the sound warming me from the inside out like rays of sunlight breaking through storm clouds. *"Trust me, you're not overstepping,"* he assures me, his words carrying that hint of playful attitude I've grown so fond of. *"I've been hoping you'd call, too. Texting is great and all, but there's something special about actually talking to someone, you know?"* His voice has this magnetic quality to it that makes me sink deeper into my leather sofa.

"Definitely," I agree, relaxing back against the sofa cushions as the initial nervousness starts to fade away. *"It's nice to put a voice to the face, so to speak."*

We fall into easy conversation then, the words flowing as naturally as if we'd known each other for years rather than weeks. Daniel tells me about his day with Jayda and Caleb and a practical joke that they played on Caleb that has me laughing so hard my sides ache. In turn, I share stories from my own life, carefully editing out any mentions of my royal status. For now, I just want to be Harald - not the Crown Prince, not the heir to the throne, just a guy talking to someone he cares about.

I open up to Daniel about my childhood with Ella, sharing cherished memories of the mischief and adventures we got into as young siblings. The laughter, the inside jokes, the music we used to listen to together just to torture our father, the unbreakable bond - it all comes pouring out as

I recount those carefree early days. But then my voice grows heavier as I describe being sent away to boarding school, ripped from the comfort and familiarity of home at such a tender age. I confess the deep loneliness that haunted me there, the anguish of realizing that no one truly wanted to know the real me hiding behind my family name and wealth. They only saw a prince, not a person. As I bare these vulnerable parts of my past to Daniel, I feel the weight of those memories lift ever so slightly, grateful to finally have someone who cares to listen.

I tell Daniel about the event I had to attend the previous night. I explain how nervous and anxious I was feeling beforehand, dreading the whole affair. But then I tell him how his encouraging words to me echoed in my mind, bolstering my resolve. I could hear his voice telling me that I was stronger than I knew, that I could handle whatever challenges came my way. And with those words of support ringing in my ears, I found the courage within myself to walk into that event with my head held high, feeling truly capable for perhaps the first time. I express to Daniel how much his belief in me has come to mean, and how grateful I am to have him in my corner.

The conversation turns to previous relationships, and as Daniel opens up to me about his past, I feel my heart break for him. His voice wavers slightly as he recounts the painful memories of his breakup with Alex, the raw emotion still evident even after all this time.

"I thought he was the one, you know?" Daniel confesses, his words heavy with the weight of his heartache. *"I gave him everything - my heart, my trust, my future. And he just...threw it all away like it meant nothing."*

I can hear the catch in his throat as he describes coming home to find Alex in bed with another man, the betrayal cutting him to the core. But it's when he starts talking about the aftermath that I feel my own eyes start to sting with unshed tears.

"I just...I couldn't see a way out," Daniel admits, his voice barely above a whisper. *"The pain was so intense, so all-consuming, that I couldn't imagine living with it for another second. I just wanted it to end."*

My chest tightens as he recounts the desperation that led him to attempt to take his own life, the hopelessness that convinced him there was no other escape from the agony of heartbreak. I want to reach through the phone and pull him into my arms, to hold him close and promise him that he'll never feel that alone again.

But even in the midst of such darkness, there were glimmers of light. Daniel's voice softens as he talks about Jayda and Caleb, the unwavering support and love they showed him in his lowest moments.

"They never gave up on me," he says, a note of wonder in his tone. *"Even when I had given up on myself, they were there, holding me up and reminding me that I was loved and needed in this world."*

I feel a surge of gratitude towards these two people I've never met, these guardian angels who helped guide Daniel back from the edge of despair. I make a silent vow to myself that if I'm ever lucky enough to meet them in person, I'll thank them from the bottom of my heart for being there when he needed them most.

As Daniel finishes sharing his story, I feel a wave of empathy wash over me. His strength and resilience in the face of such heartbreak is truly inspiring. I take a deep breath, steeling myself to open up about my own struggles with relationships.

"I've never really had a serious relationship," I confess, my voice soft and vulnerable. *"Growing up, my social status made it nearly impossible to date. I was always worried that if I did, they would just be doing it for the money or the prestige. And even more than that, I was terrified it would get back to my father."*

I pause, swallowing hard against the lump that forms in my throat at the mention of my father. Daniel waits patiently, giving me the space to gather my thoughts.

"I've never been able to come out of the closet, not publicly anyway. My father, he's... he's not exactly accepting of that kind of thing. Ella knows, of course, and she loves me just the same."

I can hear Daniel's sharp intake of breath on the other end of the line, and for a moment, I'm afraid he'll pull away, that this revelation will be too much for our fledgling connection to bear. But instead, his voice comes through, warm and understanding.

"Oh, Harald," he murmurs, his tone filled with empathy. *"I'm so sorry you've had to carry that burden alone for so long. I can't even imagine how difficult that must be, feeling like you can't be your true self out of fear."*

Tears prick at the corners of my eyes at his words, and I blink them back, grateful for his compassion. *"It's been hard,"* I admit, my voice cracking slightly. *"I want to come out, to live openly and honestly. But I'm terrified of what my father will do if he finds out. He's not exactly known for his tolerance or understanding."*

I let out a shaky sigh, running a hand through my hair as I pace the length of my study. *"Sometimes I feel like I'm suffocating under the weight of all these expectations and secrets. Like I'll never be able to break free and just be...me."*

Daniel's voice comes through the phone, soft and sincere. *"Hey, I know we haven't known each other for very long, but I want you to know that you have me now, okay? You don't have to carry all of this alone anymore. I'm here for you, whenever you need to talk or vent or just...not feel so alone in all of this."*

His words wash over me like a soothing balm, easing the ache in my chest that I've carried for so long. Tears prick at the corners of my eyes, and I blink them back, overwhelmed by the simple kindness of his offer.

"Thank you, Daniel," I murmur, my voice thick with emotion. *"You have no idea how much that means to me. I've never really had anyone to confide in about all of this before, besides Ella. It's...it's a relief to know that I have you in my corner now, too."*

I can practically hear the smile in his voice as he replies, *"Anytime, Harry. Is it okay if I call you that?"*

"Of course, Daniel. I reserve that privilege for those I truly trust and care about. And I believe you've earned a place in that inner circle."

The line goes quiet for a moment as we both take in where this conversation has gone. Sensing the need for a change of subject, Daniel clears his throat and asks in a playful tone, *"So, I have to ask...does all of this secrecy and hiding mean that you're a virgin? I mean, it's totally cool if you are, I'm just curious."*

I let out a surprised laugh, caught off guard by the sudden shift in topic. *"No, definitely not,"* I assure him, shaking my head even though he can't see me. *"I went to an all-boys boarding school, remember? Let's just say that there were plenty of opportunities for...experimentation."*

Daniel chuckles, and I can picture the mischievous glint in his eye. *"Oh, I bet there were,"* he teases, his voice dripping with innuendo. *"Care to share any juicy details?"*

I grin, feeling a blush heat my cheeks at the memories that flood my mind. *"Maybe another time,"* I demur, my tone light and flirtatious. *"A gentleman never kisses and tells, after all."*

Daniel laughs, the sound rich and warm in my ear. *"It's okay, Harry, I've had my fair share of men too. I guess we're even on that front."*

His words send a delicious thrill through my body, my mind instantly conjuring up vivid images of Daniel entwined with other men, his gorgeous tanned skin glistening with a sheen of sweat as he moves sensually against them. I can almost hear the sounds of passion, the moans and gasps filling the air. I swallow hard, my mouth suddenly dry and my pants feeling tighter, trying to push the provocative thoughts away and focus on the conversation at hand, but the tantalizing visuals linger at the edges of my consciousness.

"I wish I could meet you in person," Daniel says suddenly, his voice soft and wistful. *"I mean, I know we haven't known each other for very long, but...I feel like we have this connection, you know? Like we just...get each other."*

My heart leaps into my throat at his words, pounding so hard I'm sure he must be able to hear it through the phone. The thought of meeting Daniel in person, of being able to see his face and hear his voice without the barrier of technology between us...it's both exhilarating and terrifying.

I take a deep breath, trying to steady my racing pulse as I reply, *"What if...what if that was possible?"*

There's a pause on the other end of the line, and for a moment, I'm afraid I've overstepped, that I've misread the situation entirely. But then Daniel's voice comes through again, tentative but hopeful.

"How? I mean, you're in Denmark, and I'm in New York. It's not exactly a quick trip to the corner store."

I hesitate for a moment, my mind racing as I try to come up with a plausible excuse. I can't exactly tell him the truth - that as the Crown Prince, I could hop on a private jet and be in New York in a matter of hours. But I also can't bear the thought of letting this opportunity slip through my fingers.

"Well, my family actually owns some property in New York," I say carefully, choosing my words with deliberate care. *"I've been meaning to go check on it for a while now, make sure everything is running smoothly. I could...I could make a trip out there, if you wanted to meet up."*

I can hear the excitement in Daniel's voice as he stumbles over his words. *"That would be...I mean, yeah, that sounds great! I would love to meet up with you if you're going to be in town. I can show you the sights and we can get to know each other better...in person."*

I can't help but grin at his enthusiasm, my own heart racing with anticipation. *"Okay, let me look into it and see what I can arrange,"* I tell him, trying to keep my tone casual even as my fingers fly across the keyboard of my laptop, typing out an email to Erik.

Subject: Urgent Travel Request

Erik,

Please have the jet fueled and ready for departure to New York first thing tomorrow morning. I have some urgent business to attend to there.

Make all the necessary arrangements for my arrival and accommodations. This trip is of the utmost importance.

Regards,

Harald

I hit send on the email and turn my attention back to the phone call, my mind already racing ahead to the possibility of seeing Daniel in person. *"I'll let you know as soon as I have everything sorted out,"* I promise him, my voice soft and sincere. *"I'm really looking forward to meeting you, Daniel."*

"Me too, Harry," he replies, and I can hear the smile in his voice. *"I can't wait to see you."*

As I glance at the clock, I realize with a start that Daniel and I have been on the phone for nearly five hours. The time has flown by, lost in the depths of our conversation, our laughter, our shared secrets and vulnerabilities. It feels like we've known each other for years, not mere weeks.

My phone suddenly chirps, the low battery warning flashing across the screen. I chuckle, shaking my head in disbelief. *"Daniel, I hate to cut this short, but my phone is about to die on me. I should probably let it charge before it completely shuts down."*

Daniel's warm laughter fills my ear, sending a pleasant shiver down my spine. *"Wow, five hours? I can't remember the last time I talked to someone for that long. I guess time really does fly when you're enjoying yourself."*

"It certainly does," I agree, a soft smile playing at the corners of my lips. *"I could talk to you for hours more and never get bored."*

"Me too, Harry," Daniel murmurs, his voice low and intimate. *"I wish I could be there with you right now. I wish I could fall asleep in your arms, feeling safe and cherished and...home."*

My breath catches in my throat at his words, my heart swelling with an emotion I can't quite name. *"I wish that too, Daniel,"* I whisper, my voice rough with longing. *"More than anything."*

We lapse into silence for a moment, the weight of our feelings hanging heavy in the air between us. Finally, I clear my throat, breaking the spell. *"I should let you get some rest. It's late there, isn't it? It's already 4am here."*

"Yeah, I suppose I should try to get some sleep," Daniel agrees reluctantly. *"But I'll be dreaming of you, Harry."*

"Sweet dreams, my dear Daniel," I murmur, the endearment slipping from my lips before I can stop it. *"I'll talk to you tomorrow."*

"Goodnight, Harry," Daniel whispers, his voice soft and tender. *"Thank you for tonight. For everything."*

I hang up the phone, my heart full to bursting with the depth of my feelings for this man who has so quickly become such an integral part of my life. As I plug my phone in to charge, I can't help but smile, already counting down the hours until I can hear his voice again.

Chapter 9

Daniel

"Morning, everyone!" I say, yawning as I stumble out of my room. Jayda and Caleb are practically glued to each other on the couch watching some obscure anime flashing on the tv screen, all cuddled up under a blanket they've somehow managed to split between them.

Jayda springs up beside Caleb, planting a quick kiss on his lips, then she looks over at me. "Morning, sleepyhead! How was your night?"

I can't stop myself from smiling like an idiot. "It was fantastic, Harald and I chatted for five hours nonstop! He's incredible and his voice is absolutely dreamy and he's so thoughtful and attentive and sweet and..."

Jayda laughs and gestures to cut me off. "Hold up, let's circle back. You actually talked to Harald? Like, real-time human interaction using your phone—not some fake profile or catfish situation?"

"Five hours straight of it!" I exclaim excitedly, buzzing with energy as I step closer to the couch. Jayda's features melt into an affectionate grin when I sink onto the cushions beside her, careful to avoid the blanket draped across their laps. "But really—it was mind-blowing," I continue after a beat, my words tumbling out fast. "His voice is all rich and velvety, like melted chocolate." I pause to catch my breath, adding with a quiet chuckle, "Plus he's got that way of listening that makes you feel like you're the only person in the world."

Jayda sinks deeper into the sofa, her gaze gleaming playfully at my overflowing enthusiasm. "Sounds dreamy. So now that we've covered how amazing your chat was," she teases, smooth voice curling with amusement, "maybe we could discuss what you actually found out about the guy?"

"Right yeah, so Harald's in... like, the family corporation thing. Mega corporate environment, he spends a lot of time in stuffy budget meetings and at charitable events." I tugged a cushion into my lap, plucking loose threads from the corner. "His father's a total nightmare—sky-high demands, impossible standards. Turns out we both drew the short straw with family. He got toxic, I got..." My voice trailed off, thumb rubbing the fabric's worn spot where stuffing peeked through.

Caleb snorted into his coffee. "So you're dating a nepo baby?"

"Talking to," Jayda corrected, swatting his arm. "What else?"

I shrugged. "He's into weird Danish punk bands, apparently they really bug his dad so both him and his sister take every opportunity to use it against him. We both hate kale." My knee bounced as I fought the urge to check my phone. "And he's coming to New York soon. For work."

The porcelain mug burned my palms as Jayda leaned closer, her smirk widening in that dangerous way that always preceded a line of questioning capable of unraveling me. My stomach flipped when she drummed black-painted nails against her coffee-stained Nirvana tee.

"Work or *work*?" Her voice dripped with innuendo, crescent-moon eyebrows bouncing like she'd just cracked some secret code.

Caleb didn't bother looking up from his avocado toast. "Translation—is this rich boy swinging through JFK to sign merger papers, or dick papers?"

Coffee coated my throat like sludge, the half-trapped mouthful making me sputter and gag. "Jesus, can you two contain your collective porn brain for five seconds. Not everyone is as horny as the two of you!"

Jayda laughs and snatches my phone from my hands, quickly opening up my chat history with Harald. "Oh my would you look at these photos and these texts" she singsonged, tilting the screen for Caleb. "Danny you dog, such a shameless flirt too!"

I snatched my phone away forcefully, wincing as it left a dent in my palm. "I'll take that back, thank you very much," I retorted, trying to maintain a semblance of dignity. "And I will have you know, I am not a shameless flirt. I am a sophisticated and refined gentleman!" I added, chuckling as Jayda appraised me with a skeptical gaze and let out a snort.

"So tell me, Mr. Refined Gentleman, what's your plan if this guy turns out to be legitimate? How do you intend to handle a real relationship?" Caleb chimes in, his attention fixed on the breakfast in front of him.

"Don't know. Don't care. Just…" The pillow tumbled to the floor as I stood, suddenly needing to move. "It's nice. Not being treated like I'm made of glass for once. Let me just be happy with what I've got, at least for now."

Caleb's beanie slipped sideways as he tilted his head. "He know about what happened with Alex?"

My mouth went dry but the words kept coming, sharp and raw like picking at a half-healed scab. "Yeah, he knows everything. Not just the Alex-shaped dumpster fire.' My fingers found the edge of my sleeve, twisting the worn fabric. 'The hospital stay. The…' I made a jagged slash motion across my left forearm, thumbnail catching too hard on skin. 'The Bad Year™."

Jayda's iced coffee hit the table with a clatter. "Danny, Jesus—"

Caleb froze mid-sip, his chai latte suspended halfway to the chipped lipstick stain on the mug's rim. I watched understanding click through them both like a padlock snapping shut—Jayda's manicured hand flying to her mouth, Caleb's Adam's apple bobbing as he swallowed wrong.

The old scars itched beneath my sweater. I forced a shrug, pulse hammering where the zipper of my hoodie dug into my collarbone. "Relax, it's not like I showed him the scar collection. Yet." The joke landed like a lead balloon, my voice cracking on the last syllable. Across the room, the radiator hissed like it was laughing at me.

The radiator's metallic laughter followed me into the kitchenette. I kept my back to them as I yanked the coffee bag out of the cabinet—beans scattering across the counter like retreating cockroaches. The machine beeped its usual protest when I slammed the portafilter too hard.

Jayda's bare feet scuffed against the linoleum as she followed me tentatively. I braced for the interrogation, but her arms circled my waist instead, chin hooking over my shoulder. Her vanilla-scented curls tickled my neck.

"No disappearing into your head, okay?" Her hug tightened, trapping my arms against my sides. "Just wanted you to know…it's good. The scary kind of good. If you feel safe enough to share that with him, then he must be the real deal."

My thumbnail found a groove in the coffee grinder. "Good like kombucha or…?"

"Good like watching anime intros without skipping." She released me to spin the mug carousel, plucking out the chipped #1 Barista one from her old job. "Had to spill your darkest trauma to get me finally doing that."

The coffee maker shrieked while I fussed over a brew I had no real desire for. My mind wandered to my conversation with Harald yesterday evening, and unexpected thrill rushed through me at the prospect of his physical visit.

Jayda noticed my change in mood, and her reflection appeared in the chrome. "You're smiling."

"Am not."

"You've got that post-crush glow. Like when Caleb discovered artisanal pickles."

"Hey!" Caleb lobbed the fallen pillow at her. "Those pickles revolutionized my charcuterie boards."

I stared at the crema swirling in my cup. "Harald's different. Listens like he's actually interested instead of waiting for his turn to trauma-dump."

Jayda hip-checked me away from the machine. "Okay, lover boy. Let's get pancakes in you before you float away."

Caleb snapped his fingers. "Extra syrup for the human Disney princess."

My phone buzzed in my pocket. Three rapid vibrations—Harald's signature text pattern. I let it ring out, savoring the secret and grab my phone to see what he sent.

Jayda's eyes track my movements across the screen. "You seem serious all of a sudden," she observes, making me realize I'm probably wearing it all over my face like a neon sign.

"Maybe." The truth catches in my throat like a hairball. "I just... he says he is coming here today." I pause, running my fingers nervously through my messy curls. "He wants to meet up."

Caleb stands, moving toward me with that signature mix of warmth and protective intensity that only someone who truly cares about you can do. He places a hand on my shoulder. "You're gonna be okay, dude. Whatever happens, happens." His voice is steady but his eyes hold something else – concern wrapped in care.

Jayda joins us, sliding her arm around my waist. "And if he's the one who makes you as happy as Caleb does for me," she winks, "then that's pretty damn good news."

I nod, still staring at Harald's latest message: *"Can't wait to see you in person, for real?"* The words make something twist in my chest, somewhere between fear and hope.

Chapter 10

Harald

"Get it moving, please!" I drummed my fingers on the marble bar top as the jet crew finalized preparations. The royal insignia gleamed on every surface—mocking me, declaring my importance while I fidgeted like an impatient child. My nerves were frayed at the edges, anxiety coiling in my stomach like a restless serpent. Father would call this behavior beneath my station, another disappointment to add to his mental tally of my failings. But I couldn't help it. Every minute spent in this gilded cage of privilege only tightened the invisible noose around my neck. I watched the ground crew scurrying about outside the window, envying their simple purpose and clear direction—something I'd never truly had despite the crown that awaited me.

Erik raised an eyebrow. "Your Highness, these safety protocols exist for a reason."

"I know, I know." I ran my hand through my hair, messing up the careful styling my personal groomer had insisted upon this morning. "It's just..."

Just that Daniel was waiting. Daniel with his messy morning hair and infectious laugh that made my chest tighten with something I hadn't felt in years. Daniel who knew me as Harald, just Harald, not the Crown Prince of Denmark with all the crushing expectations that title carried—who'd helped me through that anxiety-inducing speech without even knowing it. Who'd texted me simple encouragements thinking I was just nervous about some corporate presentation, not realizing his words were steadying my hands before I addressed diplomats and dignitaries. In those moments with him, I could breathe. I could be someone other than the carefully constructed public figure my father had molded me to be.

"The pilot says ten more minutes, sir." Erik's voice softened. "Perhaps you'd like to review the itinerary for your stay?"

"I've memorized it." My voice came out more clipped than intended, the tension in my shoulders betraying my outward composure. Three days in New York. Three days where I'd pretend to be inspecting Danish investments while actually giving most of my security detail the slip to meet a man I'd never seen in person. The absurdity of my plan struck me suddenly—heir to the throne of Denmark, sneaking around Manhattan like a rebellious teenager rather than a future monarch. Yet something about Daniel pulled me toward him with a gravity I couldn't resist, couldn't explain to anyone, least of all my father or Erik. Those text conversations had become my oxygen, the only moments when the weight of the crown seemed to lift from my head, if only temporarily.

The flight attendant approached with a hesitant smile. "Would Your Highness care for a drink before takeoff?"

"No, thank you." I checked my phone again—no new messages from Daniel. Had he changed his mind? Was he as nervous as I felt?

The engines finally roared to life, and I clutched the armrests. Flying never bothered me, but this journey felt different. I wasn't traveling as Denmark's Crown Prince but as a man pursuing something real. Something honest.

"You're white as a sheet," Erik murmured, sliding into the seat across from me. "Having second thoughts?"

"Second, third, fortieth thoughts." I laughed nervously, the sound catching in my throat like a trapped butterfly. My fingers drummed against the plush armrest in an erratic rhythm that matched my pulse. "What if he's disappointed? What if he expected someone different, someone... better?" The anxiety that had been my lifelong companion twisted in my chest. I leaned forward, lowering my voice to a whisper that barely carried over the rumble of the engines. "What if he realizes who I am and everything changes? One Google search and the fairytale crumbles. The Crown Prince masquerading as just Harald from Denmark." The very thought sent a cold shiver down my spine—that moment of recognition in Daniel's eyes, wonder transforming into calculation, or worse, betrayal.

"Then he wasn't the right person." Erik's gaze held mine. "But from what little you've shared, he seems to care about the man, not the title."

I nodded, my throat tight. "I've never done this before. Met someone as... just me."

"Perhaps that's why it matters so much."

The plane began taxiing, and I closed my eyes, picturing Daniel's face from his photos—that infectious smile with a hint of mischief, those expressive dark eyes that seemed to see right through pretense. In less than eight hours, I'd see that face in person, not confined to the small rectangle of my phone screen. I'd hear his voice without the static of a phone call, clear and vibrant in the same air I breathed. My stomach fluttered with a mixture of anticipation and terror. This wasn't a diplomatic meeting with prepared statements and practiced smiles. This was me—just Harald— stepping into something real and unpredictable for perhaps the first time in my life.

I was terrified. I was exhilarated. I was finally moving toward something I wanted, not something expected of me. For once in my life, the crushing weight of duty and royal obligation wasn't dictating my actions - this was purely my heart leading the way, however reckless it might be. My pulse quickened at the thought, sending sparks of electricity through my veins that made me feel more alive than I had in years. Even the anxiety churn- ing in my stomach felt different - not the usual dread of public appearanc- es and diplomatic functions, but rather the sweet, dizzying nervousness of pursuing something genuinely meaningful to me, consequences be damned.

"You look like you need this." Erik handed me a small white pill. "Dr. Nielsen authorized it for your flight anxiety."

I studied the tablet resting in my palm. "What flight anxiety? I never take these."

"Precisely why you should now." Erik's expression softened with con- cern. "You've barely slept in days, Your Highness. You'll want to be rested when you meet him."

He was right. The thought of facing Daniel with dark circles under bloodshot eyes wasn't appealing. I'd been too wired, spending nights staring at my phone screen, rereading our conversations, analyzing every word.

"Fine." I tossed back the pill with a swig of water. "Wake me before landing. I need time to..." To what? Compose myself? Rehearse what to say? Nothing would adequately prepare me for actually seeing Daniel in person.

Erik dimmed the cabin lights. "Rest well, sir."

I reclined my seat, feeling the gentle vibration of the jet beneath me. The pill worked quickly, a gentle warmth spreading through my limbs, my eyelids growing heavy. Thoughts of Daniel drifted through my mind like clouds across the Danish sky—his laugh during our phone call, the way he'd described his tiny apartment with such animation I could almost see it, the vulnerability in his voice when he spoke about his past.

Would he see right through me? My carefully constructed facade of normalcy that couldn't possibly hold up to in-person scrutiny? Or would he see me—just Harald—the person I glimpsed in rare moments when crown and country weren't weighing me down?

The thought both terrified and thrilled me as consciousness began slipping away. In my drowsy state, I imagined Daniel's smile welcoming me, not the practiced diplomatic smile I'd perfected for cameras and public appearances, but something genuine that reached his eyes. Something real.

Something worth crossing an ocean for.

My last coherent thought before sleep claimed me was wondering if Daniel was as nervous as I was, if he too was counting hours and minutes, simultaneously afraid and eager for the moment we'd finally meet.

* * *

Erik

I leaned back in the plush leather seat of the jet, finally allowing my shoulders to slump. The morning had been a frenzy of discreet arrangements, secretive phone calls, and carefully worded emails. Organizing a royal flight without attracting the palace gossips' attention was like performing surgery with boxing gloves on.

"Everything's arranged, Your Highness," I'd told Harald earlier, handing him the itinerary. "The plane will be ready in three hours."

That's when he'd gazed at me with those eyes—the ones that had made my pulse falter since our teenage years. Eyes that never regarded me with the longing I privately hoped they might.

"Erik, I need to tell you something." His voice carried an unusual vulnerability. "I'm not just going to New York for diplomatic reasons."

I maintained my practiced neutral expression, though my stomach tightened. "Sir?"

"I've met someone. Online." His face transformed as he spoke, years of royal restraint melting away into an expression of almost boyish vulnerability that I hadn't seen since we were teenagers sneaking chocolate from the palace kitchens. "His name is Daniel. We've been talking for weeks and... I need to see him in person." The way Harald's voice softened on this stranger's name made my chest constrict with an emotion I refused to name, even as I noticed the slight tremor in his usually steady hands, the way his shoulders seemed both tense and lighter somehow, as if unburdened by finally speaking these words aloud.

"I see," I replied, my voice impressively steady despite the cold knife twisting between my ribs.

Harald sank into the chair opposite mine, relief washing over his features at having shared his secret. His shoulders relaxed as if unburdened of an invisible weight, though his fingers still tapped nervously against his knee. "He doesn't know who I really am. To him, I'm just Harald," he confessed, his voice barely above a whisper, as if speaking the words too loudly might shatter this fragile fantasy he'd constructed. The vulnerability in his eyes reminded me of when we were young, before the crown had become so heavy on his brow, before the expectations of an entire nation and an unreasonable father had carved permanent worry lines into his forehead.

"Just Harald," I echoed, swallowing hard. How I'd longed to know 'just Harald' too, beyond the barriers of crown and duty.

"I've never felt this way before," he continued, oblivious to my inner turmoil. "When I talk to him, I'm not the Crown Prince. I'm just... me."

I nodded, forcing a supportive smile that didn't reach my eyes. "That must be freeing," I managed, even as the words scraped my throat raw. Years of diplomatic training came to my rescue, allowing me to maintain this façade of calm interest while inside, my heart splintered into countless sharp-edged fragments. How many nights had I stayed late in his office, how many private moments had we shared, all while I harbored these use-less, inappropriate feelings? And now, to sit here and listen to him speak of another with such unguarded tenderness—it was exquisite torture.

"It is," he whispered, almost to himself. "For once, someone sees me clearly."

The irony burned. I'd seen him clearly for years—his doubts, his strengths, his gentle heart beneath the royal facade. I'd stood beside him through every crisis, every triumph. Yet he flew across an ocean for a con-nection formed through text messages.

Now, alone as Harald slept beside me oblivious to my inner turmoil, I allowed myself a moment of weakness. My hands trembled slightly as I organized the security protocols for his visit. I would ensure his safety, as always. I would facilitate this meeting with Daniel, whoever he was.

Because that was my role. Not the lover, but the loyal secretary. The friend who would never cross that line, no matter how much I ached to.

Chapter 11

Harald

The wheels of the jet smoothly touched down at JFK airport, sending a flutter through my stomach that had nothing to do with the landing. My hands trembled as I pulled out my phone, checking Daniel's message for the hundredth time.

"Bean There, Done That at 3. Can't wait to meet you :)"

The smile emoji both calmed and terrified me. Erik sat across from me, his face a mask of professional concern.

"Your Highness, the car is ready. With your diplomatic status you've already been precleared through customs and we've arranged-"

"Please, not now." I pressed my palms against my thighs, willing them to stop shaking. "And no 'Your Highness' in New York. Remember? Here it's just Harald or boss."

Erik nodded, though his lips tightened with disapproval. I knew he worried - it was his job to worry - but this moment wasn't about protocol or security. It was about Daniel.

The tarmac stretched before us as we deplaned. A sleek black car waited, its windows tinted against the morning sun. My security detail maintained a respectful distance, but their presence weighed on me. How could I possibly have a normal first meeting with four agents watching my every move?

My phone buzzed. Another message from Daniel: *"Already on my third cappuccino. Nervous energy is real."*

A laugh escaped me, genuine and unguarded. He was nervous too. Somehow that made everything better and worse at the same time. I typed back a quick response, telling him I'd landed safely and was on my way.

We got into the car and it smoothly pulled away from the tarmac, quickly departing the airport and weaving through traffic. The leather seats creaked as I shifted, wrestling with my tie. Through the tinted windows, Manhattan's skyline loomed closer, though traffic crawled at a snail's pace.

"Erik, hand me that bag." I pointed to the leather duffel containing my change of clothes.

He passed it over without comment, but his expression spoke volumes. The partition between us and the driver was up, giving me what passed for privacy these days.

I yanked off my suit jacket, carefully folded from years of habit. The crisp white shirt followed, replaced by a soft grey sweater that Ella had helped me pick out. It felt strange, dressing down instead of up, but I wanted Daniel to see me - just me - not some polished royal facade.

"Your High- Harald," Erik corrected himself. "Are you certain about this?"

My fingers fumbled with the button of my dress pants. "No, I'm not certain about anything." The dark jeans slid on easier than expected, though maneuvering in the back seat was awkward. "But I need to do this."

A horn blared outside, making me jump. Through the window, I watched yellow cabs weave between lanes, their drivers gesturing wildly. The chaos of New York felt fitting - my heart was racing just as frantically.

I stuffed my formal clothes into the duffel, then caught my reflection in the window. The man staring back looked almost normal. Almost like someone Daniel might want to know. My hand rose to smooth my hair, but I forced it down. Let it be messy. Let something about me be imperfect for once.

"How do I look?" I asked Erik, though I wasn't sure I wanted his answer.

"Like someone trying very hard not to look like himself."

I laughed, the sound tight with nerves. "That's exactly what I'm going for."

The traffic crawled through Queens, each red light stretching into infinity. My phone screen lit up again - another message from Daniel. My thumb hovered over it, heart pounding against my ribs.

What was I thinking? Flying across an ocean to meet someone who didn't even know who I really was? The weight of my crown had never felt heavier, even though I wasn't wearing it.

"We could still turn around," Erik said softly from beside me. "I can have the plane readied-"

"No." The word came out sharper than intended. I unlocked my phone, Daniel's last message burning into my retinas. A selfie of him at the coffee shop, hair slightly mussed, dark eyes bright with anticipation.

My fingers twisted the hem of my sweater. The fabric probably cost more than Daniel made in a month. Everything about me was a lie - my casual clothes, my vague stories about working in finance, my carefully curated photos that never showed the palace.

The Manhattan skyline loomed closer, glass towers reaching toward the clouds. Each mile marker brought me nearer to a collision between my two worlds - the carefully constructed fiction I'd built with Daniel and the suffocating reality of who I really was.

I typed out a message, deleted it, typed again. Nothing felt right. How could anything feel right when our entire connection was built on an omission so massive it felt like betrayal?

"Five minutes to destination," the driver announced through the intercom.

My stomach lurched. The phone slipped from my sweaty hands, clattering to the floor. Erik reached for it, but I grabbed it first, clutching it like a lifeline.

"What if-" The words stuck in my throat. "What if he hates me when he finds out?"

Erik's face softened with understanding. He'd been by my side through every crisis, every moment of doubt. But this time, he had no diplomatic solution to offer, no carefully worded statement to smooth things over.

The car turned onto a street lined with cafes and shops. Bean There, Done That's sign came into view further down the block. The driver parked a reasonable distance away, allowing us to remain out of sight of the cafe.

"Harald." Erik's voice cut through my thoughts. "We'll do a sweep of the location first. Standard procedure." I watched as Erik pulled out his cell and spoke softly to my security detail, giving them the go-ahead to begin their inspection while emphasizing the need to stay inconspicuous.

I found my attention fixed on the phone in my hands, scrolling through our past conversations. The easy banter, the late-night confessions, the silly selfies - would any of that translate to real life? Or would the weight of who I really was crush whatever this fragile connection might be? Was I really ready for this or was I making a massive mistake in coming here?

I closed my eyes and took several deep breaths, remembering what Ingrid had taught me. In through the nose, out through the mouth. The leather seat creaked as I shifted, focusing on why I'd flown across an ocean.

Daniel. His laugh in our late-night call. The way he'd encouraged me before that speech without even knowing who I really was. How he saw me - just me - not the crown, not the expectations, not my father's disappointment.

"I need this," I whispered, more to myself than Erik. "I need to know if someone can care about who I am underneath all of... this." I gestured vaguely at the security detail, the diplomatic plates, the whole circus that followed me everywhere.

The door opened and I stepped onto the bustling New York sidewalk. The autumn air hit my face, carrying the scent of coffee and exhaust fumes - so different from Copenhagen's carefully maintained streets.

A clothing store's window caught my eye as I walked. I stopped, studying my reflection. The grey sweater hung loose on my frame, the jeans sitting naturally on my hips. My hair, free from its usual styled precision, fell slightly across my forehead. Without the suits, without the medals and sashes, without the weight of centuries of tradition draped across my shoulders... I looked young. Normal.

A group of students pushed past me, laughing and shoving each other playfully. None of them gave me a second glance. No whispered recognition, no subtle phone cameras, no careful bows or curtsies.

For the first time in years, I was invisible. Just another face in the crowd. Just Harald.

The coffee shop's sign swung gently in the breeze ahead of me. Inside, Daniel waited, probably on his fourth cappuccino by now. My hands trembled, but not from anxiety this time.

For once, someone would meet me as myself. Not the Crown Prince.

Not the future king. Just me.

Through the cafe's window, sunlight caught Daniel's profile as he leaned against the table, hands moving nervously around a cold cappucino as he waited. My breath caught. The photos we'd shared hadn't captured the vibrant energy that radiated from him, the way his whole body participated in conversation.

He wore a dark blue sweater that complemented his warm caramel skin, his dark curls slightly disheveled like he'd been running his fingers through them. A genuine smile lit up his face as I saw him glance down at his phone and type something, moments later my phone vibrated as I received his message.

My feet refused to move. I stood rooted to the sidewalk, drinking in every detail. The way he shifted his weight when he leaned forward, intent on the messages on his phone screen. How his delicate fingers tapped against it rapidly as he sent another message. The slight scrunch of his nose when he smiled.

I needed this moment, needed to memorize Daniel as he was right now - completely himself, unguarded, before my presence complicated everything.

He checked his phone again, bottom lip caught between his teeth. Was he nervous too? The thought gave me courage. I watched as he ran a hand through his hair for probably the hundredth time, making it even messier.

My phone buzzed in my pocket - probably another message from him wondering where I was. But I couldn't look away from the real person standing just feet away from me. Daniel was no longer just pixels on a screen or a voice through my phone. He was flesh and blood and absolutely beautiful.

I tugged at my sweater one last time, heart thundering against my ribs. This was it. No crown, no title, no royal protocol. Just me, about to meet someone who had somehow become incredibly important to me without ever seeing me in person.

Daniel glanced toward the window and I ducked back, not ready to be seen just yet. One more deep breath. One more moment of being just Harald before I walked through that door.

My hand trembled as I reached for the brass door handle. The metal felt cool against my palm, grounding me in this moment. A bell chimed overhead as I pulled, and warmth rushed out to meet me.

The rich aroma of coffee enveloped me - darker and more complex than the palace's carefully curated brews. Espresso machines hissed and whirred, their mechanical symphony mixing with the lazy weekend chatter of customers. A barista called out someone's elaborate drink order over the din.

My feet crossed the threshold, and suddenly the careful distance I'd maintained dissolved. The same air Daniel breathed now filled my lungs. The same wooden floors creaked under our feet. The same sunlight that caught his profile now warmed my skin.

Someone bumped past me with a muttered "sorry," jolting me from my trance. I shifted closer to the wall, my security training kicking in as I automatically scanned the room. Two exits. Seventeen customers. Three staff members. Window seats exposed, corner tables defensible.

Stop it, I commanded myself. This wasn't a state function. No one was watching. No one cared.

Except Daniel. He hadn't noticed me yet, still focused on his phone. From this angle, I could see the way his eyelashes cast tiny shadows on his cheeks. The corner of his mouth twitched upward as he typed - probably sending me another message wondering where I was.

My phone buzzed in my pocket, but I couldn't tear my eyes away from him. The Daniel I'd imagined while texting had been a sketch, an outline, even with the photos he'd sent me. The real person before me was painted in vibrant colors - the rich brown of his eyes, the soft pink of his lips, the warm caramel of his skin.

The coffee shop's sounds faded to white noise. My heart pounded so hard I was sure everyone could hear it over the espresso machines. Just a few more steps and I'd be close enough for him to notice me. Close enough for this dream to become reality.

Daniel's head snapped up at the sound of the door chime as another person entered behind me, and our eyes locked across the room.

Everything I'd planned to say evaporated. My carefully rehearsed "Hi, I'm Harald" dissolved on my tongue. The speech I'd practiced a hundred times on the flight vanished like morning mist.

Daniel's dark eyes widened with recognition. A smile bloomed across his face - not the polite, measured smiles I was used to receiving at formal functions, but something raw and genuine that crinkled the corners of his eyes. My heart stuttered in my chest.

He stood up from his chair, the movement sending his empty cappuccino cup rattling against its saucer. A faint blush colored his cheeks as he steadied it with quick fingers. That small moment of imperfection, of human awkwardness, made my own nervousness ease slightly.

I remained frozen in the doorway, drinking in the details our phone cameras hadn't captured. The way his curls caught the afternoon light streaming through the windows. How his blue sweater hung loose at his collar, revealing a hint of collarbone. The slight tremor in his hands that matched my own.

Our gazes remained connected across the cafe, neither of us speaking. The bustling sounds of coffee grinding and customers chatting faded to background noise. In that moment, it was just us - no crowns, no titles, no expectations. Just Harald and Daniel, finally sharing the same space after weeks of digital connection.

My feet felt leaden as I took a step forward. Then another. The distance between us shrank with each movement, but the words I needed still refused to come.

Chapter 12

Daniel

I drummed my fingers against the wooden table, checking my phone for what felt like the hundredth time. The coffee shop buzzed with its usual weekend crowd, but my mind kept drifting to Harald's last message before takeoff.

"See you at 3. Can't wait to meet you properly :)"

My stomach twisted into knots, churning with a nauseating mix of excitement and anxiety that made me regret those breakfast eggs. The barista - a girl with kind eyes and a nose ring - had already given me sympathetic looks as I ordered my third cappuccino, probably thinking I'd been stood up. I couldn't blame her; I must have looked pathetic, fidgeting in my corner seat for the past hour. The foam had long since dissolved, leaving just lukewarm coffee that I couldn't bring myself to finish, the bitter liquid a perfect match for the doubts creeping into my mind. What if this was another mistake? Another Alex waiting to happen? I pushed the nearly full cup away, its ceramic base scraping against the wooden tabletop with a sound that made me wince.

The bell above the door chimed and my head snapped up, but it was just another couple seeking their afternoon caffeine fix. I slumped back in my chair, tugging at the sleeve of my blue sweater - the one Jayda insisted brought out my eyes. My heart had done this same anxious little dance at least five times now, each false alarm making my stomach twist a bit tighter. I'd spent nearly thirty minutes this morning panicking over what to wear, and then another thirty minutes ironing my entire outfit to perfection. And now here I was, probably wrinkling it beyond repair as I fidgeted nervously with the cuffs.

"You're being ridiculous," I muttered to myself, scrolling through our earlier messages for what felt like the hundredth time today. My thumb trembled slightly as I traced over Harald's words, analyzing every dot and dash for hidden meaning like some desperate teenage boy. The screen's glow illuminated my face in the dimly lit coffee shop as I obsessed over whether his casual *"can't wait"* was genuine enthusiasm or just polite small talk. After Alex, I'd gotten too good at turning innocent phrases into warning signs.

The conversation flowed so naturally between us. Harald's wit, his genuine interest in my life, the way he actually listened instead of just waiting for his turn to speak. But what if the chemistry didn't translate in person? What if-

My phone buzzed.

"Just got out of the car. Walking to Bean There, Done That now. I'm wearing a gray sweater and black jeans."

My fingers wouldn't stop shaking as I twisted the fabric of my sleeve between them. The blue cotton was going to be permanently wrinkled at this rate, but I couldn't help it. The bell chimed again and this time my heart stopped.

A tall man in a perfectly fitted gray sweater stepped through the doorway. The afternoon sun caught his blonde hair, giving him an almost ethereal glow. His eyes scanned the coffee shop, and I forgot how to breathe.

My face broke into an uncontrollable grin, all my earlier anxiety melting away at the sight of him. Those photos he'd sent hadn't done him justice - he was gorgeous in a way that made my heart skip several beats. Before I could second-guess myself, I lifted my hand and called out:

"Harry?"

His eyes found mine, and a smile transformed his entire face. The formal, almost stiff posture he'd walked in with softened, his shoulders relaxing as he weaved between the tables toward me. My pulse thundered in my ears, drowning out the coffee shop chatter. Up close, I noticed the tiny details our video calls hadn't captured - the slight crinkle around his eyes when he smiled, the way his sweater brought out flecks of gray in his blue eyes, how his fingers fidgeted with the hem of his sleeve in a gesture so familiar from our conversations about anxiety.

Gone were my rehearsed greetings and clever opening lines. Instead, I just sat there, probably grinning like an idiot, drinking in the sight of him. All those late-night conversations, all those shared fears and hopes and silly jokes - they crystallized into this moment, this person standing before me who somehow felt like both a stranger and an old friend.

The sunlight streaming through the window caught his hair, turning it to gold, and I had to resist the urge to reach out and touch it, to verify that he was real and not just another daydream born from too much caffeine and hope.

My heart raced as Harald made his way across the coffee shop. Each of his steps seemed to stretch time itself - too fast and too slow all at once. The confident stride I'd noticed when he first walked in had transformed into something more hesitant, more human.

The late afternoon sun painted shadows across his face as he weaved between tables, highlighting the sharp line of his jaw, the slight flush creeping up his neck. I caught a whiff of his cologne - something expensive and subtle that made my head spin. Or maybe that was just the effect he had on me.

Three tables away. Two. One.

I stood up, my chair scraping against the floor with an awkward screech that made several heads turn. Heat rushed to my face, but Harald's lips quirked up in that crooked smile I'd grown to adore through our countless selfies.

"Daniel." His voice was softer in person, touched with an accent that our phone call hadn't quite captured. He stopped just short of my table, close enough that I could see the tiny flecks of gold in his blue eyes, the slight tremor in his hands that matched my own.

The bustling coffee shop faded away. The whir of the espresso machine, the chatter of other customers, even the jazz music playing overhead - it all dissolved into white noise. There was just Harald, standing before me, more real than any fantasy my anxious mind had conjured up during those sleepless nights of wondering.

I wanted to say something clever, something that would break the tension and make him laugh like he did during our late-night conversations. Instead, I found myself frozen, drinking in every detail of him - the way his sweater hugged his shoulders, how his hair fell across his forehead, the nervous way he shifted his weight from one foot to the other.

We stood there, awkwardly hovering between a handshake and a hug, the coffee shop's ambient noise filling the silence between us. My usual quick wit and snappy comebacks deserted me. All those text messages, all that easy banter - none of it had prepared me for the reality of Harald standing right here, his presence both thrilling and terrifying.

"I..." My voice cracked. I cleared my throat, trying to summon my usual sass, but something in the way he looked at me - gentle, uncertain, almost reverent - stripped away my defensive armor. "I was starting to think you might not show."

Harald's fingers twisted the hem of his sweater. "I almost didn't. Not because-" He paused, swallowing hard. "I sat in the car for ten minutes, trying to convince myself to walk in."

"Yeah?" The word came out softer than I intended. "What made you do it?"

"I saw you through the window." His cheeks flushed pink. "You were checking your phone and running your hand through your hair, just like you said you do when you're nervous. It made you real."

The raw honesty in his voice knocked down another brick in my carefully constructed wall. My hand flew self-consciously to my hair - had I really been doing that?

"I'm usually better at this," I admitted, gesturing vaguely between us. "The whole meeting new people thing. I've got this whole routine - witty remarks, perfectly timed eye rolls..."

"I like this version better." Harald's smile was shy but genuine. "The real one."

My chest tightened. Here we were, two people who'd shared our deepest fears over text, now struggling to figure out how to exist in the same physical space. The vulnerability felt dangerous, like standing on the edge of something vast and unknown.

My body moved before my brain could catch up. All the tension, all the anticipation of these past weeks crashed over me like a wave. I surged forward, my hands finding purchase on his shoulders as I pulled him close. Our lips met with an urgency that surprised even me, my fingers sliding up to tangle in his soft blonde hair.

Harald made a small sound of surprise against my mouth, but his hands found my waist, steadying me as I practically melted into him. His cologne filled my senses - expensive and intoxicating - and his lips were softer than I'd imagined during all those late-night fantasies.

The coffee shop disappeared. The chattering customers, the whirring espresso machines, even my own anxieties about public displays of affection - all of it faded away. There was only Harald, his warm hands on my waist, his breath mingling with mine as I deepened the kiss.

When we finally broke apart, my heart hammering against my ribs, I noticed his cheeks had flushed a beautiful shade of pink. His hair was slightly mussed where my fingers had run through it, and his eyes had darkened to a stormy blue.

"I..." I started to apologize, suddenly aware we were in the middle of a coffee shop, but the words died in my throat. Harald's hands were still on my waist, holding me close, and the smile spreading across his face made my knees weak.

"Been wanting to do that since the night you called," I admitted, my voice barely above a whisper.

Harald's laugh - rich and warm - sends shivers down my spine. His hand reached out, fingers gently cupping my chin. The touch was electric, making my breath catch in my throat. His thumb traced along my jawline with a tenderness that made my heart stutter.

"Me too," he whispers, pulling me closer. "Every night we talked, every message..." His accent wrapped around the words like honey, making them somehow more intimate.

This time when our lips met, it was slower, deeper. No desperate crash of mouths, but a deliberate exploration. His fingers slid from my chin to the nape of my neck, threading through my hair. I melted into him, my hands finding purchase on his chest, feeling his heartbeat racing beneath that soft gray sweater.

The kiss tasted like possibility - like every late-night conversation and shared secret had been leading to this moment. Harald's other hand settled on my lower back, drawing me even closer until I could feel the solid warmth of his body against mine.

Someone cleared their throat nearby - probably the barista - but I couldn't bring myself to care. Harald's lips curved into a smile against mine, and I felt myself grinning too, both of us probably looking like love-sick teenagers in the middle of this coffee shop.

When we finally broke apart, Harald rested his forehead against mine, his breath warm on my face. Those blue eyes of his were dark with emotion, making my knees weak all over again. We stood there, wrapped in each other's arms, neither of us willing to be the first to step away.

Chapter 13

Harald

Someone cleared their throat – loudly and with the kind of pointed emphasis that suggested they'd been doing it for a while. I reluctantly pulled back from Daniel, still feeling breathless from the kiss, though our hands found each other immediately, fingers intertwining. My royal etiquette training definitely hadn't covered what to do after kissing a gorgeous man senseless in an American coffee shop.

A barista was aggressively wiping the same spot on the counter, failing spectacularly at pretending not to stare. Someone in the back of the café let out a wolf whistle, followed by scattered applause. An elderly woman in the corner shot us an enthusiastic thumbs up over her crossword puzzle, mouthing what looked suspiciously like "Get it!"

I tried not to wince as I caught sight of my security detail strategically positioned around the café – Erik by the novelty mug display, his face flushed crimson as he pretended to be fascinated by a cup that read "Bean Me Up Scotty," Agent Andersen attempting to blend in while reading yesterday's newspaper upside down, and Agent Larsen somehow making the simple act of stirring coffee look suspicious. Daniel, thankfully, seemed completely oblivious to their presence.

"So," Daniel said, his smile bright enough to power several small countries, "I usually at least make the guy buy me dinner before putting on a show like that."

I felt my own face heat up, but couldn't stop grinning. "Well, I do owe you a cappuccino that's probably gone cold by now."

Daniel scrunched up his nose, the expression making my heart skip. "After three cups while waiting for you, I'm pretty sure I can feel colors. But..." He grabbed my hand, his fingers sliding between mine. The warmth of his touch sent electricity through my arm. "How about I show you around instead? The city's gorgeous this time of day."

My security detail shifted in my peripheral vision. Erik's face tightened with concern – walking meant exposure, unpredictable variables, risk. But Daniel's eyes sparkled with such genuine excitement that the words tumbled out before I could stop them.

"Lead the way."

We pushed through the café's door into the crisp autumn air. The bustle of New York wrapped around us – car horns, fragments of conversation, music spilling from shop doorways. So different from the formal stillness of palace corridors.

"Fair warning," Daniel squeezed my hand, "I'm a terrible tour guide. I mostly know where the best food trucks are and which subway stations to avoid after midnight."

"That sounds perfect actually." I found myself matching his easy smile. The weight of crown and country felt lighter here, walking hand-in-hand down a crowded sidewalk where no one looked twice at us. Just another couple out for a stroll.

"Really? Because I was thinking we could start with Central Park. It's not far, and there's this spot by the lake that's..." He trailed off, tugging me closer as a cyclist whizzed past. "Sorry, these bike messengers are basically urban cowboys."

I laughed, allowing myself to be pulled against his side. Behind us, I knew Erik and the security team were maintaining their discrete distance, but for once I didn't care. Daniel's enthusiasm was infectious, his hand warm in mine, and New York stretched before us full of possibilities.

The autumn breeze ruffled Daniel's dark hair as we walked, and I found myself mesmerized by how the sunlight caught the subtle auburn highlights. His hand remained firmly clasped in mine, our fingers interlocked as if they'd always belonged that way. Each block we passed revealed another layer of the city – street vendors hawking roasted nuts, tourists wielding selfie sticks, locals speed-walking with determination.

"That bodega has the best coffee in Manhattan, I swear." Daniel pointed with his free hand. "And see that pizza place? They're open until 4 AM. Saved my life during some rough nights."

The casual way he shared pieces of his world made my chest tighten. No ceremony, no carefully crafted statements – just honest stories told with an open heart. Back home, every word I spoke carried the weight of centuries of protocol. Here, walking these bustling streets with Daniel, I felt that weight lifting.

"You okay?" Daniel's thumb brushed across my knuckles. "You got quiet for a second there."

"More than okay." I squeezed his hand. "It's just... nice. Being here with you."

A taxi blared its horn as we crossed the street, making me jump. Daniel laughed and pulled me closer, his shoulder bumping mine. "Don't worry, that's just how New Yorkers say hello."

The edges of Central Park came into view ahead – a green oasis rising above the concrete and glass. Daniel's eyes lit up as he pointed out different landmarks, his enthusiasm infectious. I found myself studying his profile, the way his whole face transformed when he smiled, how he gestured expressively with his free hand while never letting go of mine.

"You're staring," he said, catching my eye with a grin.

"Can you blame me?" The words slipped out before I could stop them, but Daniel's resulting blush was worth any breach of royal decorum.

We passed under the park's stone archway, leaving the city's chaos behind. The path ahead wound through trees dressed in red and gold, and for the first time in years, I felt truly present in the moment – not Prince Harald, not the future king, just a man walking hand-in-hand with someone who made his heart race.

The peaceful atmosphere of our walk shattered when I caught movement from the corner of my eye. A woman in a bright yellow coat stood frozen on the path ahead, her iPhone raised and pointed directly at us. Her eyes narrowed with the kind of scrutiny that made my stomach drop – the look of someone trying to place a familiar face.

"Wait, aren't you—"

"Let's check out the lake this way." I tugged Daniel's hand, steering us down a side path before she could finish her sentence. My pulse hammered in my throat. "I bet the view is better from the south side."

"You sure? Because I thought—"

"Trust me, I'm usually pretty good when it comes to my sense of direction." I picked up our pace, weaving between the trees. Behind us, I glimpsed Erik's tall frame intercepting the woman. His voice carried just enough for me to catch fragments.

"Delete those photos... security concern... immediately."

Daniel remained focused on pointing out a group of turtles sunning themselves on a rock, completely unaware of the close call. I forced myself to breathe normally, to keep my expression neutral even as anxiety churned in my gut. Erik would handle it. He always did.

"You okay?" Daniel squeezed my hand. "You seem tense all of a sudden."

"Just remembered something I need to tell my assistant Erik later." The lie tasted bitter, but I couldn't bring myself to shatter this perfect moment with the truth. Not yet. "Nothing important."

We rounded a bend in the path, putting more distance between us and the woman with the phone. My security detail shifted positions seamlessly, Agent Larsen taking point while Erik dealt with the situation. I hated this — the constant vigilance, the lies by omission, the way my title threatened to poison even the most genuine connections.

But when Daniel's shoulder brushed mine as he leaned in to point out a street performer in the distance, his smile bright and unguarded, I pushed the guilt aside. Just for today, I wanted to be simply Harald, walking through Central Park with a beautiful man who saw me, not my crown.

The ducks clustered at the water's edge, waddling closer as Daniel tossed bits of bread from a paper bag he'd grabbed at a nearby cart. The late afternoon sun caught the ripples on the lake, turning them to liquid gold. We'd found a secluded bench partially hidden by a weeping willow, away from the main paths.

"My therapist would probably say this is very therapeutic," Daniel said, breaking off another piece of bread. "Feeding ducks instead of overthinking life."

"Mine would agree." The words slipped out before I could catch them. Daniel's eyebrows lifted slightly, but his smile remained warm.

"You see someone too?"

I nodded, watching a particularly bold duck snatch a piece of bread from its companion. "For anxiety mainly. And... other things." The bench creaked as I shifted closer to him, our thighs touching. "It's hard sometimes, feeling like you have to be perfect for everyone."

Daniel's hand found mine, his thumb tracing circles on my palm. "Tell me about it. When I was in the system, every new home felt like an audition. Like if I just acted right, smiled enough, maybe they'd keep me."

The raw honesty in his voice made my chest ache. Here was someone who understood what it meant to live under constant scrutiny, albeit for very different reasons. I wanted to tell him everything – about the crown, the expectations, my father's disapproval. Instead, I squeezed his hand.

"You don't have to perform for me," I said softly.

Daniel turned to face me, his dark eyes searching mine. A stray lock of hair fell across his forehead, and I resisted the urge to brush it back. "Same goes for you, you know. Whatever's weighing on you, whatever you're carrying – you can just be yourself here."

The irony of his words twisted in my gut, but the genuine care in his expression soothed the sting. A duck quacked impatiently at our feet, demanding its share of bread. Daniel laughed, breaking the intensity of the moment, and tossed it a piece.

"Everybody's a critic," he said, leaning his head against my shoulder.

The weight of Daniel's head on my shoulder felt both perfect and painful. Each casual touch, each unguarded smile twisted the knot of guilt in my stomach tighter. Here, in this peaceful corner of Central Park, I could pretend to be just Harald – no titles, no duties, no expectations. But the lie grew heavier with each passing moment.

Daniel's fingers traced lazy patterns on my palm. "You know what I like about you? You actually listen. Not just waiting for your turn to talk, but really hearing what I'm saying."

My throat tightened. I did listen – because with Daniel, I could be the person receiving the confidence rather than the one always expected to have the answers. The freedom of anonymity let me focus entirely on him, on understanding his struggles and sharing my own without the weight of protocol.

"I want to tell you something," I started, then faltered as Daniel shifted closer, his warmth seeping through my sweater. The words stuck in my throat. Once I told him the truth, everything would change. The easy banter, the natural connection, the way he looked at me like I was just another person – it would all disappear behind the barrier of formality my title created.

"You can tell me anything," Daniel said softly, lifting his head to meet my eyes. The trust in his expression made my chest ache.

I opened my mouth, then closed it again as a family walked past our bench, the children pointing excitedly at the ducks. Erik's tall frame shifted in my peripheral vision, a constant reminder of the reality I was trying to escape.

Daniel deserved the truth. But selfishly, desperately, I wanted to preserve this moment – this pure connection untainted by crown and country. Just a little longer. Just one more hour of being seen for myself, not my inheritance.

"I just..." I squeezed his hand. "I'm really glad I met you."

The words were true, even if they weren't the whole truth. Daniel's answering smile lit up his entire face, and I tried to memorize it – this moment before everything would inevitably change.

Chapter 14

Harald

As the elevator doors opened with a soft ding, I followed Daniel out into the dimly lit hallway, my heart racing with anticipation. Daniel stopped just outside his apartment door, an endearing mix of nervousness and eagerness in his eyes. "Well, this is me," he said, motioning awkwardly toward his apartment, the words cascading out before he had a chance to think.

We both paused, caught in the magnetism of the moment. I felt my breath catch as our eyes locked, a profound silence enveloping us. It was as if the world had faded away, leaving just the two of us standing there, our heartbeats synchronized with the electric tension in the air.

Daniel bit his lip, glancing down briefly, battling the urge to invite me inside—to share more of himself and the space that felt so personal. I had felt so comfortable with him all day, and now, with the potential for something deeper hanging in the air, the prospect felt intoxicating yet terrifying.

"Um... would you want to come over for breakfast tomorrow? You could meet my friends Jayda and Caleb," he offered, his voice carrying a hint of hope.

I felt my eyes widen with interest, my heart lifting at the invitation. "I'd love that," I replied, a genuine smile breaking across my face. "You're sure it's okay?"

"Definitely! I think they'd love to meet you," Daniel said.

We exchanged shy smiles, neither breaking the gaze, lost in each other's eyes for just a moment longer. The world outside seemed distant and irrelevant as we relished the connection—one that felt more profound than just a casual encounter.

Finally, after what felt like an eternity, Daniel took a small step back, breaking the tension. "It's just, uh... I don't think I should be inviting you in just yet, or..." he chuckled, feeling a mix of light-heartedness and surprise.

"Yeah, me neither, I get it, really..." I admitted, still flustered, running a hand through my hair in a nervous gesture.

We both laughed lightly, the sound echoing in the corridor, dissipating some of the palpable tension. It felt right, yet there was a lingering sense of hesitation hanging in the air.

Daniel suddenly leaned in, his lips crashing against mine with an intensity that made my knees weak. The kiss was deep, passionate, filled with unspoken desires. My hands found their way to his waist, pulling him closer as the world spun around us. Time seemed to stop as I lost myself in the warmth of his embrace, my heart thundering against my chest with such force I was certain he could feel it too. The sweet taste of him, mixed with lingering traces of coffee from earlier, intoxicated me in ways I'd never experienced before. Every royal protocol, every carefully maintained barrier I'd built around myself, melted away in that moment, leaving only the raw, honest connection between us.

Daniel pulled away slightly, his warm breath caressing my ear as he murmured softly, his voice low and husky with barely restrained desire. "I can't deny that every part of me wants you to stay with me tonight," he admitted candidly as I shivered from his closeness alone.

"But I have this unbreakable rule about never letting things go too far on a first date." His fingers traced tantalizing patterns along my skin. "And I'm painfully aware that if I allow you to come in with me now," he paused for emphasis before continuing in an almost reverent whisper, "I don't think I'll be able to stick by that rule or keep these wandering hands from exploring every inch of your body."

A shiver ran down my spine, his words igniting something primal within me. My heart hammered against my chest, and I could feel the heat rising in my cheeks. The thought of staying, of following him through that door, was intoxicating.

The hallway felt too small, too intimate, too dangerous. Every fiber of my being screamed to stay, but my conscience wouldn't let me.

I forced myself to take a step back, though every cell in my body protested the movement. The loss of Daniel's warmth against me felt like physical pain.

"You're right," I breathed out, running my fingers through my disheveled hair. "We should wait."

Daniel's eyes sparkled in the dim hallway light, his lips still red from our kiss. The sight nearly broke my resolve.

"Tomorrow then?" His voice came out rough, matching the electricity still crackling between us.

"Tomorrow," I nodded, trying to ignore how the simple word held so much promise. "Sweet dreams, Daniel."

He fumbled with his keys, our eyes still locked. The metal jingled as he found the right one, sliding it into the lock. "Goodnight, Harry."

The door clicked shut between us, and I pressed my forehead against the cool wall beside it, trying to calm my racing heart. The ghost of his touch lingered on my skin, making it impossible to think straight.

Behind the closed door, I heard the soft thud of Daniel leaning against it, and imagined him standing there, just as affected as I was. After a few steadying breaths, I pushed myself away from the wall and headed toward the elevator, where Erik waited discreetly in the shadows of the building's lobby.

* * *

Daniel

I leaned against my side of the door, heart pounding in my chest. The soft thud on the other side told me Harald was doing the same. My fingers traced the wood grain, imagining his warmth just inches away through the barrier between us.

"Fuck," I whispered, closing my eyes. Every nerve in my body screamed to yank that door open, to pull him inside and forget all about my stupid first-date rule. The memory of his lips on mine in the coffee shop, the way his hands had cupped my face - it sent electricity down my spine.

A soft sigh drifted through the door. My hand wrapped around the doorknob, the metal cool against my palm. One twist and he'd be here, pressing me against the wall, those gorgeous blue eyes darkened with want...

"Get it together, Daniel," I muttered, forcing my hand to drop. The ghost of Alex's betrayal flickered through my mind - a reminder of why I had these boundaries in the first place. But Harald felt different. The vulnerability in his voice when he'd shared his struggles, the genuine way he listened...

Harald's footsteps finally retreated down the hallway, slow and hesitant. Each step echoed like physical pain in my chest. I pressed my forehead against the door, listening until the elevator dinged and the last traces of his presence faded away.

My body still hummed with unspent energy. The phantom sensation of his kiss lingered on my lips. Tomorrow couldn't come fast enough - but for now, this space between us was necessary. Even if every cell in my body disagreed.

I spun around at the sound of slow clapping behind me, my heart leaping into my throat. Caleb stood in the living room doorway, a smirk plastered across his face. Next to him, Jayda doubled over with laughter, clutching her stomach.

"That was the most dramatic door-lean I've ever witnessed." Caleb's clapping echoed through our apartment. "Oscar-worthy performance."

Heat rushed to my face. "How long have you two been standing there?"

"Long enough to see you groping the door like it was your last hope on Earth." Jayda wiped tears from her eyes, her black mascara smudging. "Girl, I haven't seen you this sprung since-" She caught herself, the name 'Alex' hanging unspoken between us.

"This is different," I crossed my arms, trying to salvage some dignity. "And I wasn't groping the door."

"Oh honey, you were one step away from making out with it." Jayda sashayed over, throwing an arm around my shoulders. "But I get it - that man is fine. Those eyes? That accent? If I wasn't taken..."

"Hey!" Caleb protested.

"You know I love you, babe." Jayda blew him a kiss. "But seriously Danny, the sexual tension was so thick in that hallway, I'm surprised the smoke alarms didn't go off."

I groaned, burying my face in my hands. "I hate you both. "

"No you don't." Caleb adjusted his beanie. "And for what it's worth, I respect the self-control. Even if it did look physically painful."

"Wait." I dropped my hands from my face, narrowing my eyes at them. "How would you two even know what happened in the hallway?" Heat crept up my neck for a different reason now. "Were you pervs spying on us?"

Jayda's guilty expression said it all. She untangled herself from my shoulders and backed away, hands raised. "Now Danny, before you get all worked up-"

"We were watching through the peephole," Caleb admitted, adjusting his glasses. "In our defense, we had to make sure this mystery man wasn't an axe murderer."

"The peephole?" My voice cracked. "Are you serious right now?"

"Girl, what did you expect?" Jayda flopped onto our couch. "You've been texting this man non-stop, then suddenly he flies across an ocean to see you? We had to make sure he was legit."

"By watching us like some discount reality show?"

"If it helps, we couldn't hear anything." Caleb shrugged. "We just saw a lot of intense staring and then that kiss that looked like it was about to set the hallway on fire. It was like watching porn gifs, lots of eye candy but no sound."

I grabbed the nearest throw pillow and launched it at his head. He ducked, laughing.

"And then there was all that dramatic leaning and sighing-" Jayda mimed swooning against the couch.

"I hate you both so much right now." I snatched another pillow. "I can't believe you were spying on me with Harald."

"Honestly I suspect half of Brooklyn was spying on you guys, from the looks of it. You two weren't exactly being discreet about it" Jayda waggled her eyebrows. "Unless you're planning to make out with the door again?"

The second pillow hit her square in the face.

"And yes, it was painful," I admitted to Caleb, dropping onto our couch. "But worth it. I think. God, is it tomorrow yet?"

"Speaking of tomorrow..." Jayda's eyes lit up with mischief. "What time is lover boy coming for breakfast? I need to know how early to start planning your outfit."

Jayda jumped up from the couch, her combat boots thudding against our hardwood floor. "Your closet is a disaster zone."

I groaned, sinking deeper into the cushions. "Can't I just wear what I have on?"

"To feed the man who flew across an ocean to see and court you? Absolutely not." She grabbed my arm, yanking me up. "Besides, these jeans have seen better days."

"They're vintage." I tried to protest, but she was already dragging me toward my bedroom.

"They're desperate, is what they are." Jayda flung open my closet doors with dramatic flair. "Now, let's see what we have to work with."

I collapsed onto my bed, watching as she started rifling through hangers. "This could take all night, couldn't it?"

"Only if you keep whining." She held up a blue button-down, then tossed it aside. "Too corporate." A sweater followed. "Too winter." Then a t-shirt. "Too casual."

"You know, some people just put on clothes without turning it into a production."

"Some people aren't trying to impress fucking gorgeous Danish men with accents that could melt butter." She paused, eyeing a pair of slim black jeans. "These might work..."

Despite my complaints, I couldn't help the smile tugging at my lips. Harald's face floated through my mind - the way his eyes had crinkled when he laughed, how his fingers had threaded through my hair when we kissed. My stomach did a little flip just thinking about seeing him again tomorrow.

"Aha!" Jayda's triumphant cry snapped me back to reality. "I found it!"

"Found what?" I propped myself up on my elbows, watching as she emerged from the depths of my closet clutching a burgundy henley I'd forgotten I owned.

"The perfect shirt. It'll make those arms look amazing, and the color will pop against your skin." She tossed it at my face. "Now we just need the right pants cause those black ones ain't it..."

I caught the shirt, running my fingers over the soft material. Maybe this fashion ordeal would be worth it, if it meant seeing that look in Harald's eyes again.

"Earth to Danny!" Jayda's shrill voice cut through my daydream. She snapped her fingers in front of my face. "You're doing it again."

Heat rushed to my cheeks as I realized I'd completely zoned out, lost in replaying that kiss with Harald. The way his stubble had scratched against my chin, how his fingers had gripped my waist...

"Look at that blush!" Jayda dropped the pile of clothes she'd been sorting and plopped down beside me on the bed. "Spill it. What exactly were you thinking about just now?"

"Nothing." I grabbed a pillow and hugged it to my chest, trying to hide my burning face.

"Mmhmm. Nothing." She poked my side. "That's why you're sitting there with that dopey smile, looking like you just won the lottery. Nothing at all to do with tall, blond, and Danish?"

"I hate that you know me so well." I buried my face in the pillow.

"Girl, please. You've got it bad." She yanked the pillow away. "Your eyes glazed over the second I mentioned finding the perfect outfit. I bet you were thinking about that hallway kiss again, weren't you?"

"Maybe." I flopped back onto the bed, staring at the ceiling. "Can you blame me though? Did you see him? Those eyes? That accent? The way he-"

"Yes, yes, we all saw Prince Charming." Jayda laughed. "Now help me pick out these clothes before you float away on cloud nine again."

"He's not actually a prince," I said, sitting up. "Just a regular guy from Denmark."

"Could've fooled me with those manners." Jayda held up another shirt. "Now focus. We've got work to do if you're going to look irresistible tomorrow morning."

I tried to concentrate on the clothes, but my mind kept drifting back to Harald's smile, his laugh, the way his eyes had darkened when we'd kissed...

"Danny!" Jayda's voice snapped me back again. "Girl, you are hopeless."

* * *

Harald

As I sank back into the plush leather seats of the black sedan, my mind was still swirling with thoughts of Daniel. The vibrancy of New York City passed by making me feel all the more alive for it. I took a deep breath, trying to center myself. The day's excitement still coursed through my veins as visions of our passionate encounter danced in my head - the warmth of Daniel's mouth meeting my own, the weight of his embrace enveloping me.

I glanced at Erik, seated beside me, and noticed the serious expression etched across his face. "You need to be more cautious, Harry," he said, his tone firm but laced with concern. "This isn't just a casual outing. You're a public figure, and the paparazzi are always lurking, waiting for a chance to capture a moment. You must keep your identity as Crown Prince under wraps. That woman in the park almost posted those photos on social media - she recognized you."

I frowned, brushing a hand through my hair in frustration. "I know that, Erik. But with Daniel, I just want to be myself... just Harald. Is that too much to ask?"

Erik sighed and turned back to the front as the driver navigated through the busy streets. "I understand how important this is to you. But you need to remember the potential consequences. If word gets out that you're—well, that you're seeing someone like him, it could lead to a media frenzy. Not to mention, the strain it would put on your relationship with him."

I leaned forward, my gaze fixed on the passing city lights, feeling trapped between my duties and my desires. "I'm trying to build something real here. Can't you see that? To Daniel, I'm just Harry. Not the Crown Prince, not someone who has to follow every royal decree."

"All the more reason to protect that connection," Erik replied, his voice softening slightly. "Trust me, I'm on your side. I want you to be happy. Just... tread carefully. Discretion is key. We need to ensure your safety and keep Daniel safe too. You don't want him caught in the storm of your world, not when he doesn't know what he's really stepping into. The last thing we need is for your father to find out by reading the newspapers."

I nodded, the weight of Erik's words sinking in. I understood the truth in them, yet my heart ached with the desire for a love unburdened by royal expectations. "I will, Erik. I promise I'll be careful. But it's hard to suppress this part of me that wants to scream it from the rooftops."

The car pulled up to the sleek entrance of our hotel, the bright lights illuminating the façade. I could feel Erik's gaze on me as he focused on one last piece of advice. "Just remember, you're not just a man in love; you're also a prince with responsibilities. Let's keep those lines separate for now."

As I exited the car, I took a deep breath, reminding myself of Erik's caution. I wanted to cherish this moment with Daniel, but I knew I would have to navigate it cautiously—one step at a time.

Chapter 15

Daniel

I woke at dawn, my nerves crackling with anticipation. The kitchen needed to be spotless before Harald arrived. Empty takeout containers vanished into the trash. Dishes that had lounged in the sink found their way into cabinets. The coffee maker sputtered to life as I wiped down every surface twice.

My phone buzzed. A message from Harald lit up the screen: *"Good morning handsome. Can't wait to see you again."*

My heart skipped. I typed back: *"Morning! Before you come over, fair warning about my roommates..."*

"Should I be worried?"

"Let's just say Jayda and Caleb are... unique. She's a goth punk rocker with a heart of gold, and he's the world's most sarcastic hipster. They're also ridiculously protective of me."

"After everything you've been through, I'd expect nothing less from true friends."

I smiled, touched by his understanding. *"They might interrogate you. Especially after Alex."*

"I welcome the challenge. I'll win them over with my charm and good looks."

"Cocky much?" I snorted, arranging fresh flowers in a vase - a touch Jayda would definitely notice and tease me about later.

"Only stating facts. But seriously, I promise to be on my best behavior. Your friends matter to you, so they matter to me too."

The sincerity in his words warmed my chest. *"Just be yourself. That's who I..."* I backspaced, hesitating. Too soon for that word. *"That's who I like spending time with."*

"Same here. See you soon x"

I tucked my phone away and surveyed the apartment one last time. Everything gleamed. The coffee table magazines aligned at perfect right angles. Fresh pastries from the bakery downstairs waited on a plate. Now I just had to survive the next hour without completely losing my mind over what was to come.

The sound of Jayda's bedroom door opening made me jump. "Danny! Is that coffee I smell?"

Here we go.

"Okay, ground rules for breakfast." I planted myself in front of Jayda and Caleb, who lounged on the couch with matching smirks. "No embarrassing stories. No death threats. And absolutely no mention of-"

"Alex?" Jayda arched an eyebrow. "You mean the walking trash fire we warned you about?"

I winced. "Yeah. That one."

"We hated that snake from day one." Caleb adjusted his beanie. "Remember when he 'forgot' his wallet that time at dinner? And made you pay for his fancy wine?"

"Or how about when he kept blowing off our game nights?" Jayda's dark lips pressed into a thin line. "Always with some lame excuse about work."

The memories stung. They'd tried so hard to show me Alex's true colors, but I'd been too love-blind to see it. "I know, I know. I should have listened to you both."

"Damn right you should have." Jayda softened her tone. "We're just looking out for you, baby."

"Which is why we need to properly vet this Harald guy." Caleb grinned. "Make sure he's worthy."

"Please don't scare him away." I dropped onto the couch between them. "He's different. He actually listens when I talk. And he's genuine and kind and-"

"And we still need to test him." Jayda patted my knee. "That's non-negotiable."

"What kind of best friends would we be if we didn't put him through his paces?" Caleb nudged my shoulder.

I groaned. "Can you at least promise to be somewhat nice?"

They exchanged a look.

"We promise to be..." Jayda paused.

"Thorough in our evaluation," Caleb finished.

"That's not reassuring at all." But I couldn't help smiling. Their protective streak might be annoying, but after Alex, I understood why they needed to be sure. This time, I'd trust their judgment.

* * *

Harald

My palms feel clammy as I stand outside Daniel's door, the hallway's fluorescent lights casting harsh shadows. The bouquet of fresh sunflowers I picked up this morning trembles slightly in my grip. Back home, I've faced rooms full of dignitaries without breaking a sweat, but meeting Daniel's friends feels infinitely more daunting.

The door swings open. Daniel's face lights up, and my breath catches at the sight of him in a burgundy henley that hugs his chest and arms perfectly.

"You brought flowers?" His eyes sparkle as he leans in for a tantalizing kiss that leaves the promise of more later. "Come in, come in."

I step inside, hyper-conscious of my movements. Did I walk too stiffly? Should I have worn something more casual than this blue cashmere sweater?

"These are lovely." Daniel inhales the sunflowers' scent. "Let me grab a vase."

The apartment unfolds before me - mismatched furniture arranged with care, a wall covered in polaroid photos, the lingering aroma of coffee and something sweet baking. It's everything my stark palace quarters aren't - warm, personal, alive with memories.

Two people emerge from the kitchen - a tall man with close-cropped hair and a woman with box braids cascading down her back. Daniel's roommates. My throat tightens.

"Jayda, Caleb, this is Harald." Daniel's voice carries a hint of nervousness that matches my own.

I extend my hand, praying they can't see it shake. "It's wonderful to meet you both. Daniel speaks of you often."

The scrutiny in their gazes makes my skin prickle. They're protective of him - as they should be after what his ex did. I straighten my shoulders, channeling years of diplomatic training while trying not to seem too formal.

The sound of Daniel dropping something in the kitchen breaks the tension. "Shit! Don't worry, vase is okay!"

A genuine laugh escapes me, and for a moment, I forget to be nervous. This is Daniel's world - messy, real, wonderful. I want so badly to belong in it.

Jayda and Caleb exchange a look that speaks volumes - the kind of silent communication that comes from years of being in love. My heart pounds against my ribs as I wait for their verdict.

"Come help me with breakfast," Jayda says, jerking her head toward the kitchen. "Daniel's hopeless with pancakes."

"I heard that!" Daniel calls out, still fussing with the vase.

"You were meant to," Caleb shoots back, dropping onto their worn leather couch with a knowing smirk.

I follow Jayda into their compact kitchen, where the scent of coffee mingles with vanilla and cinnamon. She hands me a whisk and slides a bowl of batter across the counter.

"So, Harald from Denmark," she says, measuring coffee grounds into a filter. "What brings you to New York?"

The whisk moves smoothly through the batter as I consider my response. The truth - that I'm here specifically to see Daniel - feels both too simple and too loaded.

"Work, primarily," I say, which isn't entirely a lie. "But meeting Daniel has definitely been the highlight."

"Mhmm." Jayda's rings click against the coffee pot as she fills it. "And what kind of work do you do?"

Before I can fumble through an answer, Daniel swoops in and wraps his arms around my waist from behind. "Stop interrogating him, J."

"I'm just making conversation." Jayda's stern expression cracks into a warm smile. "Besides, anyone who brings flowers and knows how to properly whisk pancake batter can't be all bad."

"Thank you, I try." I keep my tone light as I continue whisking. "Though I must confess, my culinary skills are limited to breakfast foods and the occasional pasta dish."

"And what do you do when you're not making breakfast?" Jayda measures out another scoop of coffee, her dark eyes intent.

"I work for the family business in government administration primarily." The familiar half-truth rolls off my tongue. "Lots of meetings, policy reviews, public relations. Rather dull stuff, actually." I pour the batter onto the hot griddle in careful circles, grateful for something to focus on besides her piercing gaze.

"And your family? They're all back in Denmark?"

My hand tightens on the spatula. "They are, yes." I flip a pancake with perhaps more force than necessary. "Daniel mentioned you're into punk music? He showed me some of the bands you've introduced him to."

Jayda's eyes narrow slightly at my obvious deflection. She sets down the coffee pot with deliberate care, and I can feel her reassessing me. The kitchen fills with the sizzle of pancakes and an undercurrent of tension.

Daniel slides his arms around my waist again, resting his chin on my shoulder. "These smell amazing."

I lean back into his embrace, grateful for the interruption. The warmth of his chest against my back grounds me, helps steady my racing thoughts.

"You're right," Jayda says after a moment, though her tone suggests she's filing away my evasiveness for later consideration. "The Ramones are always a good place to start for newcomers to punk."

"The Ramones are classic, but I've always had a soft spot for The Clash," I say, flipping another pancake. "London Calling got me through some particularly tedious state dinne- meetings, I mean."

"Oh, we've got ourselves a proper punk fan here." Jayda's eyes light up, her earlier suspicion momentarily forgotten. "What's your take on Dead Kennedys?"

"Holiday in Cambodia is brilliant." The tension in my shoulders eases as we drift into safer territory. "Though I suppose it hits different when you actually work in government."

Daniel snorts against my neck. "Harald's got jokes."

"Speaking of musical taste," Caleb pipes up from the doorway, pushing his thick-rimmed glasses up his nose. "Have you heard the new indie folk band from Portland? They only released twelve copies of their album on recycled vinyl-"

"No." Jayda points her coffee mug at him. "We are not doing this. Not everyone needs to know about your obscure bands that recorded their albums in abandoned grain silos."

"It was actually an old lighthouse," Caleb mutters.

"Even worse." Jayda turns back to me. "So, The Clash? Tell me you've got Better Living Through Chemistry on your playlist."

"Of course." I plate up the last pancake, grateful that my hands have stopped shaking. "Though I have to admit, Spanish Bombs speaks to me more."

"Decent taste." Jayda nods approvingly. "We might keep you around after all."

Daniel squeezes my waist, and I catch the relief in his expression. We've cleared the first hurdle, even if there are countless more ahead. For now, though, I'll take this small victory - standing in this cozy kitchen, talking punk rock with Daniel's chosen family while breakfast sizzles on the griddle.

I settle onto their worn leather couch, balancing my plate of pancakes on my knee. The living room buzzes with comfortable chaos - mismatched cushions, books stacked on every surface, and that wall of memories that keeps drawing my eye.

"Your home is wonderful," I say, meaning every word. "It feels truly lived in. My place back home is all straight lines and antiques nobody dares touch."

Daniel plops down beside me, close enough that our thighs touch. "Rich people problems?" He grins, nudging my shoulder.

"Something like that." I take a bite of pancake to avoid elaborating.

"Oh, you're looking at our wall of shame?" Jayda points with her fork toward the polaroids. "That's from our road trip to New Orleans last summer."

"The one where Danny tried to convince us he could speak French to that bartender?" Caleb snorts.

"Hey, I got us free drinks didn't I?"

"Because he felt sorry for you butchering his language." Jayda reaches up to tap a photo of the three of them, faces flushed and happy, holding hurricane cocktails. "But that weekend was epic."

Daniel leans forward, pointing to another snapshot. "And that's from when we drove to Maine for lobster rolls. Caleb got chased by seagulls."

"Those birds were organized," Caleb protests. "They had a battle plan."

I study each photo, drinking in these glimpses of Daniel's life - his real, messy, beautiful life. There he is laughing in front of the Grand Canyon, sprawled on a beach in Miami, pulling faces at a Christmas party. Such a contrast to my own carefully curated photo albums, full of formal events and practiced smiles.

"You all seem to have such adventures together," I say softly.

Daniel's hand finds mine, squeezing gently. "Well, now you can be part of our next one."

The warmth of his touch spreads through my chest, even as guilt twists in my stomach. How many more memories can we make before the truth of who I am changes everything?

* * *

Jayda

I stack the breakfast plates while watching Caleb scrub the frying pan, admiring how his long fingers work methodically at a particularly stubborn bit of egg. My chunky boots squeak against the linoleum as I shift my weight, trying to appear casual despite my burning curiosity. "So... what's your read on Harald?" I ask, fiddling with the silver rings on my fingers while waiting for my boyfriend's inevitably shrewd assessment.

"He's hiding something." Caleb doesn't look up from his scrubbing, his wrist moving in tight, focused circles that make the metal wool pad squeak against the non-stick surface. "Did you notice how he dodged every question about his work or family? Like, he'd give these vague non-answers about 'working in government' and 'having a complicated family situation.' Classic deflection tactics if you ask me." His tone carries that analytical edge I've come to know so well - the same one he uses when he's piecing together the plot twists in those mystery novels he loves so much.

"Mhmm." I methodically wipe down the counter with slow, deliberate strokes, my mind replaying Harald's carefully constructed responses about 'consulting' and 'family business' from earlier. The practiced way he'd redirected questions reminded me of politicians I'd seen on TV. "But the way he looks at Danny though—that's real." I say it with absolute certainty, because I've seen enough people feign interest in my best friend to know the difference. When Harald gazes at Danny, his eyes soften with a warmth that no amount of social polish could fake, like he's seeing something precious and rare. It's the kind of look that makes my protective instincts war with my romantic heart.

"Yeah, not like Alex's greasy little snake eyes." Caleb's jaw tightens at the mention of Danny's ex, and I can practically feel the tension radiating off him. Neither of us can forget how broken Danny was after that betrayal. Caleb rinses the pan with more force than necessary, the water splashing against the metal like his barely contained anger. "Harald seems... I don't know, genuine? Despite the mystery act. And I know that doesn't make sense." He pauses, scrubbing at a particularly stubborn spot as if it personally offended him. "There's something almost vulnerable about him when he thinks no one's watching, you know what I mean?"

"The sunflowers were a nice touch. I'm not sure if he even realized that those are Danny's favorite flowers," I smile, glancing at the bright yellow blooms now sitting in our best vase. The cheerful petals seem to glow in the late afternoon light streaming through our kitchen window, making the whole room feel warmer somehow. "And he actually listened when Danny talked. Didn't try to make it all about himself. You could see it in his eyes, the way he was completely focused on every word, like Danny's stories about his terrible job were the most fascinating things he'd ever heard."

"True." Caleb dries his hands methodically on our striped kitchen towel and leans his lanky frame against the counter, adjusting his ever-present beanie with still-damp fingers. "Plus, he laughed at my jokes. That's major points right there."

"You mean your terrible puns?" I bump his hip playfully with mine as I pass by. "But seriously, I haven't seen Danny this happy in ages. The way his whole face lit up when Harald walked in..." I trail off, remembering how Daniel's eyes had sparkled with genuine joy, something I hadn't witnessed since well before the Alex disaster. It was like watching a flower bloom after a long winter - subtle but unmistakable, the kind of transformation that makes your heart squeeze with hope.

"I know." Caleb wraps an arm around my waist. "Just hope Harald doesn't break his heart. Danny's been through enough."

"We'll break his legs and drown him in concrete if he does." I rest my head on Caleb's shoulder, feeling the soft fabric of his well-worn cardigan against my cheek. The familiar scent of his sandalwood cologne wraps around me like a comfort blanket. "But I've got a good feeling about this one. Did you see how nervous he was meeting us? Like our approval actually mattered to him." I can't help but smile, remembering how Harald had fidgeted with his watch strap and kept smoothing down his perfectly pressed shirt. It was endearing, really - this polished, clearly wealthy man so concerned about impressing Danny's ramshackle found family. After the nightmare with Alex, seeing someone treat Daniel with such genuine respect feels like a breath of fresh air.

"Yeah, not exactly giving off rich asshole vibes despite the fancy watch and that tailored suit that probably costs more than our monthly rent." Caleb kisses my temple, his lips lingering there for a moment as I lean into his familiar touch. "Though what kind of government consultant needs a security detail? I mean, those two guys hovering near the elevator entrance in the hallway weren't exactly subtle with their earpieces and stern faces. Kind of weird for someone who just helps companies restructure or whatever it is he said he does."

"You noticed that too hey?" I straighten up.

"Hard to miss. But hey, maybe Harald's just important in Denmark or whatever." I shrug, trying to play it casual even though my curiosity is definitely piqued. The whole setup does seem a bit excessive for a regular business consultant, but who am I to judge how they do things in Europe? Still, something about this situation niggles at the back of my mind, like a song lyric I can't quite remember.

"You think Danny even registered them, or was he too busy gazing at Sir Handsome von Panty-Dropper?"

Caleb exhales sharply through his nose. "Danny wouldn't have noticed if I moonwalked butt-ass naked through the living room serving waffles. His eyeballs might as well have been surgically attached to Harald's jawline."

"Should we loop him in?"

"Let him connect the dots. Anyway, Harald's babysitters mean Dan gets free protection by proxy." He brushes crumbs from his jeans. "Upside: our boy stays safe. Downside: I lose my new evening entertainment."

Chapter 16

Harald

The cacophony of sounds hits me all at once—carnival music, the screams from roller coasters, hawkers calling out to passersby. Coney Island stretches before us in a colourful blur of movement, smells, and noise unlike anything I've experienced.

"This is..." I struggle to find the right words, my eyes wide as I take it all in.

"Too much?" Daniel asks, a flicker of concern crossing his face.

I squeeze his hand. "No, it's incredible. We don't have anything quite like this in Denmark."

"Wait, you've never been to an amusement park?" Daniel's eyebrows shoot up.

Heat rushes to my face. "Not like this. The royal fam—" I catch myself. "I mean, my family doesn't really do things so... public."

Daniel tugs me toward a cotton candy vendor, his eyes sparkling with excitement. "Then we're doing everything today. Cotton candy, the Wonder Wheel, hot dogs—the works."

The vendor hands me a massive pink cloud of spun sugar. I stare at it, perplexed.

"Just pull a piece off and eat it," Daniel demonstrates, his fingers coming away sticky.

I follow his lead, surprised when the sugar dissolves instantly on my tongue. "It's just... gone! How do they make this?"

Daniel laughs, the sound warming me from the inside. "You're like an alien discovering Earth for the first time."

We wander past game booths where people throw balls at bottles and toss rings onto pegs. A carousel spins nearby, children laughing as painted horses bob up and down. Everything feels wonderfully ordinary and extraordinary at the same time.

"Look," Daniel points toward the massive Wonder Wheel dominating the skyline. "We have to ride that."

I nod, though a flutter of nervousness passes through me. In Denmark, I always have security protocols, risk assessments. Here, I'm just a man on a date, about to trust my safety to a massive spinning wheel that's probably older than my father.

Daniel notices my hesitation. "Hey, we don't have to if you don't want to."

I straighten my shoulders. "No, I want to experience everything. Lead the way."

As we join the queue, I can't help wondering what Erik would think seeing me here. I'd manage to convince him and my security detail to stay behind at the hotel, promising to be on my best behaviour. Meanwhile I'm the Crown Prince of Denmark, standing in line for a carnival ride, fingers sticky with cotton candy, without a care in the world beyond the beautiful man beside me.

The line for the Wonder Wheel moves steadily forward, and I find myself studying the massive structure with both awe and trepidation. Its steel frame reaches toward the sky, swinging cars dangling from its circumference.

"Is this safe?" I ask, immediately regretting how sheltered I sound.

Daniel chuckles. "Totally. This thing's been running since 1920. It's survived wars, storms, everything. Classic New York landmark."

"So it's very old, that's what you're saying," I deadpan, but squeeze his hand to show I'm joking.

We climb aboard one of the blue cars that Daniel explains are the "swinging" ones. As we ascend, the car sways gently, offering breathtaking views of the beach, boardwalk, and sprawling city beyond.

"This is magnificent," I breathe, taking in the panorama. The vastness of the ocean stretches to the horizon on one side, while New York's concrete jungle rises on the other. It's a perspective I've never seen before—not from royal helicopters, not from diplomatic viewpoints carefully curated for state visits.

When our car pauses at the top, I turn to Daniel. "Don't you have work today? It's Monday, isn't it?"

A mischievous grin spreads across his face. "Called in sick."

"You did? For me?"

"Of course for you." Daniel straightens in his seat, clears his throat, and adopts a pitiful, croaking voice. "Hi Cassandra? It's Daniel. I'm so sorry cough cough but I seem to have caught something sniffle and I don't think I'll make it in today."

He clutches his stomach dramatically, hunching over. *"Yes, ma'am, I know the Taylor account needs processing wheeze but I'm afraid I might be contagious. Wouldn't want to infect the whole office. I think it might be strep."*

Daniel finishes with a theatrical sneeze and returns to his normal voice. "She totally knew I was faking, but what could she do?"

Something warm unfurls in my chest. No one has ever skipped responsibilities for me before. People rearrange entire schedules to accommodate my royal duties, but no one has ever simply chosen to be with me over their obligations.

"You risked the wrath of your tyrant boss for me?"

"Worth it," Daniel says simply, his eyes meeting mine. "Every second."

I lean forward, bridging the small gap between us in our swinging car atop the Wonder Wheel. My lips find Daniel's, soft and warm against mine. This isn't just a kiss—it's everything I can't say with words: how much this ordinary day means to someone who's never known ordinary, how his simple act of calling in sick for me touches something profound in my royal, regimented heart.

My fingers brush his cheek as I deepen the kiss, trying to pour every ounce of gratitude and wonder into this moment. The car sways gently beneath us, suspended between earth and sky, just as I'm suspended between two worlds—the crown prince and just Harald, the man who gets to experience cotton candy and Ferris wheels and playing hooky on a Monday.

When we finally part Daniel's eyes are bright, his cheeks flushed and his lips puffy. The wind tousles his dark hair, and behind him stretches the vast Atlantic—the same ocean that connects his home to mine, though he doesn't yet know how far that distance truly is.

"What was that for?" he asks, his voice slightly breathless.

"For being the first person who's ever chosen just... me." The words come out more vulnerable than I intended. "Not for duty or obligation or appearances. Just me."

Daniel's expression softens. He takes my hand, running his thumb across my knuckles. "Well, get used to it. I'd choose you over spreadsheets and Cassandra's jowly disapproval any day."

I laugh, the sound carried away by the sea breeze. For this perfect moment, I'm not thinking about the crown, the responsibilities waiting across the ocean, or the truth I still haven't told him. I'm just a man, kissing another man at the top of a Ferris wheel, feeling more alive than I have in years.

I step off the Wonder Wheel with Daniel, our fingers interlaced, feeling lighter than I've felt in years. The midway stretches before us, a gauntlet of carnival games with barkers calling out to passersby.

"Step right up, test your skill! Three balls for five dollars!"

Daniel tugs me toward a booth where milk bottles are stacked in pyramids. The attendant, a man with weathered skin and a faded Coney Island cap, grins at us.

"Wanna win something for your boyfriend?" he asks, nodding toward the oversized plush animals hanging from the ceiling.

I feel a pleasant warmth spread through me at the word "boyfriend." Is that what we are now? The thought makes me stand a little taller.

"I'll try," I say, pulling out my wallet.

Daniel leans close, his breath tickling my ear. "These games are totally rigged, you know."

"Are they?" I hand over a five-dollar bill. "We don't have these exact games in Denmark."

The attendant passes me three baseballs. They feel heavier than they look.

"Just knock down all the bottles in one throw," he explains, gesturing toward the stack. "Simple as that."

I weigh the ball in my hand, studying the pyramid. In reality, I've had some training in various sports—part of my royal education—but never specifically in knocking down milk bottles at carnivals.

My first throw misses completely.

Daniel bursts out laughing. "That was... spectacularly bad."

I feel my cheeks flush. "I'm just warming up."

The second ball clips the edge of the pyramid, sending one bottle wobbling but not falling.

"Close!" the attendant encourages, though his expression suggests he's seen this play out thousands of times.

I take a breath, focusing on the center of the bottom row. The ball leaves my hand in a clean arc and—

CRASH!

The entire pyramid collapses, bottles scattering across the back of the booth.

"We have a winner!" the attendant announces, sounding genuinely surprised.

Daniel's mouth drops open. "How did you—"

"Lucky throw," I shrug, unable to hide my grin.

"Which prize do you want?" the attendant asks, pointing to the hanging plush animals.

I turn to Daniel. "You choose."

Daniel points to a ridiculously fluffy blue penguin with oversized eyes. The attendant unhooks it and hands it to me, and I present it to Daniel with a small bow.

"Your penguin, sir."

Daniel hugs it to his chest, his eyes bright. "I shall name him Harald Junior."

I laugh, imagining what my father would say about my namesake being a carnival penguin. "An honor I don't deserve."

The afternoon sun beats down on the boardwalk as Daniel and I stroll past souvenir shops and food stands. The weight of his hand in mine feels right, like something I've been missing my whole life. We pass a group of teenagers playing music from a portable speaker, and Daniel starts bobbing his head to the beat.

"Dance with me," he says suddenly, pulling me toward the makeshift dance floor where a few other couples are swaying.

"Here? Now?" I glance around, years of royal protocol screaming in my head about public appearances and dignity.

Daniel reads my hesitation and squeezes my hand. "No one's watching.

No one cares. We're just two guys having fun."

He's right. No palace photographers, no royal observers, no Erik anxiously checking his watch. Just us.

I let him lead me into a ridiculous twirl, and then we're both laughing, dancing terribly to a song I don't know. Daniel's movements are fluid and uninhibited, while I'm stiff and awkward, but it doesn't matter. The freedom of it—the sheer joy of being able to make a fool of myself in public without it becoming a national headline—is intoxicating.

As the afternoon stretches on, we walk along the weathered wooden planks of the boardwalk, our fingers intertwined. Seagulls swoop overhead, and the rhythmic crash of waves against the shore provides a constant backdrop to our adventure.

"Ice cream?" Daniel suggests as the sun begins its descent toward the horizon, painting the sky in dramatic pinks and oranges.

We queue at a small stand advertising "Brooklyn's Best Ice Cream" and order a large cone with two scoops—chocolate for Daniel, vanilla for me.

"Here," Daniel says, handing me the cone first. "You start."

I lick the vanilla side, savoring the rich, creamy sweetness. This isn't the carefully presented desserts of royal banquets or the delicate confections of palace kitchens. It's simple and perfect.

Daniel takes the cone next, his tongue darting out to taste his chocolate scoop. A small bit dabs onto his nose, and I reach up to wipe it away with my thumb.

"Messy," I tease.

"Part of the experience," he replies with a grin.

We find a bench facing the ocean and sit close together, passing the ice cream cone back and forth as the sun sinks lower, casting long shadows across the beach. The day crowds are thinning, leaving just scattered couples and families enjoying the evening.

"This has been the best day," I say softly, watching the golden light play across Daniel's features. "Just... normal. Perfect."

I hold the ice cream cone back out to Daniel, watching the sunset catch in his dark eyes as he takes another small bite.

"I know exactly what you mean," Daniel agrees, leaning into my shoulder. "I haven't felt this relaxed and safe in a long time." His voice trails off for a moment before recovering. "Being with you feels easy. Natural."

This hits me right in the chest—how something so simple for others is extraordinary for me. A day without protocol, without crown or country weighing on my shoulders. Just ice cream and laughter and Daniel.

"Look, they're starting to turn off the lights on some rides," I note, gesturing toward the darkening carnival. "I think the park must be closing soon."

Daniel nods, finishing the last bite of our cone. "Yeah, they close earlier on weekdays." He stands and extends his hand to me. "Shall we?"

I take his hand, our fingers interlacing naturally now. We stroll toward the exit, my thumb absently brushing over his knuckles. The crowds have thinned considerably, leaving the boardwalk peaceful as the first stars appear overhead.

"Next time we should—" Daniel begins, but his words cut off abruptly.

I follow his gaze to see a tall man with blond hair and a smirk heading directly toward us. Daniel's hand tightens in mine, his entire body tensing.

"Well, well," the man calls out, his voice carrying a mocking edge. "If it isn't Daniel. Already found someone new to trick?"

Daniel's face drains of colour. "Alex," he says, barely above a whisper.

So this is Alex. The man who broke Daniel so thoroughly he ended up in hospital. I straighten my posture instinctively, royal training kicking in as I assess this unexpected threat.

"Thought I recognized that laugh," Alex continues, looking me up and down with obvious disdain. "Well would you look at that Danny, how'd you manage to trick this guy who is totally out of your league into a date?"

Alex's smirk widens as he steps closer, his eyes darting between Daniel and me.

"I'm surprised you're even out and about," Alex says, his voice dripping with venom. "Last I heard you were in the loony bin after your little... episode." He makes a slashing motion across his wrist. "How's that working out for you? Still collecting scars?"

Daniel flinches beside me, his hand trembling in mine. I feel a surge of protective rage rise in my chest. This man knows exactly where to strike to cause maximum pain.

"Let's go," Daniel mutters, trying to pull me away.

Alex steps directly into our path. "Oh no, don't leave on my account. I'm just catching up with my ex." He turns to me with mock concern. "Has he told you everything? About how he completely lost it when he found me with someone else? Drama queen couldn't handle that I needed more than just him."

The casual cruelty in his tone makes my blood boil. I've faced down hostile dignitaries and aggressive press, but never have I felt such immediate, visceral disgust for another human being.

"You know, Danny," Alex continues, "that guy I was with when you walked in? He wasn't even the first. Or the tenth." He laughs, a hollow sound. "I was hooking up with guys from Grindr our entire relationship. Even that weekend we went to the Hamptons—remember when I said I was going for a run? Yeah, I was actually—"

Something snaps inside me. Before I fully realize what I'm doing, my fist connects with Alex's jaw with a sickening crack. Boxing lessons paying off in a way my instructors never intended.

Alex crumples to the boardwalk, a look of shocked disbelief on his face as he clutches his jaw and spits blood.

"You had no right," I hiss, standing over him, my voice low and controlled despite the fury coursing through me. "No right to hurt him then, and certainly no right to hurt him now." White-hot rage fractures my self-control. My knuckles smash into Alex's cheekbone again with a wet crunch before my mind catches up—those princely sparring sessions honing reflexes meant for defence, not this.

He collapses onto weathered planks, hands scrambling to cradle his face. The whites of his eyes gleam with animal panic beneath smeared glasses.

I'm vaguely aware that I've just committed assault in public—something that would cause an international incident if anyone knew who I was—but in this moment, I couldn't care less. It doesn't matter that there are people watching us and laughing at Alex on the ground, or that there are camera flashes as people record us and our fight. All that matters is Daniel.

I stand over Alex, my chest heaving, a strange calm settling over me despite the chaos of the moment. This isn't the measured diplomacy I've been trained in since birth—this is something rawer, more primal. The protection of someone I care about.

"Listen carefully," I say, my voice dropping to a dangerous whisper as I lean closer to where Alex sprawls on the boardwalk. "Daniel deserves better than the air you pollute by breathing it."

Alex's eyes widen. There's something in my tone—perhaps the absolute certainty that comes from generations of royal command—that makes him shrink back.

"If you ever so much as look in his direction again," I continue, each word precise and measured, "I will personally ensure you regret it for the rest of your miserable existence. "

I straighten up, smoothing my sweater with the practiced motion of someone accustomed to maintaining appearances. "I have resources you can't begin to imagine, connections that could make your life very difficult with a single phone call. Your job, your apartment, your future prospects—all of it could just…disappear overnight."

The threat rolls off my tongue with terrifying ease, as if the prince in me knows exactly how to wield power, even when the man in me is shaking with rage.

"Is that perfectly clear?" I ask, my voice eerily calm.

Alex nods rapidly, scrambling backward before staggering to his feet. He opens his mouth as if to say something, then thinks better of it and hurries away, casting one last fearful glance over his shoulder.

Only when he's gone do I turn to Daniel, suddenly uncertain. I've just revealed a side of myself I didn't know existed—the ruthlessness that perhaps comes with royal blood after all.

Daniel stands frozen, his lips slightly parted, eyes wide. There's shock there, certainly, but something else too—a heat, an intensity that makes my heart race faster. He stares at me as if seeing me for the first time, his breath coming quick and shallow.

"Are you okay?" I ask softly, reaching for his hand.

I step toward Daniel, my heart hammering. The adrenaline from confronting Alex still courses through my veins, but now it's mingled with dread. What have I done?

Chapter 17

Harald

"Daniel, I'm so sorry," I start, my voice unsteady. "I shouldn't have—"

I don't finish my sentence because suddenly Daniel launches himself at me, his arms wrapping around my neck as his body collides with mine. For a split second I think he's attacking me—until I feel his lips crash against mine with bruising intensity.

He kisses me with a desperate hunger, his hands gripping my hair, my shoulders, my back. I respond instinctively, my arms encircling his waist and pulling him closer. The taste of him—salt air and ice cream and something uniquely Daniel—floods my senses.

When we finally break apart, we're both breathing hard. Daniel's eyes are liquid fire, his pupils blown wide with desire.

"Thank you," he whispers against my mouth, his fingers tracing the line of my jaw. "Nobody's ever stood up for me like that."

"I was afraid I'd frightened you," I admit, searching his face. "I don't usually... I've never actually punched someone outside of training before."

Daniel laughs, a sound of pure delight. "Frightened me? Harald, that was the sexiest thing I've ever seen in my life." He presses another kiss to my lips, gentler this time. "You defended me. You made him stop."

His hand slides down to rest against my chest, right over my thundering heart. "Nobody's ever cared enough to protect me before."

The vulnerability in his voice breaks something open inside me. I cup his face in my hands, brushing my thumbs across his cheekbones.

"I will always protect you," I promise, the words carrying more weight than he can possibly know. It's a vow not just from a man, but from a prince.

Daniel smiles up at me, his eyes shining. "My hero," he murmurs, and there's no mockery in it, only wonder.

"That's all I want to do from now on."

Daniel leans forward, and I feel his lips meet mine again, but this time there's something different—a hunger, an urgency that wasn't there before. His hands cradle my face, then slide into my hair, pulling me closer with a need that makes my breath catch. The gentle exploration of our previous kisses transforms into something more primal, more desperate.

I respond instinctively, my arms tightening around his waist as I pull him against me, eliminating what little space remained between us. The heat of his body pressed against mine sends electricity racing through my veins. My royal training—years of restraint and proper decorum—dissolves beneath the fire of Daniel's touch.

His teeth graze my bottom lip, a gentle nip that draws a surprised sound from my throat. Then his tongue slides against mine, deepening the kiss as his fingers tangle in my hair. I've never been kissed like this—like I'm essential, like I'm something precious and desired for myself alone, not for my title or my position.

"Harry," he breathes against my mouth, the word half-plea, half-prayer.

I'm dimly aware that we're still standing on the boardwalk, that there are people around us, that everyone is probably watching us nearby, horrified at this public display. But I can't bring myself to care. For once in my life, I'm not thinking about consequences or appearances or duty. I'm simply feeling—Daniel's hands in my hair, his chest against mine, his heartbeat matching the frantic rhythm of my own.

His kisses grow more insistent, more demanding. One of his hands slides down my back, pulling me impossibly closer as he deepens the kiss further. I feel myself respond, a low sound escaping me as my fingers press into his hips. There's something liberating about this moment—about being wanted so openly, so honestly by someone who has no idea of my royal status. Daniel wants just me, Harald the man, not Harald the Crown Prince.

I'm lost in Daniel's burning gaze when he suddenly grabs my wrist, tugging me away from the boardwalk with urgent purpose.

"We need to get out of here. Now," Daniel says, his voice thick with desire. He's practically dragging me toward the main street, his grip firm and insistent. My body follows automatically, pulse racing as I struggle to keep pace with him.

"Where are we—" I start to ask, but Daniel cuts me off with a look that steals my breath.

"How far is your hotel?" he demands, his eyes dark with intention. He flags down an approaching taxi with his free hand, never loosening his grip on me.

"About twenty minutes," I manage to say as the yellow cab pulls to the curb. "Midtown. The Peninsula."

Daniel yanks open the door and practically shoves me inside before sliding in beside me. He gives the driver the address, then turns to me with a fierce intensity that makes my stomach drop.

"I know I said I have rules about this," he says, his voice low enough that only I can hear. "Second date, no sleeping together on that one too, all that..." His hand finds mine in the space between us, our fingers interlacing with a desperate strength. "But after what just happened? Those rules are officially broken."

I swallow hard, feeling heat crawl up my neck. "Are you sure?"

The taxi pulls away from the curb, and Daniel shifts closer, his thigh pressing against mine. "Very sure," he whispers, his breath warm against my ear. "The way you stood up for me back there..." His free hand moves to my knee, squeezing gently. "I need you. Right now. Hotel room. As soon as humanly possible."

The certainty in his voice, the raw want in his eyes—it's intoxicating. No one has ever looked at me like this before, like I'm essential, like I'm worth breaking rules for.

"Twenty minutes," I repeat, my voice rough with anticipation.

Daniel's fingers tighten around mine. "That's nineteen minutes too many."

I stare at Daniel's lips, already missing their warmth against mine. Something primal stirs in me as I watch him unbuckle his seat belt and mine with deliberate slowness, his eyes never leaving mine. The click of the release echoes in the small space of the taxi.

"What are you—" I begin, but my words dissolve into a sharp intake of breath as Daniel shifts across the seat and slides onto my lap in one fluid motion. His knees bracket my hips, his weight settling against me as he takes my face in his hands.

"I can't wait nineteen minutes," he murmurs, before capturing my mouth with his.

Daniel's body melds against mine, his scorching heat searing my very soul. His fingers entwine themselves in my hair, tugging just enough to send shivers of exquisite pleasure cascading down my spine. I grip his hips, digging my nails into his firm, toned ass, desperate to bring him even closer as our throbbing lengths meet and grind together through the thing fabric of our pants. Each slick, electric friction between us sends a delicious avalanche of sensation crashing through me, obliterating all thought and reason. All that remains is the intoxicating heat of his skin against mine and the need to possess him completely.

"Hey! HEY!" The taxi driver's voice cuts through the haze of desire. "This ain't that kind of cab! Save it for the hotel!"

Daniel reluctantly breaks the kiss, his heated breath ghosting against my lips as we both struggle to catch our breath. I can feel his frustration—a palpable, primal ache that matches my own—as we yearn to be closer, to feel every inch of each other's bodies.

Without thinking, I reach into my pocket and pull out my wallet. Royal instinct takes over—problems have solutions, and sometimes those solutions are monetary.

"Two hundred and fifty dollars if you just drive and ignore us," I say, my voice rough with desire as I hold up the bills.

The driver's eyes widen in the rearview mirror, darting between the money and us. For a moment, I think he might refuse—might throw us out of his cab for the impropriety.

Then he snatches the bills from my hand, tucks them into his shirt pocket, and adjusts his mirror so he can no longer see the backseat.

"Fifteen minutes to the Peninsula," he announces, then cranks up the radio to an almost deafening volume.

Daniel's wicked, triumphant smile sends a shiver down my spine. "Resourceful," he purrates against my lips. "I've always had a weakness for resourceful men."

His mouth claims mine once more, hungrier this time, as if the knowledge of our stolen privacy has lit a fire within him. My hands slip under the hem of his shirt, fingertips trailing along the hot, slick skin of his lower back. He arches into my touch with a needy moan, his hips grinding against mine in silent invitation.

"I want you," I groan into his ear between kisses, unable to keep the desire from my voice any longer. "I've wanted you since the moment I laid eyes on you."

Daniel's hips roll against mine, creating a delicious friction that sets every nerve ending in my body on fire. His lips brush my ear, his breath hot and heavy against my skin. "Harry," he moans, his voice ragged with need, "I need you so badly I can't even think straight."

The sound of my name—my nickname, not my title—on his lips sends a wave of heat through me. This isn't about the Crown Prince of Denmark. This is just about us—Harald and Daniel—two people consumed by desire.

"I've been aching for this since that first call," Daniel whispers, his fingers tightening in my hair. His confession sends my heart racing even faster. "I've wanted you, Harry. God, I've wanted you so much."

My hands trail up his back, sliding under his shirt to explore the contours of his heated skin. His flesh is impossibly soft, like silk against my fingertips. Each touch elicits a breathy moan or whimper from him—sounds that I yearn to capture with my lips, sounds I want to etch into my memory.

"I've wanted you too," I breathe against his ear, trailing open-mouthed kisses along the column of his neck. "Thought about this more than I should admit."

"Prove it," he challenges, arching his back in anticipation. "Show me how much you've wanted me."

Daniel rolls his hips against mine again, creating a friction that tears a groan from deep in my chest. His movements become more insistent, more deliberate, as if he's determined to drive me to the edge of control right here in this taxi.

"Tell me," he demands, his voice low and urgent. "Tell me what you've fantasized about."

In the royal household, desire remains unspoken—a weakness to be managed, not expressed. But here, with Daniel's weight anchoring me, with his hands mapping my body like uncharted territory, I find the courage to voice what I've kept locked away.

"Everything," I confess, my accent thickening with desire. "Your mouth, so warm and wet on mine. Your hands, roaming over my body, setting every inch of my skin on fire." I trail a line of kisses down his jawline. "The sounds you might make when I touch you... when I'm inside you," I whisper into his ear, my voice husky with need.

Daniel's answering groan vibrates against my lips as I press them to his throat. His head falls back, exposing more of his neck to my exploration.

"The real thing is even better," he manages, his voice breaking as my teeth graze his pulse point.

Daniel's hips rock against mine with mounting urgency, his breathing ragged in my ear. The world outside the taxi cab fades away—the blaring radio, the flash of passing streetlights, the honks of impatient drivers—all of it melts away until there's only us, our bodies a tangle of need and desire.

"Harry," Daniel pants against my neck, his voice strained. "I'm close—I can't hold on much longer."

I grip his hips tighter, guiding his movements as I grind up into him. "Me neither," I manage through gritted teeth. "I want to see you come apart for me."

Daniel moans low in his throat as he kisses me messily, roughly, biting at my lower lip before moving down to my jawline. His fingers dig into my hair, angling our bodies together just so, sending delicious shivers of pain-laced pleasure down my spine. The dual sensations push me closer to the edge, and I know I won't last much longer either.

"Look at me," I command in a husky voice. "I want to see your face when you come."

Daniel reluctantly pulls back just enough to meet my gaze, his eyes dark with lust and desire. The vulnerability in those chocolate orbs undoes me completely. I watch as he teeters on the edge, his face contorting with pleasure as he reaches climax, and it's all it takes to send me over the edge as well. We both moan out our releases together, our bodies shuddering in unison as we ride out our orgasms together.

I bury my face against Daniel's neck to muffle my moan as waves of intense pleasure crash over me. He holds me through it, his body trembling with the aftershocks of his own climax.

For several moments, we stay like that—Daniel's weight on my lap, our foreheads pressed together, our breath mingling as we slowly return to ourselves. His hands cup my face with a tenderness that makes my heart ache, his thumbs brushing gently across my cheekbones.

"That was..." Daniel trails off, seemingly at a loss for words.

I laugh softly, feeling lighter than I have in years. "Yeah," I agree, pressing a gentle kiss to his lips. "It was."

Daniel shifts slightly on my lap, grimacing a bit at the mess we've made. "Not exactly how I planned this day to go," he admits with a sheepish grin.

"Me neither, but I wouldn't change it for the world," I respond, cradling Daniel's face in my hands. "That was so much better than anything I could have imagined."

His smile—soft and slightly dazed—makes my chest tighten with emotion. This moment feels perfect in its imperfection: both of us disheveled, slightly sticky, and completely unconcerned with appearances. It's a freedom I haven't felt in a long time, if ever.

"So," Daniel says after a moment, his voice still hoarse from our passionate encounter. "I think we might need to... uh, clean up a bit before we get back to the hotel." He smirks at me as he adjusts his pants, which are visibly dampened in the crotch area.

I blush and follow suit, discreetly trying to hide the evidence of our tryst in my own pants. "You're right," I agree, running a hand through my hair self-consciously. "We don't want to cause any more of a stir than we already have."

Daniel chuckles and reaches for his jacket, draping it over my shoulders. "Here, use this as a shield," he says with a wink. "And for what it's worth? I think you look pretty damn hot with your hair all messy like that."

The taxi driver abruptly turns down the blaring music, clearing his throat loudly. "Peninsula Hotel," he announces, pointedly not looking in the rearview mirror. "We're here, gentlemen."

Daniel scrambles off my lap, a flush creeping up his neck as reality crashes back. I smooth my hair, acutely aware of how we must look— clothing rumpled, lips swollen, and the evidence of our passion still visible between our legs. Anyone who glances our way would know exactly what we've just done.

"Come on," I say, reaching for Daniel's hand and giving it a squeeze.

We exit the taxi with as much dignity as we can muster, which isn't much. I linger by the driver's window, pulling out my wallet and extracting another two hundred dollars. The exchange of money is something I understand— the universal language of discretion.

"For your trouble," I say, passing the bills through the window. "And your... understanding."

The driver takes the money, tucking it into his shirt pocket alongside the first payment. He gives me a knowing nod and wink.

"Enjoy the rest of your night," he says with a knowing grin before pulling away from the curb.

I turn to find Daniel watching me, his expression a mix of disbelief and admiration. The doorman of the Peninsula approaches, offering to assist us, but I wave him off with a polite smile.

"Do you always carry that much cash?" Daniel asks in a low voice as we head toward the entrance.

"Force of habit," I reply, guiding him through the revolving door with my hand at the small of his back. I don't mention that as Crown Prince, I've been trained to always have cash available for unexpected situations— though admittedly, this particular situation wasn't covered in my royal education.

The lobby of the Peninsula is every bit as opulent as I remember it— marble floors and crystal chandeliers casting a warm glow over the space. Daniel takes it all in with wide eyes, leaning closer to whisper, "Just how rich are you exactly?"

I step closer to Daniel, acutely aware of our disheveled state in this opulent lobby. His question hangs between us, genuine curiosity in his eyes.

"Honestly? I've never really... considered it," I admit, keeping my voice low. "Money is just there."

Daniel's expression shifts subtly—a flash of something that looks like envy crosses his face before he can mask it. It's a familiar look I've seen countless times before, the moment when someone realizes the vast gulf between their financial reality and mine.

"Must be nice," he says, his tone light but with an undercurrent I can't miss.

I reach for his hand, threading our fingers together. "It's not perfect, you know," I say gently. "Even with all the money." The words sound cliche, even to my own ears—the wealthy man claiming wealth doesn't bring happiness. But it's true in ways Daniel can't possibly understand yet.

"The money comes with... expectations. Responsibilities. Limitations." I think of my father, of the crown, of the future that's been mapped out for me since birth. "I can't just do what I want or be who I want to be." Daniel's eyes soften as he studies my face. "That sounds lonely." "It was," I say, squeezing his hand tightly. "But it's a lot better now that you're in my life."

The simple truth of this statement catches me off guard. I've known this man such a short time, yet he's already changed something fundamental in my existence. With Daniel, I've felt more like myself than I have in years—perhaps more than I ever have.

Daniel's answering smile is tentative but genuine, the earlier flash of envy completely gone now.

"I make your rich boy life better, huh?" he teases, lightening the moment.

"Much better, especially in taxi rides" I confirm, tugging him toward the elevators. "Though right now, I think we both need to clean up before we scandalize the entire hotel staff."

I hear Daniel's laugh—a sound that's already becoming addictive to me—as we wait for the elevator.

"Yes, we absolutely should clean up," he agrees, stepping closer until his lips brush against my ear. "Though I was thinking... maybe we could clean up together? In your shower?"

My jaw drops slightly at his boldness. The mental image his words conjure—Daniel's naked body glistening with water, his hands sliding over my skin—sends a jolt of renewed desire straight through me. Despite what just happened in the taxi, I feel my pants growing tight again with embarrassing speed.

"I... um..." My usual eloquence abandons me completely. The Crown Prince of Denmark, trained in five languages and diplomatic speech, reduced to stammering by one suggestive comment.

Daniel notices my reaction immediately, his eyes darkening as they flick down to the front of my trousers. "Is that a yes?" he asks, a smirk playing at the corners of his mouth. The elevator arrives with a soft chime, doors sliding open to reveal an empty car. Daniel steps in first, turning to face me with an expectant look. The space suddenly feels charged with possibility. I follow him inside, reaching past him to press the button for my floor—the penthouse suite, of course. As the doors close, sealing us into this private space, I find my voice again. "That's definitely a yes," I manage, my accent thickening as desire overrides my careful English pronunciation. "Though I can't promise how much actual cleaning will happen."

Daniel's answering smile is wicked as he moves toward me, backing me against the elevator wall. "Good," he murmurs before claiming my lips in a searing kiss that leaves no doubt about our intentions once we reach our destination

His boldness awakens something primal in me—something far removed from the reserved, proper prince I've been trained to be. I want to match his confidence, his openness about desire. I want him.

Chapter 18

Daniel

The Peninsula presidential suite door clicks shut behind us, and Harald's hand is still warm in mine. I can't help but stare at the ridiculous luxury surrounding us - the room is surrounded in windows probably taller than my entire apartment, casting long shadows from the city's lights below us across carpet that probably costs more than I make in a year.

"This is..." My voice trails off as I try to find words that won't make me sound like the poor foster kid I am.

Harald squeezes my hand gently. "Too much?"

"No, it's just... different," I reply softly, my voice carrying a hint of wonder as I drink in the opulence surrounding us. Turning to face Harald, I find my nerves gradually settling into something more tranquil as our gazes meet. Those earnest blue eyes seem to sparkle with an inner light, their depths inviting and reassuring. "Good different," I continue, a small smile tugging at the corners of my mouth as I give his hand a gentle squeeze. The warmth of his skin against mine is comforting, grounding me.

My fingers tremble slightly as I let go of his hand and slowly begin to unbutton my shirt, revealing tantalizing glimpses of my skin beneath. The air between us feels electric, charged with anticipation as I step back from

Harald's embrace. I need him to see every inch of me - scars and all - laid bare before him like an offering.

"Let me," I murmur softly when he instinctively moves to follow me. My voice is barely audible over the pounding of my heart in my ears. "Just... watch."

I savor each second our eyes are locked, drinking in the hunger and desire reflected back at me from those blue depths. With deliberate slowness, I slip my shirt off one shoulder and then the other, letting it fall to pool on the plush carpet at my feet.

I stand before him now in nothing but my pants - utterly exposed yet strangely empowered by his ardent gaze roaming over my body like a reverent caress. Every nerve ending tingles with sensitivity as the cool air kisses my newly bared skin.

Arousal coils hot and tight in my core as Harald's eyes darken with lust. My cock twitches against my fly at the sight of him watching me so intently. The knowledge that he desires me just as much - if not more so - than I crave him sends a shiver racing down my spine straight to my groin.

I wet my suddenly dry lips with the tip of my tongue and hold his molten gaze as my hands drift down to the button of my pants. With agonizing slowness, I pop it open, letting the fabric part just enough to reveal the top of my hip bones and the trail of dark hair leading downwards.

"Daniel..." The way he says my name, like a prayer, gives me confidence I didn't know I had.

Emboldened, I slide the zipper down, tooth by torturous tooth. The sound is obscenely loud in the otherwise silent room. I shrug the pants off my hips, letting them fall and pool around my ankles before stepping out of them completely.

I'm laid bare before him now, clad in nothing but my black boxer briefs. The thin fabric does little to hide my obvious arousal straining against it.

"Your turn," I whisper huskily, my voice barely audible over the pounding of my heart. I close the distance between us until mere inches separate our bodies. "I want to see you too."

My hands find the soft, luxurious hem of his cashmere sweater, gently sliding underneath to feel the warmth radiating from his skin. I look up at him from beneath my lashes, silently begging him to let me undress him as he did for me.

"Can I?" I ask softly yet urgently yearning for Haralds response; my desire evident by my ragged breathing; Haralds eyes lock onto mine; blue meeting brown; both filled intense neediness; raw sexual energy crackling between us; an almost tangible force drawing our bodies together despite ourselves

Harald nods, lifting his arms as I pull the sweater over his head. I can't help but run my hands down his firm muscular chest, my fingers trailing along his taut stomach tracing each defined ab muscle sending electric shivers through both our bodies, feeling his heart racing beneath my fingertips. His skin is impossibly soft, and I lean in to press my lips against his collarbone.

I feel Harald's breath tickling my ear as he murmurs, "You're driving me crazy," his accent thicker than usual.

I grin, feeling powerful. "That's the idea." I say. I run my hands up his arms, feeling the muscles tense beneath my touch. His skin is so warm, practically burning against my palms. I trail my fingers down to the button of his designer jeans, popping it open with deliberate slowness.

"Daniel..." His voice is rough, desperate, a deep rumble that reverberates through my very core. I love that I can affect him like this, that with just a few simple touches, a mere caress along his arms, I can reduce him to such an urgent need. It's intoxicating, heady stuff - the power I hold over him in this moment, the knowledge that his desire is entirely because of me.

"Patience," I tease, though my own heart is racing like a runaway train, thumping so hard against my ribs that I'm sure he can hear it. My breath catches in my throat as I slide his zipper down with agonizing slowness, the metallic rasp echoing through the charged silence between us. I let my knuckles brush against him teasingly through the thin fabric of his boxer briefs, savoring the intoxicating feel of him already so rock hard and ready for me. Harald's sharp intake of breath at that intimate contact sends a shiver down my spine, and the firmness I feel through his underwear is all the encouragement I need to keep going.

I can't help but marvel at the trust he's placing in me, allowing me this close, revealing this vulnerable side of himself. Slowly, as if unraveling a precious gift, I slide his pants down over his hips, revealing the boxers that leave little to the imagination. His erection presses against the fabric, straining for release, and it takes every ounce of self-control not to moan aloud at the sight of him.

Steam continues to curl from the bathroom, fogging the mirrors and filling the air with warmth. But the heat between us has nothing to do with the running shower.

"You're gorgeous," he whispers, pressing a kiss to my shoulder. His lips trail up my neck, and I tilt my head to give him better access. "Perfect."

I turn in his arms, pressing our chests together. "Shower's going to get cold," I murmur against his lips, though we both know I couldn't care less about the water temperature right now.

His hands span my waist, thumbs stroking over my hipbones with tantalizing gentleness, igniting a trail of goosebumps in their wake. The delicate touch makes me shiver, making me acutely aware of every nerve ending in my body that yearns for his caress.

"We should do something about that," he murmurs, his voice low and husky with desire. The words hang heavy in the air between us like an unspoken promise.

I hook my fingers into his waistband, the fabric soft against my skin as I tug him closer. I start walking backwards toward the bathroom, pulling him along with me as I go. My heart pounds in my chest with anticipation, the sound echoing loudly in my ears.

Harald follows willingly behind me, his eyes never leaving mine for an instant. In their depths, I see a hunger that mirrors my own - a longing so intense it takes my breath away. He moves with a predatory grace. Every step he takes brings him closer to me until finally he reaches out and pulls me flush against his chest.

In the bathroom, surrounded by steam and the soft sound of running water, I finally let myself really look at him. His chest is flushed, his hair messed up from where I pulled off his sweater. He's the most beautiful thing I've ever seen.

"Last chance to back out," I murmur softly, my voice husky with anticipation, though deep down I know neither of us has any intention of stopping what's about to happen. The air between us crackles with unspoken desire, our bodies gravitating together as if drawn by an irresistible force.

Harald's response is a searing kiss that ignites a fire within me, his lips moving against mine with a hunger that sends electric shivers racing through my body. The marble beneath my feet, warm from the heated floors, seems to melt away as I lose myself in his embrace. His breath mingles with mine, hot and sweet, carrying the whispered promise: "Never." A shudder ripples through me at the intensity of his words. "I want this," he murmurs, his voice rough with desire. "Want you."

The shower beckons behind us, but for a moment we just stand there, holding each other, breathing the same air. Harald's fingers trail down my spine, leaving goosebumps in their wake as they dance across the sensitive skin of my lower back. I arch into his touch, craving more of that delicious pressure against my aching body. His hands slide lower still, cupping my ass and pulling me flush against him as he nips at my neck.

I moan softly, tilting my head to give him better access as his lips work magic on my skin. But then Harald's fingers slip beneath the waistband of my tight boxers and all thoughts of waiting disappear in a haze of steam and desire as he frees my straining erection from its confines.

My hips buck forward reflexively into his touch, seeking more of that electrifying friction against my sensitive flesh. Harald chuckles low in his throat at the reaction before slowly stroking me from root to tip. Pleasure shoots through me like liquid fire with each drag of his hand over my throbbing length.

Emboldened by the breathy sounds spilling from my lips, I reach down to return the favor and free Harald's own impressive cock from the prison of his boxer briefs. It springs out eagerly, slapping against our abdomens with a fleshy thwack that reverberates through the charged air between us. The sound is obscene yet utterly arousing as I gasp sharply at the feeling of my throbbing shaft pressed up hotly against Harald's own arousal. His is larger than mine, longer and thicker with a delicious weight that promises so much pleasure to come. Seeing what Harald has to work with sends a surge of masculine pride coursing through me along with the liquid fire of desire searing my veins.

The shower spray is hot against my back as I step in and as Harald steps in after me, his hands finding my waist in the steam. Water runs down his face, catching on his eyelashes, making him look somehow younger, more vulnerable. I reach up to brush a droplet from his cheek.

His voice is a low, honeyed murmur. "Is this okay?" he asks softly, thumbs drawing circles on my hip bones with a feather-light touch that ignites sparks under my skin. I feel like molten lava is flowing through my veins at his tentative exploration, every nerve ending alive and tingling with anticipation. The gentle friction of his thumbs tracing lazy spirals on either side of my pelvis makes me ache to arch into his touch, to press closer and feel the hard planes of his body against mine.

I answer by pulling him closer, pressing our foreheads together. The heat of his breath mingles with mine, a promise of the passion to come. "More than okay," I murmur against his lips before capturing them in a scorching kiss. The warm water cascades over both of us like a tropical rainforest deluge, creating our own private world where time stands still - a cocoon of steam and sensation that blocks out everything except the feeling of his body pressed against mine. "I trust you," I breathe into the kiss before trailing hot kisses along his jawline and down the column of his throat.

His breath catches at that, and I know he understands what those words mean coming from me. After Alex, after everything, trust doesn't come easily. But with Harald, it feels as natural as breathing.

"Let me take care of you," he murmurs, reaching for the hotel's fancy body wash. The scent of sandalwood fills the air as he pours some into his palm.

His hands are gentle as they move across my shoulders, down my back, leaving trails of silky lather in their wake. Each touch feels like a promise, like healing, erasing the ghosts of past hurts with every careful caress. The steady pressure of his fingers works out knots of tension I didn't even know I was carrying. I close my eyes, letting myself feel completely safe for the first time in years, surrendering to the absolute trust I have in him. The warmth radiating from his body and the rhythmic sound of the shower create a cocoon of security that makes my chest ache with emotion.

"You're trembling," he notices, his voice thick with emotion.

"Good trembling," I assure him, opening my eyes to meet his worried gaze. "I just... no one's ever touched me like this before. Like I matter."

Harald's eyes darken with a mix of desire and protective anger. "You matter," he says fiercely. "You matter so much, Daniel."

I reach up and gently cup Harald's strong jaw with my hand, guiding his lips towards mine. The moment our mouths meet in an intimate embrace under the cascading water droplets showering us from above creates such an electrifying sensation all through my body it makes every single nerve ending tingle and buzz. The kiss is deep and sensual as we lose ourselves in this perfect intimate moment together sharing our raw emotions with each other.

I pull Harald flush against me and wrap my arms around his neck pulling myself closer as we pour our hearts out into the kiss that conveys all the unspoken feelings building up inside us both. Even with the water running down between us I've never felt more connected, more attuned, more in sync with another person than this instant right here wrapped up together locked in each other's loving arms kissing passionately underneath the soothing hot stream.

His strong, skilled hands glide sensually down the curves of my body until they reach my firm buttocks. He grips them tightly, his fingers digging into my supple flesh as he pulls me flush against him. I let out a sharp gasp against his soft lips at his bold touch sending jolts of electricity racing through my body straight to my core.

"Harry..."

The tender words caress my ears as his breath tickles the delicate skin of my neck. "I've got you," he whispers, and I believe him. The sincerity in his voice resonates deep within my soul, a soothing balm to the raw, exposed places that have been so long denied such simple yet profound affirmation. In this moment, wrapped securely in his strong embrace, I feel an overwhelming sense of safety wash over me like a wave of liquid warmth. "I've got you," he repeats softly, as if to drive home the reality of it, and I lean into him, pressing myself against the firm contours of his body, feeling his firm desire pressing against me. With those three simple words spoken against my skin like a lover's caress, he has claimed me in a way no one else ever has before.

In the steam and warmth, surrounded by his touch and his care, I let myself fall apart in his arms, knowing he'll catch me.

Harald's skilled fingers leave a trail of fire in their wake as they tease my entrance, sending shivers of pleasure coursing through my entire body. I can't help but moan out his name in response, the sound muffled by the steady spray of water cascading around us. The sensation is both exhilarating and terrifying, but with Harald's strong arms wrapped around me, I feel a sense of safety I never thought possible.

Emboldened by the trust we've built between us, my own hands begin to roam as well. My fingertips glide over his hard length, tracing the veins and contours of his long thick shaft. The way he groans into my ear at my touch sends a thrill straight to my core, and I can't help but smile to myself. It feels empowering to know that I have this effect on him - that I can make him feel even a fraction of the desire he stirs in me with just a simple touch.

"Oh God, Daniel," he pants against my neck, his grip on my hips tightening ever so slightly as if he's trying to maintain control. "You feel so good."

His words are like gasoline on the flames of my arousal, and I find myself grinding back against him, desperate for more contact between us. His fingers slip further inside me, and I gasp at the intrusion - not from pain but from the overwhelming sensation of being filled by him in such an intimate way. It feels right somehow - like two puzzle pieces finally coming together after years of searching for their match.

"Harry," I moan breathlessly as he begins to move his fingers in and out in time with the rhythm of our kisses - slow at first but quickly picking up speed as our passion ignites white-hot between us like kindling waiting for a spark...

Harald's fingers inside me feel so good, but I want more. I need more. I can't get enough of him. I look into his deep blue eyes, my own reflecting the same desire and need that I know must be written all over my face.

"Harry," I pant, my voice hoarse with lust. "I-I want... God, I want you so bad."

He stares at me for a moment, his eyes searching mine as if he's trying to read my thoughts, gauge my sincerity. Then, as if he's made up his mind about something, he leans in and captures my lips once more in a searing kiss that leaves me breathless. His fingers withdraw from me all too soon, but before I can even think to protest, he's scooping me up in his strong arms and pressing me against the cold tiled wall of the shower stall. The contrast between the cool wall and our heated bodies only serves to heighten my arousal further.

"Are you sure about this?" he asks again, his voice low and rough with desire.

"Yes," I moan back desperately, wrapping my legs around his waist and pulling him closer still. "Please, Harry... I need you."

He doesn't say another word but instead reaches for the bottle of lube perched on the ledge nearby. Slicking up both himself and me in practiced motions that send shivers down my spine, he positions himself at my entrance. Our eyes lock as he begins to push forward - slow at first - stretching me open around his thick girth until we are connected in the most intimate way possible.

As Harald's thick length begins to push inside me, I feel a rush of emotions I'd never experienced before. Heat and pleasure courses through my veins, but it's more than just the physical sensation of our bodies joining together. It's the way he looks at me, as if I'm the only person in the world that matters to him in that moment. The way his hands grip my hips so gently, as if I might break under his touch but at the same time, as if he can't get close enough.

He fills me completely, stretching me in ways Alex never had - both physically and emotionally. With each slow thrust, I feel myself opening up to him in ways I never thought possible. This was different from anything I'd ever known before; this was real and raw and messy and perfect all at once.

"God, Daniel" he pants against my neck as he starts to move inside me with a slow, deliberate rhythm that has my toes curling into his back. "You feel so good... so damn good."

His words sends shivers throughout me and straight to my core and I feel my hole opening up for him, spurring him on even more. His hips picked up speed ever so slightly until we were moving together like two halves of a whole - our breaths mingling together in the steamy air between us. The sound of our bodies slapping against each other echoed off the tiled walls of the shower stall around us but all I could focus on was him... on us... on this moment suspended in time where nothing else mattered but us finally being together after what felt like an eternity of waiting.

"Harry," I moaned out his name like a prayer on shaky exhale as wave after wave of pleasure began crashing over me like ocean waves against a rocky shore line - relentless yet oh so sweetly agonizing at once.

"Please Harry," I beg breathlessly against his ear as he continues to move inside me at that same steady, maddening pace. "I need... I need it harder."

He groans at my words and kisses along my jawline making me writhe, even as he plunges deeper into me, stretching me open more and more.

"I've got you Daniel," he murmurs back reassuringly, even as he obliges my pleas by increasing his speed just a fraction - enough to send sparks shooting through every nerve ending in my body like fireworks exploding across a night sky on the fourth of July.

"Oh God Harry!" I cry out involuntarily as he hits that sweet spot deep inside me dead on with each perfectly aimed thrust of his hips against mine. Pleasure and pain blend together until they become indistinguishable from one another and all I can focus on is the feeling of him moving within me so perfectly.

"Yes Daniel, yes," Harald pants into the shell of my ear before trailing open-mouthed kisses down the column of my neck in between thrusts. "You're so hot and tight, you're doing so good..."

His praise sends a surge of masculine pride racing through me along with the overwhelming pleasure building at my core until I can feel myself coming closer and closer to that inevitable edge of ecstasy... but something about his words also sends a fresh wave of arousal coursing through me like molten lava and suddenly I find myself bucking up to meet him thrust for thrust.

"Harry!" I cry out sharply at the intensity of sensation overwhelming my entire being. My head thunks back against the cool tiles behind us as my eyes flutter closed and I arch into him completely - offering myself up fully to whatever he wants from me in this moment.

"I've got you!" Harald's voice cuts through my haze of lust as he tightens his grip on my hips, holding me steady while he drives us both relentlessly towards the edge of ecstasy. "Come for me... let go..."

His command sends me over the edge, and I cry out Harald's name over and over again, my voice a primal, impassioned prayer as we hurtle together into the abyss of orgasmic bliss. My hands are free to grasp at anything to anchor myself as I surrender completely to him and the intense pleasure that crashes over me in endless waves, like a tidal wave engulfing every fiber of my being.

Harald's thick cock doesn't falter as he continues to pound into me through my climax, and I can feel his hot seed spurting deep inside me as he moans out his own release. His powerful thrusts send me over the edge once more, and I spill myself onto our stomachs, our combined essences mingling together in a sticky mess that serves as a testament to our shared passion.

"Oh fuck, Daniel," he gasps against my sweat-soaked skin. His voice is thick with emotion and post-orgasmic bliss as he presses feverish kisses along my face before claiming my mouth in a deep, possessive kiss. Our tongues dance together in a sensual tango that echoes the raw passion we just shared.

"That was... unbelievable..." he pants against my lips when we finally break apart for air, his words barely audible above the still-running shower spray cascading around us both.

But I hear them loud and clear even as my heart swells with emotion at their sincerity... and know without a doubt that they are true.

"It was…" I answer back softly - smiling up at him from beneath lowered lashes and cupping his stubbled jaw affectionately between my palms. "It's never felt like that before with anyone."

His eyes darken at those words and suddenly Harald is kissing me again deeply - passionately pouring all of his own emotions into each press of our mouths together until we're both left breathless once more...

But this time it has nothing to do with sex and everything to do with how much we mean to one another on a fundamental level of human connection. And somehow that means even more than any physical act could possibly convey between us.

Chapter 19

Daniel

The bathroom is filled with steam as Harald reaches past me to turn off the shower. He grabs one of the ridiculously fluffy hotel towels, but instead of drying himself, he wraps it around me first. The gesture is so tender it makes my chest ache.

"Such a gentleman," I tease, trying to hide how much these little acts of care affect me. But Harald sees right through me – he's gotten good at that in such a short time.

"Only the best for you," he says with a soft smile, grabbing another towel for himself. His hair is darker when wet, curling slightly at the ends, and I can't resist reaching up to run my fingers through it.

"Your accent gets stronger when you're..." I hesitate, my cheeks flushing with embarrassment. "When you're... aroused."

Harald chuckles. "Really?" he asks, a playful glint in his eyes. "I didn't realize that." He leans in to nip at my earlobe teasingly. "I'll have to keep that in mind for next time, then."

We dry off leisurely, stealing glances and touches as we go. It should feel awkward, this in-between moment, but it doesn't. Even when Harald's towel slips and he scrambles to readjust it, we both share a laugh.

"I... uh, brought sleepwear," he says, blushing slightly as he ducks out of the bathroom and returns with a bag. He pulls out two sets of pajamas, handing one to me. "I thought... well, I hoped..." His cheeks turn a deeper shade of pink as he trails off, unable to meet my eyes.

"You planned ahead," I say, touched by his thoughtfulness. The pajamas are soft silk, probably cost more than my entire wardrobe, but I don't even care about that right now. I'm too moved by the fact that he hoped I'd stay, that he wanted me to be comfortable.

Once we're dressed, Harald leads me to the massive bed. The sheets are turned down – someone must have done that while we were at Coney Island – and more rose petals are scattered across the pillows.

"I didn't arrange this," Harald says quickly, his cheeks flushing with a hint of embarrassment. He looks at me apologetically, his blue eyes widening slightly as if anticipating my reaction. "The hotel must have..." His voice trails off uncertainly. I can sense a mix of emotions playing across his handsome features - a touch of self-consciousness at the lavish display, perhaps a dash of hope that I'll find it romantic despite his protests. The vulnerability in his expression tugs at something deep within me, a reminder that beneath all the wealth and privilege lies a complex man with his own set of insecurities and desires.

"It's perfect," I cut him off, my voice warm and sincere as I squeeze his hand. "A little cheesy, maybe," I admit with a playful smirk dancing across my lips, "but perfect."

We slide under the plush covers, sinking into the soft mattress. After a moment of shifting, I settle with my head on Harald's chest, his arms enveloping me. The steady thrum of his heart pulses against my ear, the soothing rhythm resonating deep within my soul. Cocooned in luxurious sheets scented with rose petals, I'm shielded from the world's harsh realities, safe in Harald's tender embrace.

I'm acutely aware of every point of contact between us - his chest rising and falling with each breath, warmth seeping through our thin layers wherever we press together. His hand caresses my back in gentle circles, each stroke igniting tingles of pleasure across my skin. Nuzzling into the crook of his neck, I breathe in his intoxicating scent, a mix of cologne and natural musk.

"Is this okay?" Harald whispers.

"Mmm, more than okay," I hum drowsily. "You're comfy."

"Sleep, kæreste," he murmurs, lips brushing my hair.

"What's it mean?" I ask through a yawn.

A pause, his arms tightening. "Dearest."

Harald's fingers thread through my hair as he hums what sounds like a lullaby, the soft notes chasing me into slumber. For the first time in years, I fall asleep completely safe, cherished. Home.

* * *

Harald

The city lights paint soft patterns across Daniel's sleeping face, his dark lashes casting shadows on his cheeks. His breathing is deep and even, one hand curled loosely grasping onto my chest like he's making sure I won't disappear. The sight makes my chest tight with emotion.

I shouldn't be here. I shouldn't be falling for this beautiful, brave man who has no idea who I really am. But watching him sleep, so trusting in my arms, I can't bring myself to regret any of it.

Daniel shifts slightly, mumbling something in his sleep, and I automatically tighten my hold on him. He settles immediately, pressing his face into my chest. The simple trust in that unconscious movement nearly undoes me.

"Jeg er ved at forelske mig i dig," I whisper in Danish, because I'm not brave enough to say it in English yet, even while he's sleeping. *I'm falling in love with you.*

The weight of my crown has never felt heavier than in this moment. Daniel deserves someone who can be completely honest with him, someone who won't have to hide their relationship. But the thought of letting him go makes it hard to breathe.

His curly hair is still slightly damp from the shower. I can't resist running my fingers through it, marvelling at how something so simple can feel so intimate. He makes a soft sound of contentment that makes my heart skip.

"What am I going to do about you?" I murmur, pressing a kiss to his forehead.

The city continues its endless symphony outside – car horns, distant sirens, the rush of traffic – but in here, in this moment, it's just us. No crown, no royal duties, no lies between us. Just Daniel in my arms, trusting me completely.

I know I'll have to tell him the truth soon. I know this bubble we're in can't last forever. But for now, I let myself imagine a world where I'm just Harald, where I can keep him safe and happy in my arms, where loving him doesn't mean potentially destroying both our lives.

Daniel stirs again, this time blinking up at me sleepily. "You 'kay?" he mumbles, accent thick with sleep. "You're thinking too loud."

I smile, smoothing his hair back. "I'm perfect, kæreste. Go back to sleep."

He hums contentedly, already drifting off again. "Stay?"

"Always," I promise, knowing I shouldn't but unable to stop myself. "I'll be right here."

As his breathing evens out again, I send up a silent prayer to whoever might be listening. *Please let me keep him. Please let him forgive me when he learns the truth. Please let this be enough.*

Chapter 20

Harald

Sunlight streams through the floor-to-ceiling windows, painting Daniel's skin in golden hues. I've been awake for hours, unable to stop watching him sleep, cataloguing every perfect detail. The way his dark curls spill across the pillow, how his hand stays pressed against my chest even in sleep, the slight part of his lips.

My phone buzzes on the nightstand - another message from Erik about palace business requiring my attention. I ignore it. This precious moment with Daniel feels stolen, fragile as spun sugar.

He stirs beside me, stretching like a cat before his eyes flutter open. A sleepy smile spreads across his face. "Morning."

"God morgen, skat." The Danish endearment slips out before I can catch it. Another small betrayal to add to my growing list.

Daniel props himself up on one elbow, studying my face. "You look worried. Everything okay?"

My chest tightens. How do I tell him that our love is both perfect and doomed? That each moment I fall deeper for him, I'm also deceiving him? How can I express this sinking feeling that everything we've found together could be ripped away in an instant?

"Just thinking about work," I deflect, running my fingers through his sleep-mussed hair.

"Mm, the mysterious Danish business empire?" He grins, clearly teasing, but the words hit like a physical blow.

I force a smile, hating how easily the lies come now. "Something like that."

Daniel leans in, pressing a soft kiss to my jaw. "Well, whatever it is, it can wait. You're in New York now."

If only he knew how complicated it really was. The Danish press will already be speculating about my absence. Father will be furious about me skipping meetings. Every minute I spend here puts my secret - and Daniel's privacy - at risk.

But when Daniel kisses me properly, warm and sweet and perfect, I can't bring myself to care about any of it. I pull him closer, losing myself in the feel of him, trying to quiet the voice in my head warning me that this can't last.

Daniel jerks away from our kiss as my phone's shrill ring pierces the morning calm. Ella's name flashes across the screen, and my stomach drops - she wouldn't call unless it was important.

"Sorry, I need to take this. It's my sister, it must be important. "Ella?"

"Harry, turn on CNN now!" Ella's trembling voice sends ice through my veins, dread settling in my stomach. With shaking hands, I fumble for the remote, my heart pounding as I click through channels. Daniel sits up, confusion clouding his features. I can't answer him, can't find the words as my world threatens to shatter.

The bold text scrolling across the screen makes my fingers go numb, the remote slipping from my grasp. "Harald?" Daniel's concerned voice cuts through the rush of blood in my ears. "You're scaring me. What's wrong?"

I remain frozen, unable to look away from the devastating news that threatens to destroy everything we've built. The anchor's detached voice fills the room, each word another nail in the coffin of my carefully constructed life. I can practically hear my father's rage already, see the headlines that will flood every newspaper, all because I dared to find happiness with the man beside me.

I see footage of me punching Alex, our private moments now broadcast for the world to dissect. The anchor announces my identity as the first openly gay member of Danish royalty. More photos flash across the screen, each one another violation.

"Harald?" Daniel's voice cracks. "Crown Prince?"

I can't bear to face the betrayal in his eyes. "I was going to tell you," I whisper. "I just wanted a chance to be myself first."

Daniel's emotions crash across his features - shock, hurt, betrayal, anger. The warmth drains from his eyes, replaced by something cold and distant. The wall he'd torn down is suddenly towering between us.

"Everything was a lie?" His question hangs heavy, each syllable striking me like my father's harshest condemnations.

"No, Daniel, please-" I reach for him desperately, but he flinches away. My chest constricts as I watch him retreat, everything we've built crumbling.

"The mental health site? Was that even real?" His words drip with venom, burrowing deep. "God, I'm such an idiot."

"The site was real. Everything I told you about myself was real-" My voice cracks with desperation. "Every confession, every vulnerable moment - it was all genuine."

"Except the tiny detail that you're the fucking Crown Prince?" Daniel springs from the bed, pacing. "My face is all over international news. Everyone will see this!"

Horror dawns on his face, my stomach churning with guilt. I've exposed him to exactly the scrutiny I was trying to escape. The weight of my title has come crashing down on this innocent man who trusted me.

"I never meant for this to happen," I whisper, the words inadequate. "I just wanted..." My voice cracks. For once, I had dared to reach for something real, but even that has transformed into another royal mess.

"What you wanted?" Daniel's laugh holds no humor. "That's all this has ever been about, hasn't it? Did you ever think about what this would do to me?" His words strike with devastating accuracy, each one a reminder of my selfishness. The bitterness in his voice makes my stomach churn with guilt, knowing he has every right to his anger.

"You lied to me! You told me you wanted something real, that this was serious!" His voice cracks, the sound splitting my chest wide open. "Now I see you've been hiding who you are, and I can't trust anything you said! Everything we built feels like a lie, and I don't know if I can feel safe with you anymore!"

Each word hits like a physical blow. My throat constricts as I watch him wrap his arms around himself - a protective gesture I recognize from when he talked about Alex. The realization that I've made him feel as vulnerable and betrayed as his cheating ex did makes bile rise in my throat.

I want to reach for him, to pull him close and promise that everything will be okay, but I've lost that right. My hands clench uselessly at my sides as I watch the man I love retreat into himself, building walls I'd spent weeks carefully dismantling. The distance between us spans more than just the few feet of plush hotel carpet - it's a chasm of broken trust and shattered expectations.

"Daniel, please - I was terrified!" My voice cracks as emotions surge through me. "Every person who's ever known who I am has treated me differently. They see the crown, the title, the wealth - never just me. Never Harald." I run my trembling hands through my hair, my chest tight with panic. "I couldn't bear the thought of you looking at me the way everyone else does."

The words pour out of me now, raw and desperate. "Do you know what it's like? Having every interaction, every relationship tainted by who you're born to be? I just wanted one person - one person who could see me for who I really am, not what I represent."

Daniel's eyes flash with hurt and anger. "You should have trusted me with the truth! I can't believe I let myself fall for you, only to find out you kept the most important part of yourself hidden! How could you do this to me?"

His words strike deep, and I feel tears burning behind my eyes. "Important? Being Crown Prince isn't who I am - it's what I was born into! The man who held you last night, who listened to your stories, who fell in love with your smile - that's the real me." My voice breaks. "The Harald who struggles with anxiety, who feels crushed under his father's expectations, who finally felt like he could breathe when he met you - that's who I am."

I take a shaky breath, watching him through blurred vision. "I know I should have told you sooner. But every day I waited, I grew more terrified of losing this - losing you. For the first time in my life, someone saw me as just Harald, and I couldn't... I couldn't bear to watch that change."

The CNN broadcast continues in the background, each new photo of our private moments together driving home the magnitude of my betrayal. I see Daniel flinch as they show footage of our kiss on the Wonder Wheel, that perfect moment now tainted by my deception.

My heart races as Daniel retreats, when the door bursts open. Erik rushes in, disheveled and sweating.

"Harald! We need to go now! Your father is demanding you return home—the situation is out of control!"

The words hit me like a blow. Of course Father would demand my return - the scandal of his son with another man would be intolerable. My stomach churns imagining his rage and disgust.

Daniel's eyes widen at Erik's entrance. "Your secretary... more lies."

"Daniel, please-" I reach for him, but Erik cuts through my plea.

"Your Highness, there's no time. The press is surrounding the hotel. Security is preparing the exit, but we must move."

The title makes Daniel flinch. He backs away, trapped and betrayed. Seeing him pressed against the wall, trying to shrink, breaks me. This is what I tried to prevent - him feeling cornered, exposed, vulnerable.

My phone buzzes - Ella's number. Father must be livid if she's calling back so soon. The walls close in, trapping us in this nightmare of my own making.

Erik hovers, his mask cracking with concern. "Harald, please. We need to leave now."

"Daniel, wait!" I cry out, but my plea falls on deaf ears as he tears off the silk pajamas I'd given him - the intimate gift now a symbol of my deception. The soft material drops to the floor like discarded trust, my heart clenching as he roughly pulls on yesterday's wrinkled clothes.

His movements are jerky, desperate, like a wounded animal seeking escape. I recognize this behavior - the same defensive posture he described after finding Alex with another man. Only this time, I'm the one who's caused this pain.

The transformation in his face cuts deeper than any of Father's disapproving glares. Those expressive eyes that had looked at me with such warmth now turn cold and distant. His features shut down completely - a mask sliding into place that I recognize from my own royal training. The irony isn't lost on me.

"Daniel, please, just let me explain, don't leave like this-" I step forward, but Erik's hand on my shoulder holds me back. Daniel doesn't even look at me as he yanks open the door, his shoulders rigid with tension.

The slam of the door echoes through the suite like a gunshot, leaving behind a deafening silence broken only by the continued murmur of news coverage detailing our exposed relationship.

My legs give out, and I sink to the floor, my breath coming in short gasps. My fingers dig into the plush carpet as I try to ground myself, but the panic rises like a tide.

"Your Highness..." Erik kneels beside me, his voice gentle. "Harald, breathe."

I shake my head, tears burning my eyes. "I've ruined everything. He trusted me, Erik. He let me in, showed me his vulnerabilities, and I..." My voice breaks. "I betrayed him just like everyone else in his life has."

Erik's hand rests on my shoulder, steady and familiar. "You were trying to protect yourself. To have something real."

"And look what it cost him!" I gesture wildly at the TV still broadcasting our private moments. "I exposed him to exactly what I was hiding from. The press, the scrutiny, the judgment - I've thrown him into the spotlight without any warning or protection."

"We can help protect him now," Erik says softly. "But first, we need to get you somewhere safe. Your father-"

"To hell with what Father wants! When has Father ever given a flying fuck about what I want!" The words explode from me with surprising force. "I need to find Daniel. I need to explain-"

"Harald." Erik's grip tightens on my shoulder, his voice stern. "He needs time. And right now, you have responsibilities that can't wait. We need to go."

The weight of my title settles back onto my shoulders like a lead cape, suffocating and drowning me. But all I can see is Daniel's face, twisted with hurt and betrayal, as he realized the extent of my deception.

Act III

Chapter 21

Daniel

I stumble out of the Peninsula's revolving doors, my legs trembling beneath me. The morning sun feels too bright, too harsh against my tear-stained face. My phone vibrates non-stop in my pocket – a constant reminder of the nightmare unfolding around me.

A crowd of photographers materializes, their cameras clicking like insects. Flashes burst in my face.

"Daniel! Over here!"

"Are you Prince Harald's boyfriend?"

"How long have you been dating the Crown Prince?"

My chest constricts. The air feels thick, impossible to draw into my lungs. I duck my head and push through the wall of bodies, their questions becoming a deafening roar. My hands shake so violently I can barely pull up my hood to shield my face.

My phone won't stop. Notifications flood the screen – texts from coworkers, Instagram tags, Twitter mentions. CNN's headline glares up at me: *'Danish Crown Prince's Secret Gay Romance Exposed.'* There's a photo of us kissing on the Wonder Wheel, another of us walking hand in hand on the boardwalk. My stomach lurches.

Harald's name lights up my screen. Again. Again. Again.

"Daniel, please let me explain."
"I never meant to hurt you."
"Pick up, kæreste. Please."

I silence the phone and shove it deep in my pocket, bile rising in my throat. The sidewalk swims before my eyes as I break into a run, desperate to escape the pursuing cameras. My heart pounds so hard I think it might burst. Every breath comes in short, painful gasps.

I duck into the first subway entrance I find, practically falling down the stairs. The fluorescent lights flicker overhead as I collapse against a pillar, sliding to the ground. My whole body trembles, fingers tingling with pins and needles. The phone keeps buzzing against my thigh – Harald's desperate attempts to reach me. I squeeze my eyes shut, but the tears leak out anyway.

Crown Prince. He's the fucking Crown Prince of Denmark. And I'm just... me. The foster kid. The insurance drone. The fool who fell for another beautiful lie.

I pull my hoodie tighter around my face as I emerge from the subway, scanning the street for cameras or curious eyes. A woman walking her dog does a double-take, staring at me with dawning recognition. I duck into a bodega, pretending to browse magazines while my heart hammers against my ribs. The cashier glances up from his phone, his eyes widening.

"Hey, aren't you—"

I bolt before he can finish, abandoning any pretense of normalcy. Three blocks from my apartment, a group of teenagers point phones in my direction. I cross the street abruptly, taking a circuitous route through back alleys I've never used before. By the time I reach my building, sweat soaks through my shirt despite the cool morning air.

The moment I unlock our apartment door, I hear the TV blaring. My stomach drops.

"—Crown Prince Harald of Denmark seen in New York City with a man now identified as Daniel Ramirez—"

I freeze in the doorway. Jayda and Caleb sit on the couch, their faces illuminated by the flashing images on the screen. My face. Harald's face. Our kisses played on repeat for the world's entertainment.

"Danny!" Jayda jumps up, rushing toward me. Her black-painted nails reach for me, her face twisted with concern. "Oh my god, we've been trying to call you!"

Caleb's already grabbing the remote, shutting off the TV. "Dude, what the actual fuck?" His voice is soft, stunned. "He's a fucking prince?"

"Are you okay?" Jayda's hands hover near my shoulders, afraid to touch me. "What happened? The news is saying—"

"I don't want to talk about it." My voice sounds hollow, distant, like it's coming from someone else.

"Danny, come sit down." Caleb moves toward me, his lanky frame unfolding from the couch. "We're here for you, man."

Something inside me snaps. "I said I don't want to talk about it!" The words explode from me, raw and jagged.

Jayda flinches. "We're just worried—"

"Don't." I push past them both, heading straight for my bedroom. "Just... leave me alone."

"Daniel, wait—" Caleb calls after me.

I slam my door shut, the sound cracking like thunder in our apartment, cutting off their voices mid-sentence. The cool wood presses against my back as I slide down against it, my body feeling impossibly heavy, until I hit the floor with a dull thud. My knees automatically pull tight against my chest, a defensive position I've assumed countless times since childhood— my body's way of making itself smaller, less of a target. The pressure builds inside me until I can't hold it back anymore, and I let myself sob, ugly, gasping cries that rip from my throat and shake my entire frame. Tears burn hot trails down my cheeks, dripping onto my t-shirt, and I taste salt when I try to breathe through my mouth. My fingers dig painfully into my shins, anchoring me to something solid while everything else feels like it's crumbling away.

After what feels like forever, I get up and lie back on my unmade bed, staring up at the ceiling. The blinds are drawn, plunging the room into a dim twilight that matches my mood. My phone screen glows harsh and blue in the darkness as I scroll through our messages, each word now tainted with deception.

"Tell me about your job," I'd asked him.

"I work with the government for my family's business," he'd replied. *"Foreign affairs, budget, consulting. Lots of meetings and paperwork. Nothing exciting."*

The truth hides in plain sight, mocking me with its cruel simplicity. All those "meetings" he mentioned so casually were royal engagements with diplomats and dignitaries. The "work travel" that kept him away for days at a time wasn't some corporate drudgery but official state business—negotiations and ceremonies that impacted an entire nation. The "family business" he'd described with such practiced nonchalance wasn't some inherited company but literally running a country—a monarchy with centuries of history behind it. How could I have been so blind? The clues were scattered throughout our conversations like breadcrumbs, but I'd been too caught up in my feelings to notice the trail leading to the truth.

I scroll further back.

"Nice place," I'd texted when he sent a photo from his balcony.

"Just the family home," he'd answered.

Family home. A fucking palace. His "assistant" Erik wasn't just his assistant at all but his royal handler—probably some high-ranking official with an impressive title and job description that included managing the Crown Prince of Denmark's day-to-day affairs and keeping his royal ass out of trouble. I bet Erik had been hovering in the background of every video call, strategically out of frame, making sure Harald didn't reveal too much to the random American guy he'd met online. God, it was all so obvious now.

My thumb hovers over a selfie he sent—Harald standing beside a portrait of some stern-faced man in military dress.

"Who's the guy in the painting?" I'd asked.

"Just a distant relative," he'd written back. *"Family likes to keep the old portraits up."*

The "distant relative" was probably his great-grandfather or something. The King of Denmark.

God, I'm such an idiot. The security detail. The luxury hotel. The way people stared at him on the street. The evasiveness about his family. How could I have been so blind? So fucking stupid?

I throw my phone down on the bed, pressing the heels of my palms against my burning eyes until I see white spots dancing in the darkness. First Alex, now this. What is it about me that makes men lie? Is there something fundamentally broken inside me that attracts deception? Some cosmic joke where the universe decided I should be everyone's favourite punching bag? The familiar weight of betrayal settles in my chest, constricting my lungs until each breath becomes a struggle. I thought I'd learned my lesson after Alex, but apparently, I'm still the same naive idiot who believes what people tell him. Maybe Jayda's right—maybe I should just get a cat and call it a day. At least cats are honest about their indifference.

My phone buzzes again. Harald's name flashes on screen.

"Daniel, I know you're angry. You have every right to be. But please give me a chance to explain."

Three missed calls. Seventeen unread texts. Two voicemails.

Another text appears: *"What we have is real. That wasn't a lie."*

I grab the phone, thumbs hovering over the keyboard. For a split second, I consider responding. Then I remember his words at the hotel: "There's another part of my life I haven't told you about."

Yeah. The part where he's literal fucking royalty.

I toss the phone aside again and curl onto my side, pulling the blanket over my head as fresh tears burn my eyes.

* * *

I've been holed up in my bedroom for days now. The blinds stay drawn, letting in just enough light to see the mess I've become. My phone chimes with another notification—probably Jayda trying to coax me out for dinner again. I ignore it and continue scrolling through yet another news article about *"The Crown Prince and His American Lover."*

My reflection in the dark phone screen startles me. Bloodshot eyes stare back, surrounded by dark circles. My patchy stubble has grown into an uneven beard that itches constantly. I haven't showered since... I honestly can't remember when.

"Denmark's playboy prince slums it in New York with American escort boy" reads the headline. The article includes photos of us on the Wonder Wheel, Harald's arm wrapped around me. What felt intimate and special is now splashed across the internet for everyone to dissect.

I switch to Twitter, which is even worse.

"Who is Daniel Ramirez? Royal insiders say the Crown Prince's latest fling has a troubling past."

"Sources confirm Prince Harald met commoner on mental health support website. Palace in crisis mode."

"Does anyone else think this Daniel guy is just after royal money? #GoldDigger #RoyalScandal"

My stomach twists as I scroll through the comments:

"He looks trashy. Denmark deserves better than this nobody."
"Just another attention seeker. Bet he leaked the photos himself."
"Look at his eyes—total psycho. No wonder he was in a mental hospital."

They've found everything. My hospitalization. The suicide attempt. Photos from high school. Even shots of me leaving work at Insuricarica. Every private moment between Harald and I has been picked apart and analyzed by people who know nothing about us.

I click on a Danish news site translated to English and see photos of Harald I've never seen before—in military uniform, at state dinners, shaking hands with the Queen of England. There's an entire slideshow titled *"The Life of Crown Prince Harald,"* showing him growing up in the palace, attending boarding schools in Switzerland and England, graduating from university with honors in international relations.

A photo shows Harald standing beside his father, both in formal royal attire with medals and sashes. The caption reads: *"Crown Prince Harald and King Magnus at the 2023 New Year's Royal Reception."*

This man—this entire life—was hidden from me. The person I thought I was falling for doesn't even exist.

* * *

I drag myself out of bed Monday morning after refusing to go to work for a week, knowing I need to face the music eventually. My phone's been buzzing non-stop—Harald's texts, calls, and voicemails piling up. I switch it off completely, tossing it on my bed before heading out.

The subway ride is excruciating. People stare, some even take photos. A teenage girl whispers to her friend, "That's the prince's boyfriend." I pull my hoodie tighter around my face.

At Insuricarica, the security guard eyes me suspiciously before reluctantly letting me through. The office falls silent as I walk to my desk. Coworkers pretend to work while sneaking glances.

"Daniel Ramirez." Cassandra's saccharine voice cuts through the silence. "My office. Now."

Her office feels smaller than usual. She sits behind her desk, jowls quivering with barely contained glee.

"Well, well. Quite the celebrity, aren't we?" she drawls, her southern accent stretching each word like taffy. Her smile doesn't reach her eyes, which glitter with malicious delight. The family photos on her desk—all featuring her array of cats in different holiday-themed outfits—seem to judge me alongside her.

I stare at the carpet as Cassandra's words hammer into me like nails into a coffin.

"The board has decided to terminate your employment, effective immediately." Her lips curl into a smile that reminds me of a cat who's finally cornered its prey. The fluorescent light glints off her too-white teeth as she savours each syllable. "Your... escapades have damaged our company image. We can't have someone so publicly scandalous representing Insuricarica. The insurance industry is about trust and integrity, Daniel, and you've become a liability."

My stomach drops to my feet, a cold wave of panic rushing through my veins. Two years of mind-numbing work, of forcing myself out of bed each morning to face her torment—gone in a single sentence. I can already feel the anxiety clawing at my chest, wondering how I'll make rent next month.

"You can't fire me for my personal life."

"Oh, but we can. Page 47 of the employee handbook clearly states employees must maintain professional conduct outside of the workplace that reflects company values." She slides a folder across the desk. "Your final paycheck and termination papers. Security will escort you out."

As I empty my desk into a cardboard box, memories of Alex flood back. Finding him in our bed with another man. His pathetic excuses. "It didn't mean anything, baby." The same hollow feeling settles in my chest now.

Harald's betrayal cuts deeper somehow. Alex was upfront about who he was—a cheater. Harald built an entire relationship on lies. Pretending to be someone else. Tricking me into thinking he understood me.

A security guard hovers as I pack. Everyone watches, even Piper who doesn't want to look me in the eye. I hear whispers—"royal plaything," "fifteen minutes of fame."

Walking out of the building, box in hand, I realize this is what I deserve. People like me don't get fairy tales. Foster kid who nobody wanted, mental case who couldn't even kill himself properly, fool who falls for men who lie.

Some people are meant to be alone. I'm one of them. Harald's deception just confirms what I've always known—I'm not worth the truth. Not worth staying for. Not worth loving.

Chapter 22

Harald

I step off the private jet into a nightmare of flashing cameras and shouting voices.

"Crown Prince Harald! How much did you pay the American escort for his services?"

"Your Highness, what does your father say about your gay relationship?"

"Is this a royal scandal or a love story?"

Questions ricochet around me like bullets. Erik and my guards form a human shield, guiding me toward the waiting car. I can't focus on any single face in the churning sea of reporters. They're vultures circling, sensing the carrion of my shattered heart.

"Keep moving, sir," Erik murmurs, his hand firm against my back.

Inside my chest, something vital has collapsed. Daniel's face when he discovered the truth—the betrayal washing over his features, wiping away the warmth I'd come to crave—plays on endless loop in my mind.

The car door slams shut, muffling the chaos outside. I lean my forehead against the cool window, watching Denmark welcome home its disgraced prince.

"Your father expects you at the palace immediately," Erik says, his voice professionally neutral.

I nod mechanically. What does it matter now? Everything important lies across an ocean, in a Brooklyn apartment where I'm no longer welcome.

My phone sits heavy in my pocket. No new messages. I've sent dozens—explanations, apologies, pleas—each one meeting silence. The Daniel who trusted me, kissed me, held me close in those hotel sheets exists no more. I've killed him with my lies.

"I should have told him," I whisper, not realizing I've spoken aloud until Erik shifts uncomfortably beside me.

"Perhaps," he answers carefully. "But what's done cannot be undone."

Outside the window, Copenhagen slides past—beautiful, ancient, indifferent to the implosion of my personal life. These streets will someday be my responsibility. These people will look to me for leadership. The thought, once merely daunting, now seems impossible. How can I guide a nation when I couldn't even be honest with the one person who saw me as just Harald?

The palace gates loom ahead, promising judgment and consequence. I straighten my spine by instinct, royal training overriding my grief. But inside, I remain shattered.

The palace doors stand imposing and cold as we approach. I can't feel my legs beneath me—they move autonomously while my mind remains trapped in a New York hotel room, watching Daniel's face crumble with betrayal.

Ella rushes through the entrance before I've even fully emerged from the car. Her blonde hair catches the afternoon light as she flies down the steps toward me.

"Harald!" She crashes into me, wrapping her arms around my rigid frame. The warmth of her embrace barely penetrates the numbness enveloping me.

"It's going to be okay," she whispers fiercely against my ear, squeezing tighter. "We'll figure this out."

I can't bring myself to respond. Nothing feels okay. Nothing will ever be okay again.

Erik clears his throat softly. "His Majesty awaits in the study, Your Highness."

Ella's arms tighten protectively. "Father can wait five minutes."

"No," I manage, my voice sounding distant and hollow. "Let's get this over with."

The walk to Father's study stretches endlessly. Each step feels like marching toward execution. Ella keeps her hand firmly clasped around mine, but even her steadfast presence can't quell the dread building in my chest.

The heavy oak door swings open to reveal Father standing by the window, ramrod straight in his immaculate suit. The evening sunlight casts half his face in shadow, sharpening his already severe features.

His eyes—cold blue identical to mine—lock onto me. The disappointment radiating from them hits me with physical force.

"So." The single syllable slices through the silence with the precision of a surgeon's blade. "The Crown Prince of Denmark, cavorting with a man in public. Splashed across international tabloids like some common celebrity scandal."

I remain mute, unable to form words in my defense.

"Do you have any concept of what you've done?" Father's voice rises, sharp as broken glass. "Generations of careful diplomacy, royal dignity—and you destroy it for what? A flight of fancy with some American nobody?"

Daniel isn't a nobody. The thought flares briefly then dies, unspoken.

"This disgrace reflects on all of Denmark." Father paces toward me, each word calculated to wound. "You've proven every criticism true—you are weak, selfish, and entirely unfit for the crown you'll inherit."

I stand motionless. My father's condemnation washes over me in waves. I should defend myself. Defend Daniel. Explain that for once I found someone who saw me—the real me. Instead, I remain silent, a perfect royal statue carved from ice, while inside, everything crumbles.

"You will remain within your chambers until this scandal subsides," Father declares, each word a nail in my coffin. His eyes, so like mine yet devoid of warmth, fix on me with the cold precision of a sniper. "No public appearances. No interviews. No contact with anyone outside this household."

I stare at the intricate pattern of the carpet beneath my feet. The ornate swirls blur as I force myself to breathe evenly.

"You've embarrassed the monarchy enough," he continues. "Your staff will bring meals. Erik will filter all communications. You are to speak to no one outside these walls—especially not to that American."

Daniel's name remains unspoken, as if Father can't bear to acknowledge his existence. The thought of being cut off from even attempting to reach Daniel makes my chest constrict painfully.

"Father, this is—" Ella begins, her voice rising in protest.

"Necessary," he cuts her off sharply. "The damage control has already begun. The official statement is that the Crown Prince has returned to attend to pressing royal duties. You will be seen by no one while we determine how to proceed."

I finally find my voice, though it emerges hollow and small. "For how long?"

"For as long as it takes." His mouth sets in a grim line. "Perhaps this time of reflection will remind you of your responsibilities to this crown, this country, and this family."

The word "family" twists in my gut like a knife. What family? A father who sees only my failures, a mother long dead, and a sister who alone stands between me and complete isolation.

"Is that understood?" Father demands.

I raise my eyes to meet his. "Yes, Your Majesty."

The formality pleases him. He gives a curt nod and turns away, my punishment delivered, my sentence pronounced. I am to become a ghost in my own home, haunting rooms that suddenly feel more like prison cells than the chambers I've known since childhood.

Ella squeezes my arm, her touch an anchor in this storm. "I'll visit you," she whispers fiercely as we exit.

I nod mechanically, but my mind remains fixed on a Brooklyn apartment thousands of miles away, where the only person who made me feel truly alive now believes I am nothing but a liar.

* * *

I wake each morning to sunlight filtering through curtains I don't bother to open, pale fingers of dawn intruding despite my wishes for continued darkness. My chambers—once my sanctuary—have transformed into my prison, gilded and suffocating in equal measure. Every ornate fixture, every priceless painting, every velvet cushion mocks me with its perfection while I crumble, a fraud of a prince housed in splendour I haven't earned. The ceiling's elaborate mouldings seem to press down on me each day, centuries of royal expectations weighing on my chest before I've even risen. I trace the sunbeam's path across my silk sheets and wonder how something so free can visit something so trapped.

The palace staff moves around me like I'm made of glass, delicate crystal that might shatter at the slightest touch or careless word. They leave trays outside my door rather than risk interaction, porcelain rattling as they hastily depart—their footsteps always quicker going away than coming. Sometimes I hear them whispering, their voices dropping to nothing when I approach, conversations smothered mid-sentence with painful obviousness. The sudden silence burns worse than whatever words they might have spoken. Even the servants judge me now, these people who have known me since childhood, who once smiled warmly and snuck me extra pastries. Their eyes slide away from mine, focusing on some fascinating spot on the wall behind my shoulder, and I wonder what rumours about the fragile Crown Prince have reached their ears. What version of Harald do they see when they peek through keyholes or pass my chambers with downcast eyes? Not their future king, surely. Something less. Something broken.

"Your breakfast, Your Highness," Erik says, placing a tray on my desk. Steam rises from the porridge, carrying the scent of cinnamon and apples. My favorite.

I turn away. "Thank you."

Erik lingers, searching my face with quiet concern. His green eyes— steady, loyal—scan the hollows beneath my cheekbones that have grown more pronounced this past week.

"You haven't eaten properly in days," he says, voice pitched low enough that the guards outside won't hear this moment of impropriety, of someone speaking to the Crown Prince as if he were merely human. There's a gentle reproach there, wrapped in genuine worry that makes my chest tighten with guilt.

"I'm not hungry." The words barely carry across the room, a whisper so fragile it might disintegrate in the space between us. My stomach betrays me with a hollow ache that I've grown accustomed to ignoring these past several days. It's easier to feel empty than to face what awaits me beyond the prison of my chambers.

After he leaves, I lift the silver cover and stare at the perfectly arranged meal. My stomach churns with emptiness, but I can't bring myself to eat. The food grows cold, untouched, like yesterday's meal and the day before.

I wander the restricted sections of the palace during off-hours when fewer eyes might catch me. The grand ballroom, usually alive with light and sound, stands empty and cavernous. My footsteps echo across the polished floor where dignitaries and royalty once danced. Now there's only me, moving like a ghost through memories.

The library offers some escape. I run my fingers along leather-bound spines, pulling books at random. The words swim before my eyes, meaningless. I've read the same page sixteen times. The ancient texts that once transported me to different worlds now fail to pull me from my own suffocating reality. Father's collection of historical biographies—kings and conquerors who never seemed to doubt themselves as I do—mock me from their shelves. I sink deeper into the wingback chair by the window, where afternoon light streams through centuries-old glass, illuminating dust motes that seem more purposeful in their drifting than I feel in my existence. Even here, surrounded by the accumulated wisdom of generations, I cannot find answers to questions that plague me. The silence, usually comforting, presses against my temples like an unwanted crown.

Sometimes I find myself in the portrait gallery, staring up at generations of faces with my same blood. Stern kings and solemn queens look down from gilded frames, their eyes following me with silent reproach. Did any of them ever feel this hollow? This trapped?

At night, I lie awake remembering Daniel's eyes when the truth hit him. The hurt. The betrayal. I've replayed the moment a thousand times, imagining different words, different outcomes. The memory haunts me like a persistent ghost, refusing to grant me peace. His gaze—once warm and trusting—had turned cold with disbelief, each blink of his eyes like another door closing between us. If only I'd found the courage to tell him who I really was before he discovered it himself. If only I'd trusted him with Crown Prince Harald instead of the fabricated wealthy Dane he thought he knew. Now I stare at the ornate ceiling, counting the elaborate mouldings as if they were sheep, while my mind tortures me with alternative scenarios where honesty had prevailed and perhaps, just perhaps, he had stayed.

My phone sits dark and silent on my nightstand, its sleek surface reflecting the dim light of my bedchamber like a cruel mirror to my own emptiness. Daniel doesn't respond to any of my dozens of messages, all begging him to respond—desperate pleas typed with trembling fingers, each one more pathetic than the last. *"Please talk to me." "Let me explain." "I never meant to hurt you."* The words blur together after a while, an endless stream of regret sailing into a void. I ignore my father's orders to "compose myself befitting a future monarch" and his cold instruction to "cease this undignified pursuit immediately," delivered through Erik's uncomfortable, pitying glance. I can't stop trying, though every unanswered text carves another sliver from my already fractured heart. The royal seal on my signet ring catches the light as I reach for my phone again, a heavy reminder of the crown that stands between us.

I catch glimpses of myself in mirrors and windows—a paler, thinner version of the man who flew to New York. Large black bags under my eyes that seem flat and dull. The Crown Prince of Denmark dissolving into nothing before the kingdom's eyes.

* * *

I fumble for my phone on the nightstand, squinting at its harsh glow in the darkness. Three in the morning in Copenhagen—what time is it in New York? I calculate quickly—Daniel might be getting home from work now. My thumb hovers over our message thread, the last dozen texts all blue bubbles from me, each one unanswered. The sight makes my chest ache with a physical pain I can't push away.

A soft knock at my door startles me. I slip the phone under my pillow like a guilty teenager.

"Your Highness?" Erik's voice, hushed but concerned.

"Come in," I say, not bothering to sit up.

Erik enters, his silhouette framed by the dim hallway light. Even at this hour, his posture remains perfect, though his eyes betray his exhaustion. "I heard you were awake and wanted to check in. You need to rest."

"I can't sleep."

"Shall I call Dr. Nielsen for a sleeping aid?"

I shake my head. "I don't want to be medicated. I want—" My voice catches. What do I want? Daniel back? My life before this mess? Some alternate universe where I wasn't born into this gilded cage?

Erik's gaze falls to where my hand still clutches the edge of my pillow, my phone hidden beneath like some pathetic teenage secret. The slight shift in his posture tells me he knows exactly what I've been doing—staring at Daniel's number, drafting messages I'll never send. His expression softens with understanding, the rigid formality he maintains crumbling just enough to reveal the genuine concern beneath. The moonlight filtering through my curtains catches the tired lines around his eyes.

"Perhaps... perhaps a clean break would be kinder to you both, Your Highness," he suggests, his voice gentle in a way that makes my chest ache. There's something unspoken in those words—the wisdom of someone who understands sacrifice all too well, who has perhaps made similar choices himself in service to the crown I never asked to inherit.

I feel a flash of anger—not at Erik, but at the circumstances that force him to give such advice. "I can't just let him go without trying one more time."

Erik hesitates, then nods, his shoulders slumping almost imperceptibly. "I'll leave you, then." He pauses at the door, fingers lingering on the handle as though weighing something heavy in his mind. The moonlight catches the soft concern in his expression as he turns back to me. "For what it's worth, I thought he was..." His voice trails off, and I see him swallow hard before continuing. "I thought he was good for you. I haven't seen you smile that way in years, Harald. Not since we were boys at least."

After he's gone, I pull out my phone again and stare at our message thread. My fingers tremble slightly as I begin to type.

"Daniel, I know you probably won't read this. I've lost the right to expect anything from you. But I need to say that meeting you was the first time I felt real—not the Crown Prince, not the heir, just Harald. A person, not a title. I never meant to lie, but I've lived so long behind masks that I was terrified to remove the last one. I understand your anger. I deserve it. But please know that everything else was real. Every laugh. Every touch. Every kiss. It was all me—the real me I've never been brave enough to show anyone else."

I pause, swallowing hard before finishing:

"I don't expect forgiveness, but I wanted you to know: Jeg elsker dig. I love you. Always, Harald."

I press send, watching the message deliver into silence, my chest hollow with a fragile, desperate hope that somewhere across the ocean, he might still care enough to read my words.

Chapter 23

Ella

I pace the marble floor of the east wing corridor, my nerves still raw from the past week. The memory of that CNN alert makes my stomach clench even now. I'd been midway through my morning coffee when my phone buzzed with breaking news.

"Danish Crown Prince Harald's Secret Gay Romance Exposed."

I remember how my coffee mug slipped from my fingers, shattering against the tile. My hands trembled so badly I could barely tap Harald's number. When he finally answered, his voice had already shattered into pieces.

"Ella?" he'd whispered, terror threading through that single word.

"Harry, turn on CNN right now! You need to see what's happening!" My voice had risen with each word, panic taking hold as I realized what this meant.

The sounds that followed still haunt me—the raised voices in the background, Daniel's shout of betrayal, my brother's desperate pleas, Erik crying out that they needed to go. I'd clutched my phone so tightly my knuckles went white, listening helplessly as Harald's world collapsed in real time.

"I need to fix this—I need—" Harald's voice had broken, and I'd never felt more useless than in that moment, thousands of kilometres away while my

little brother's heart splintered.

The moment his plane landed, I broke every protocol to meet him at the front entrance of the palace. I'll never forget how Harald looked stepping out of that car—hollowed out, his eyes haunted, shoulders curled inward as if trying to disappear. Not the Crown Prince of Denmark, just my broken little brother.

It's been three weeks since Harald returned, and I barely recognize my brother anymore.

This morning, I find him at the breakfast table, staring vacantly at an untouched plate of food. His cheekbones jut sharply beneath pale skin, the hollows beneath his eyes dark as bruises. When did he get so thin?

"Harry," I say, sliding into the chair beside him. "You need to eat something."

He blinks slowly, as if waking from a dream. "I'm not hungry."

His royal blue sweater, once fitted, now hangs from his frame. I reach across and push the plate closer, but he just shakes his head.

"I saw the staff removed the television from your chambers," I mention, trying to keep my voice casual.

"I asked them to." He runs a finger around the rim of his untouched coffee mug. "I'm tired of seeing my face everywhere. Tired of the speculation. Tired of seeing the reminder."

Each day, he withdraws further into himself. The few times he's ventured from his rooms, I've caught him checking his phone, that brief flicker of hope followed by crushing disappointment when there's nothing from Daniel.

Last night, I heard him through the wall—crying. Not the quiet, controlled tears of a prince, but the raw, gasping sobs of someone coming apart. I sat outside his door, my own tears falling, feeling helpless.

"Father wants me to issue a formal statement." Harald's voice brings me back to the present. "About my 'indiscretion'."

I reach for his hand, alarmed by how cold his fingers feel. "What did you tell him?"

"Nothing. I just walked out." A ghost of a smile touches his lips, then vanishes. "Probably the first time I've ever done that."

He stands abruptly, chair legs scraping against marble. For a moment, he sways slightly, and I wonder when he last slept properly.

"Council meeting in twenty minutes," he mumbles, though his eyes are unfocused, distant.

I watch him shuffle away, shoulders hunched, each step heavy as if gravity pulls at him with extra force. My brother is disappearing before my eyes, fading like a photograph left too long in sunlight. Something essential is being bleached from him, day by empty day.

I slip away from breakfast to my private sitting room, hand trembling as I dial Ingrid's number. Three rings, four—please answer.

"Hello, Ella." Ingrid's warm voice usually brings comfort, but today I'm too frayed.

"I don't know what to do anymore," I blurt, pacing the length of my room. *"It's getting worse. He's not eating, barely sleeping. This morning he could hardly focus on a simple conversation."* The words tumble out, my voice pitching higher. *"I'm scared, Ingrid. I've never seen him like this, not even after—"*

I can't bring myself to say it—after the hospital. After those terrifying weeks when we nearly lost him.

"Has he been responding to your messages?" I ask. *"He mentioned you'd reached out."*

Ingrid sighs, the sound heavy. *"I've called several times, sent texts. He responds with single words, if at all. He's cancelled our last three appointments."*

My stomach drops. *"He's not seeing you either? I thought—I assumed he was at least talking to you."*

"I'm afraid not. From what you're describing, this is deeply concerning, Ella. His pattern of isolation, refusing food, emotional withdrawal..." She pauses, her professional tone faltering slightly. *"These are warning signs we can't ignore."*

The words I've been afraid to speak crystalize in my throat.

"Do you think... do we need to consider the hospital again?" My voice cracks. *"I can't bear the thought, but I'm watching him fade away right in front of me."*

"It may come to that if he continues on this path," Ingrid says gently. *"Self-neglect at this level can become dangerous quickly. His history means we need to be particularly vigilant."*

I sink onto my sofa, a cold dread washing over me. *"He would never forgive us."*

"This isn't about forgiveness, Ella. It's about keeping him safe until he can find his way back."

I press my fingertips to my temples, fighting back tears. The memory of Harald's face the last time—hollow-eyed, betrayed—as security escorted him to the private psychiatric facility haunts me still. How he'd looked at me like I was a stranger.

"I'll try again today," I whisper. *"But I don't know how much longer we can wait."*

* * *

Erik

I fold the measuring tape between my fingers as Harald stands motionless before the mirror. The numbers shrink with each visit. Another centimetre gone from his waist. Two from his chest. The sharp angles of his collarbones push against skin that once filled his suits properly.

"We'll need to take these in again, Your Highness." I keep my voice neutral, professional. The tailor scribbles notes, casting concerned glances my way.

Harald doesn't respond. He stares at his reflection without seeing it, the way he does everything these days. When the tailor leaves, I help him out of the jacket that hangs from his shoulders like a child playing dress-up.

"Perhaps we should order a new set instead of these constant alterations." I suggest, folding the offending garment.

He shrugs. The gesture lacks the energy to be dismissive.

Later, in my office, I place an order for three new suits. Size 46 instead of 52. Shirts with smaller collars. Trousers that won't pool around his thighs. Each click of the mouse feels like an admission of my failure to help him. I've been useless in the face of his heartbreak.

The order confirmation arrives in my inbox alongside another calendar alert: the Climate Council wishes to reschedule their meeting with the Crown Prince. The third postponement this week. I open the shared royal calendar and my stomach tightens at the sea of red. Crossed-out engagements. Rescheduled appearances. Cancelled charity visits.

I add the Climate Council to the growing list of disappointments and make a note to craft another polite excuse. *"His Royal Highness regrets that he is indisposed at present..."* The same words in different arrangements, a diplomatic way of saying he lacks the strength to leave his rooms.

The phone rings. It's the Danish Medical Association. Their gala dinner is next week, and they're hoping to confirm the Crown Prince's attendance. I glance at yesterday's untouched dinner tray outside Harald's chamber door.

"I'm afraid His Royal Highness's schedule is currently being reassessed," I hear myself say, adding another red mark to the calendar. *"I'll contact you when we have more certainty regarding his availability."*

Another cancellation. Another day Harald retreats further into himself. Another moment I stand by, arranging his shrinking clothes and diminishing life, wondering if there's anything I could have done differently.

* * *

I watch him from the doorway as he fumbles with his belt, thin fingers struggling with the leather strap. The sound of it sliding through the loops echoes in the cavernous dressing room. One notch. Two. Three. Each click of the prong finding a new hole pierces my heart. That belt—I'd had it custom-made in Florence last year as a birthday gift. Now he's run out of pre-punched holes and uses the rough one he made himself with a letter opener.

"Harald," I say, my voice barely carrying across the room. "Your break-fast—"

"I'm not hungry." He doesn't look up, just continues dressing with the methodical emptiness that's become his daily ritual.

My eyes trace the hollow of his cheeks, the shadows beneath his eyes that never seem to fade. I remember the Harald from before—the one whose laughter would fill a room, whose eyes sparkled with mischief during tedious state functions, who would steal pastries from the kitchen and share them with me while we reviewed his schedule.

This skeletal figure before me is a stranger wearing his face. I can barely reconcile him with the vibrant prince I've served for years. His collarbones jut beneath his crisp shirt, and the royal garments that once fitted perfectly now hang loose on his frame. It's as if some hollow doppelgänger has replaced my Harald, stealing away not just his flesh but the light that once animated his features. Each morning I find myself searching his eyes for some flicker of the man I've devoted my life to.

When he turns to reach for his watch, I notice how his shirt collar gaps around his neck, how his trousers bunch awkwardly despite the overtightened belt. The royal tailors have taken in his clothes three times in as many weeks, and still they hang from him like borrowed garments.

A wave of tenderness crashes over me, washing away any lingering jealousy. Whatever romantic feelings I've harboured for years seem trivial now, mere footnotes in the margins of a story that was never meant to be mine. My heart aches with a strange mixture of longing and resignation as I watch him waste away. I'd gladly watch him love Daniel forever if it meant seeing him healthy again, seeing him care about something—anything. I would trade every secret daydream, every accidental brush of our hands over state documents, every private smile he's ever given me, if only to see colour return to his hollow cheeks and purpose light those eyes that once commanded a room simply by glancing into it. Harald's happiness has always meant more to me than my own impossible wishes—this is the bargain I made with myself long ago when I chose to stay by his side.

"You need to eat something," I try again.

He glances up, and for a brief moment, I catch a glimpse of the old Harald—vulnerable, present—before the shutters come down again.

"I said I'm not hungry, Erik." His voice is soft but firm, that familiar stubbornness threading through each word. It's the same tone he's used since we were young men, when he would refuse royal banquets after particularly harsh criticism from his father. I recognize the gentle dismissal for what it is—another small wall erected between himself and anyone who might care enough to worry.

The click of his belt being fastened to that makeshift hole haunts me. It sounds like failure—my failure to protect him, to help him heal, to bring him back from wherever he's retreated.

* * *

Ella

I can't stop pacing the hallway outside Harald's room. My hands won't stop shaking as I watch the medical team enter—Ingrid leading them, her usual composure shattering the moment she sees my brother.

"Oh, my dear boy," Ingrid whispers, and my heart breaks at the tears welling in her eyes. My brother lies there, barely conscious, drowning in blankets that can't hide how skeletal he's become. The hospital gown they've put on him makes him look smaller, more fragile than I've ever seen him.

I want to scream, to fight, to do something—anything—but I know this is necessary. I've tried everything else. Watching the paramedics carefully transfer Harald onto the stretcher feels like I've failed him, even though I know deep down this is the only way forward.

Ingrid touches Harald's hand, her fingers gentle against his protruding bones. "We'll take care of him," she promises me, but her voice wavers. In all the years we've known her, I've never seen Ingrid cry. The sight of those tears rolling down her weathered cheeks tells me more than any medical report could about how serious this has become.

"I'm coming with him," I announce, my tone leaving no room for argument. Nobody tries to stop me as I fall into step beside the stretcher. Harald's eyes flutter open briefly, finding mine in a moment of clarity.

"Ells?" His voice is barely a whisper.

"I'm here, Harry. I'm right here." I grab his hand, so thin and cold, as they wheel him toward the waiting ambulance. The same hospital as before—the place that helped him once, that needs to help him again. "I'm not going anywhere."

The lights in the corridor feel too bright, too harsh, highlighting every sharp angle of my brother's face. Staff members pause and turn away, unable to watch their Crown Prince being taken out on a stretcher. I hold my head high, daring anyone to whisper, to judge. Let them see. Let them know that even princes can break, can need help.

As they load Harald into the ambulance, Ingrid places a hand on my shoulder. "He's stronger than he knows," she says softly, though her eyes are still wet. "And he has you."

I climb into the ambulance, taking my place beside my brother. As the doors close and the engine starts, I think of all the times I've protected Harald—from our father's harsh words, from society gossip, from his own demons. But this time, I have to trust others to help fight this battle.

I squeeze his hand gently, watching his chest rise and fall with shallow breaths. "We're going to get through this," I whisper, as much to myself as to him. "Just like last time. I promise."

The ambulance moves through the night, carrying us both back to the place where Harald once found his way back to himself. I pray it can work its magic again, that somewhere in my brother's too-thin frame, that fighting spirit still lives.

In the meantime, there's something I have to do. Save my brother.

Chapter 24

Daniel

I'm lying in bed, staring at my phone for the thousandth time, re-reading the message I've memorized by heart. I love you. I'm sorry I couldn't tell you before. The words blur as my eyes unfocus. Five weeks, and I still can't make sense of it.

The sound of our front door bursting open startles me from my daze.

"Excuse me, you can't just—" Jayda's voice rises in alarm.

"I need to see Daniel. Now." The unfamiliar voice carries a Danish accent.

"Lady, I don't care who you are, you can't just barge in here," Jayda snaps. "Caleb, call the police."

"Hold on, let's all just take a breath," Caleb says, ever the mediator. "Maybe we can—"

"I'm not leaving until I speak with Daniel," the voice interrupts. "I've flown across an ocean to be here."

"I'm dialling 911 right now," Jayda warns, and I hear her phone beeping.

"I'm Ella, Harald's sister, and if you call the police, I'll have diplomatic immunity anyway. Now where is he?"

The name 'Harald' jolts through me like electricity. I hear Jayda's sharp intake of breath.

"Wait," Caleb says. "Harald's sister? The Harald?"

"The same Harald who broke our best friend's heart?" Jayda's voice turns ice cold. "Give me one good reason why we should let you anywhere near Daniel."

"Because my brother is dying," Ella's voice cracks. "And Daniel is the only one who can save him."

"Dying?" Caleb echoes. "What do you mean dying?"

"He's in the hospital. He's stopped eating, barely sleeping. He's...he's given up."

"Good," Jayda spits, but I hear the uncertainty in her voice. "After what he did to Daniel—"

"What he did?" Ella's voice rises. "You mean falling in love with him? Being forced to choose between his heart and his duty to an entire country? Do you have any idea what this has done to him?"

I force myself to sit up, my body protesting after days of barely moving. My reflection in the bedroom mirror shows a stranger—unwashed hair, dark circles under my eyes, wearing the same sweater for what might be a week.

"Daniel!" Ella calls out. "Daniel, please!"

When I open my bedroom door, the scene in our living room freezes. Jayda stands with her phone still in hand, Caleb's arm around her waist as if holding her back. And there, in the middle of it all, stands a small blonde woman whose fierce blue eyes are exactly like Harald's.

"Finally," she says, her voice softening as she takes in my appearance. "Oh god, you look as bad as he does. You and Harald are more alike than you know."

"Daniel," Jayda moves toward me protectively. "You don't have to talk to her. Say the word and she's gone."

"Let him decide," Caleb murmurs, squeezing Jayda's shoulder.

"What do you want?" My voice is rough from disuse.

"I want you to listen." Ella steps forward, and despite her size, her presence fills the room. "My brother is in the hospital. Again. He's not eating, barely sleeping. He's..." her voice catches. "He's destroying himself."

I stare at Ella, trying to make sense of her words. Harald? In the hospital? A part of me wants to tell her it's not my problem anymore, but something in her desperate expression stops me.

"He lied to me," I say, my voice barely above a whisper. The words taste bitter on my tongue. I clench my fists until my knuckles ache, trying to anchor myself against the rising tide of betrayal flooding my chest. "He let me believe he was just...normal. Not a goddamn prince." I nearly choke on the last word, the absurdity of it all hitting me anew. All those quiet moments, those shared secrets—and he'd been hiding the biggest secret of all. The memory of his gentle smile twists something painful inside me.

"He is normal," Ella insists, taking another step toward me. "That's what you gave him—the chance to just be Harald, not the Crown Prince, not the heir, just... himself."

Jayda scoffs, crossing her arms over her chest. The black polish on her nails catches the light as she drums her fingers impatiently against her forearm. "Very touching," she says, voice dripping with sarcasm that I've grown all too familiar with over the years. "He still deceived Daniel." The way she says my name—protective, fierce—makes my throat tighten with emotion.

Ella's eyes flash with an intensity that makes me take a half-step back, her small frame suddenly radiating an almost palpable energy. Her blonde hair catches the light as she tilts her chin up defiantly.

"And what would you have done? Tell a stranger you just met online that you're royalty? Who would believe that?" She spreads her hands wide in frustration, her voice rising with each question. "Who wouldn't immediately change how they treated him? Do you have any idea what it's like for him? Everyone—absolutely everyone—wants something from the Crown Prince. Nobody sees Harald, just the title."

I feel my jaw tighten as her words hit home, conjuring unwanted images of Harald alone. Even as my stomach churns with anger, I can't completely silence the voice whispering that I might have done exactly what she's describing—treated him differently, or worse, assumed he was playing some elaborate joke and ignored him from the beginning.

I sink onto our couch, suddenly exhausted and feeling lost. "How bad is it?"

"They've put him on IV fluids." Ella's voice trembles. "He's lost so much weight. The doctors are talking about feeding tubes if he doesn't improve soon." She pulls out her phone, taps a few times, then hands it to me. "This was taken yesterday."

The photo knocks the wind out of me. Harald—my Harald—looks like a skeleton. His cheekbones jut out sharply, dark hollows beneath his eyes, his hospital gown hanging off his frame. He's staring out a window, not even aware of the camera, with such emptiness in his expression that my chest tightens in physical pain. I can't reconcile this gaunt figure with the man whose smile lit up my screen for weeks. His once vibrant eyes seem sunken into his skull, lifeless and dull. My fingers tremble against the phone screen as I trace the outline of his face, fighting the urge to pull the image closer as if I could somehow reach through it and touch him. The same hands that held me close in bed now lie limp and thin against sterile white sheets. My throat constricts around a sob I'm desperately trying to hold back. This isn't just weight loss—it's like he's disappearing altogether, fading away while I sit helplessly an ocean apart.

"Jesus," Caleb mutters, looking over my shoulder.

"Please, Daniel," Ella kneels in front of me. "I'm not asking you to forgive him. I'm not even asking you to love him. I'm just asking you to talk to him. To tell him to his face whatever you need to say, even if it's goodbye. Because right now, he's just... waiting to die."

"That's not fair," Jayda protests, her voice rising as she steps between Ella and me. "Danny's not responsible for—"

"I'll go," I cut her off, still staring at the photo. My voice comes out raspy, barely audible even to my own ears. The image of Harald—so frail, so utterly defeated—burns itself into my retinas. I swallow hard against the lump forming in my throat. "I'll go to Denmark."

The words hang in the air between us, surprising even me. After everything that's happened, after all the pain and betrayal I've suffered, here I am volunteering to fly across the ocean for someone I barely know. But that hollow-eyed ghost in the hospital gown isn't a stranger anymore. He's someone who understands the darkness I've walked through, perhaps even better than I do.

"Daniel, are you sure?" Caleb asks gently.

I look up at Ella, seeing Harald in the determined set of her jaw, the pleading in her eyes. The family resemblance strikes me so forcefully it's almost painful—that same Nordic stubbornness etched into the corners of her mouth, the identical shade of vulnerability swimming in her blue eyes. Even the way she holds herself, shoulders squared against invisible burdens, mirrors her brother's posture on better days. Before the hospital. Before the darkness dragged him down into that hollow shell I saw in the photos.

"When do we leave?

* * *

As I pack, I hear the conversation continue in the living room.

"I still don't trust this," Jayda says. "How do we know this isn't some elaborate trick?"

"You think I faked these hospital photos?" Ella asks wearily, her voice tinged with a blend of exhaustion and disbelief. "That I came all this way to hurt him more? Flew across an entire ocean just to pile on additional trauma?"

I pause my packing, straining to catch every word. The way her accent lilts slightly on certain syllables reminds me of Harald, her heightened emotions causing the accent to strain through. Something in her tone—a raw, protective quality—resonates with me.

"Jay," Caleb's voice is gentle, carrying that rare tone he reserves for moments of genuine concern rather than his usual sarcasm. "Look at Daniel. Really look at him. When was the last time you saw him smile? When was the last time he even left his room? He doesn't eat, and he's losing weight too. Soon enough he's going to look just like Harald does, and then what are we gonna do? He doesn't have a job, no health insurance, just us and nothing else…he'll die."

I freeze mid-fold, a shirt crumpled in my hands as his words pierce through me. The quiet tenderness in Caleb's question makes something in my chest constrict painfully. Even from the hallway, I can feel the weight of what he's asking Jayda to see—to really see me, not the version of myself I've been desperately trying to project. It's terrifying being dissected like this, having someone point out the emptiness I've been trying to disguise with snark and attitude. The fact that hipster-boy Caleb, with his ridiculous beanie and ironic t-shirts, can read me this clearly makes me want to crawl under my bed and disappear. But there's something almost relieving about being seen, truly seen, even as I continue pretending I can't hear them discussing me like I'm some fragile artifact on the verge of shattering.

"I just…" Jayda's voice wavers. "I can't watch him get hurt again. I'd never allow him to harm himself that way, you understand, right? If it came down to forcing a feeding tube into his mouth myself and restraining him to the bed, you know I wouldn't hesitate for a second."

"Then help me fix this," Ella pleads, her voice cracking with emotion that makes my chest tighten. "Because right now, they're both hurting, and it's killing them both. I can see it eating away at Harald every day, and Daniel—" She gestures in my direction with a helpless wave of her hand, "—Daniel looks like he hasn't truly slept or eaten in weeks."

I hear Jayda sigh. "If this goes wrong..."

"You have my permission to hunt me down and kick my ass," Ella says, and I hear Caleb chuckle.

"I'm holding you to that," Jayda warns, but there's a hint of warmth in her voice now. "And you better have room on that fancy royal jet for us too, because there's no way in hell we're letting him go alone."

"Jay..." I call out from my room, emotion thick in my throat.

"Don't even try to argue with me, Daniel. We're coming with you, and that's final."

For the first time in five weeks, I feel my lips curve into something resembling a smile. "Okay."

* * *

I stand in front of the massive oak doors leading to the King's office, straightening my tie one last time. The royal guard nods, opening the door without announcement. King Magnus sits behind his desk, his silver hair combed back perfectly, not a strand out of place—unlike the chaos he's about to unleash.

"Your Majesty," I bow slightly. "You summoned me?"

He doesn't look up from the papers in front of him, making me wait as he has countless times before. The grandfather clock in the corner ticks, each sound like a hammer in my chest.

"Erik." He finally acknowledges me, his voice cold as a Danish winter. "I've come to a decision regarding my son."

My stomach drops. I keep my expression neutral, years of practice serving me well. "Yes, Your Majesty?"

"I intend to disinherit Harald." He states it plainly, as though discussing the weather rather than destroying his son's life. "I've consulted with my advisors. Prince Oskar—Harald's cousin—will be named heir to the throne instead."

The room spins slightly. I grip my hands behind my back to steady myself.

"I see, Sir."

"Do you? Because Harald certainly doesn't." Magnus stands, walking to the window overlooking the palace gardens. "He's proven himself utterly incapable. Weak. Emotional. And now this... disgusting display with that American boy."

The bile rises in my throat as he spits the word "disgusting." I taste copper as I bite the inside of my cheek hard enough to draw blood. It's a physical pain that momentarily distracts from the emotional one tearing through my chest. Years of diplomatic training haven't prepared me for standing here, listening to a father speak about his own son with such contempt. My loyalty to Harald screams inside me, demanding I defend him, but my position demands silence.

"His... proclivities," Magnus continues, the word dripping with contempt, "have no place in this monarchy. Denmark needs strength, tradition. Not a king who weeps and falls apart over some homosexual affair."

My stomach twists into a nauseating knot as the King's words hang in the air between us, each syllable laced with poison. I feel my fingernails digging crescents into my palms, the small pain a desperate anchor to keep me from showing the rage building inside me. The royal office suddenly feels airless, the ornate Danish furniture and centuries of tradition pressing down like a physical weight on my shoulders. The portrait of Harald's grandfather stares down from behind Magnus's desk, his stern expression seeming to echo the current king's sentiments across generations.

"Homosexual affair," he says, as if speaking of some disease rather than his own son's identity. The casual cruelty makes my throat constrict. I've witnessed Magnus's coldness for years, but this naked hatred towards Harald – towards people like us – slices deeper than I can bear. My loyalty to the Crown Prince burns even fiercer in response, a protective flame that threatens to consume my professional composure. I swallow hard, tasting blood again, and shift my weight slightly, the leather of my shoes creaking against the polished floor – a small reminder that I must remain steady, remain useful to Harald, no matter how much I long to defend him.

Every word is a dagger. I nod mechanically, forcing my face into what I hope appears as sympathetic agreement.

"You've always been loyal to the Crown, Erik. You understand what I'm saying, don't you?" The King's voice drops to a conspiratorial rumble, like distant thunder promising a storm. His eyes—Harald's eyes but without their warmth—fix on mine, demanding agreement, demanding complicity.

I feel sweat gathering at my collar, my throat constricting with the effort of maintaining this charade. Of course I understand. He wants me to be his spy, his informant, his tool to further bend Harald to his will and utterly destroy him. The irony burns—my loyalty being wielded as a weapon against the very person to whom I am truly devoted.

"Yes, Your Majesty," I manage, the words like chalk in my mouth. I nod again, the movement stiff and unnatural, as though my body itself rebels against this betrayal. But is it betrayal to agree while intending to protect Harald? The moral calculus makes my head ache, another pressure building behind my temples to join the mounting tension in my chest.

Inside, I'm screaming. I want to tell him that Harald shows more strength in his vulnerability than Magnus has shown in his entire reign. That Harald's compassion makes him more qualified to rule than this cold, heartless man could ever comprehend.

Magnus seems satisfied with my betrayal. "Good. The announcement will come after Harald's...recovery." He pauses on the word with deliberate condescension, as if Harald's struggle is nothing more than an inconvenient delay in his political machinations. "I'm told he's gaining strength. Perfect timing to strip him of his birthright, don't you think?"

My stomach twists violently at his words, bile rising in my throat. The clinical detachment with which he speaks of destroying his own son's future makes my hands tremble slightly where they rest at my sides. Behind my carefully constructed expression, I'm mapping out contingency plans, desperately searching for any legal precedent, any political ally, any strategy that might protect Harald from this coldly orchestrated downfall.

I bow again, rage boiling beneath my careful exterior. "As you wish, Your Majesty."

The King dismisses me with a casual wave of his hand, turning his attention back to the papers on his desk as if he hasn't just revealed plans to destroy his son's life. I bow stiffly and exit, pulling the heavy oak door closed behind me with careful control, though every muscle in my body screams to slam it.

The corridor stretches before me, portraits of past monarchs watching as I walk with measured steps despite the hurricane inside me. Only when I reach the empty stairwell do I allow myself to stop, gripping the marble banister until my knuckles turn white.

"Breathe, Erik," I whisper to myself. My lungs expand painfully against my ribs as I force air in and out.

I can't let this happen. Not to Harald. Not after everything he's endured.

The law is clear—succession can only be altered through Parliament with royal consent. But Magnus has allies everywhere, constitutional loopholes at his disposal, and the power of public opinion. And Harald, Gods help him, is in no position to fight back.

I glance at my watch. Two hours until I'm expected at the hospital to brief Harald on today's correspondence. Two hours to formulate a plan.

My decision crystallizes as I descend the stairs. Magnus thinks I'm his loyal servant, that I'd help dismantle Harald's future because I "understand." His arrogance will be his undoing.

The palace gardens blur around me as I walk briskly across the grounds, nodding mechanically at staff who greet me. My mind races through options, connections, possibilities.

Only one person has both the power and motivation to help me stop this. Someone who will understand exactly what needs to be done.

I reach for my phone, sending a brief, encoded message requesting an immediate meeting.

The door opened without a sound, revealing Anja Christensen, Denmark's new Prime Minister. She didn't extend a hand or offer a smile, her steel-grey eyes fixing on me with unnerving intensity.

"Erik. I assume this isn't a social call regarding the Crown Prince."

I took a steadying breath. "No, Prime Minister. King Magnus plans to disinherit Prince Harald in favor of his cousin Oskar."

Something flickered across her face - not surprise, but sharp calculation. "Bold move, considering that would require parliamentary approval and a constitutional amendment."

"The King believes he has the necessary support."

Anja's eyes narrowed slightly, the only sign my news unsettled her. "The recent scandal with the American has shifted public sentiment. Harald's suffering made him more popular, not less. Magnus is a relic who's clinging to power in a changing world."

Her words confirmed my own assessment. "Harald would be a better monarch. One suited for a modern Denmark."

"Agreed. Which is why we must act." She paced deliberately, heels clicking. "I can block the King's petition in Parliament easily enough. But we need to be proactive in dismantling his support and forcing abdication."

Relief mingled with unease at her ruthless efficiency. "What do you propose?"

She smiled, and I understood why opponents underestimated her only once. "Accelerate his political isolation. Leverage allies who owe me favors. If needed, I have information about his private affairs that would shock the nation."

An unsettled feeling twisted my gut. "There's a price for your cooperation, I assume."

Her gaze pierced through me. "Naturally. The days of the monarchy as a symbolic relic are over. Harald keeps his crown at my discretion, ruling in service to the people, not tradition."

"You'd make him a puppet king."

"I'd make him a partner in progress." Her tone brooked no argument. "This is the cost, Erik. Uphold a dying institution or preserve the man you love to be an agent of change."

The words hit like a physical blow. In Anja's unflinching presence, I realized the impossibility of separation between heart and crown. The choice lay bare - tradition or Harald. Power or love.

I flinched, my carefully constructed facade cracking. "He will understand the parameters."

Anja's smile widened, a predator scenting weakness. "Then we have an agreement. You've made the right choice—for Harald and for Denmark."

As we shook hands, I felt the weight of my decision settle heavily on my shoulders. In Anja's unflinching presence, I realized the impossibility of separating my heart from the crown.

For Harald, I reminded myself. Always for Harald.

Chapter 25

Daniel

I followed Jayda up the steps of the private jet, barely registering the royal crest emblazoned on its side. My best friend's hand remained firmly clasped around my wrist, guiding me forward like a lifeline through fog. Everything felt distant, unreal—my mind fixated on the image of Harald in that hospital bed, looking so fragile.

"Danny, sit here." Jayda's voice cut through my thoughts as she guided me into a cream-coloured leather seat. The luxury surrounding me might as well have been cardboard for all I noticed. My hands trembled slightly as I fumbled with the seatbelt until Jayda reached over and clicked it into place.

"When was the last time you ate something?" Her question floated somewhere in the background of my consciousness. I couldn't remember. Time had become meaningless since Ella had shown up at our door with that photo. Harald's sunken cheeks and pallid skin haunted me, making my stomach twist into knots.

A flight attendant approached with offers of champagne and snacks, but her words washed over me like white noise. Jayda handled everything, her protective presence shielding me from the need to respond.

As the jet took off, I pressed my forehead against the cool window, watching New York disappear beneath the clouds. Somewhere across the ocean, Harald was lying in a hospital bed because of me. Or was it because of his lies? The thoughts swirled together until they became indistinguishable, a tempest of worry and hurt that consumed everything else.

I don't know how long I've been staring out this window. Time stretches and compresses like an elastic, measured only by the steady thrum of the engines and Jayda's occasional gentle touches on my arm.

"Here." Jayda presses a bottle of water into my hands. "You need to drink something."

I lift the bottle mechanically to my lips, the water tasteless as it slides down my throat. My reflection in the window catches my eye—dark circles under hollow eyes, skin sallow against the darkness beyond the glass. I look almost as bad as Harald did in that photo.

Harald. My chest tightens at the thought of him. Five weeks of silence between us, and now this. Now he's lying in a hospital bed, refusing food, barely conscious. And here I am, racing across an ocean because his sister showed up at my door with pictures that made me feel terrified.

"You should try to sleep," Jayda murmurs, draping a cashmere blanket over my shoulders. The soft fabric probably costs more than my monthly rent, but luxury means nothing when my mind keeps circling back to Harald's vacant eyes in that hospital photo.

"I can't." My voice cracks. It's the first thing I've said since we boarded.

"I know, babe." Jayda squeezes my hand. "But we've got eight hours until Copenhagen, and you're going to need your strength."

Copenhagen. The word alone sends a fresh wave of anxiety through me. What will I even say to him? 'Sorry I ghosted you after finding out you were secretly a prince, but could you please start eating again?' The absurdity of it all hits me, and I might have laughed if I wasn't so scared.

Across the aisle, I catch Ella watching me with concern in her eyes. She looks away quickly, tapping something on her phone, probably handling whatever royal crisis our impending arrival will cause.

I pull the blanket tighter around my shoulders and close my eyes, not to sleep but to escape the pitying looks and the weight of what waits for us in Denmark. But even in darkness, I can't escape the image of Harald in that hospital bed, or the crushing guilt that maybe, just maybe, I'm partly responsible for putting him there.

The flight attendant approaches again, this time with a tray of food that makes my stomach turn. Jayda intercepts her before she can reach me, murmuring something I can't quite catch. I'm grateful—the thought of eating anything right now seems impossible.

"Daniel." Ella's voice startles me. I hadn't noticed her move to the seat across from us. "The doctors say he asks for you, when he's lucid enough to speak."

My throat constricts. I stare at my hands, unable to meet her gaze. "How long has he been...?" I can't finish the question.

"Two weeks since he stopped eating entirely." Her voice wavers slightly. "The medical team had to intervene three days ago when he tried to—" She breaks off, composing herself. "We almost lost him. They've put him into a medical coma and have him on feeding tubes now."

Jayda's hand finds mine again, squeezing tight. I'm glad she's here; I don't think I could handle this alone.

"Your Highness," a man in a dark suit—one of the security detail, I think—approaches Ella with a tablet. "The Prime Minister is requesting an update."

Ella sighs, rising from her seat. "Excuse me," she says, but pauses before leaving. "Daniel... thank you for coming. I know this isn't easy."

Easy? Nothing about this is easy. Not the way my heart feels like it's being squeezed in a vice, not the guilt churning in my stomach, not the memory of Harald's last text message that I never answered. I close my eyes again, but the words are burned into my memory: *I don't expect forgiveness, but I wanted you to know: Jeg elsker dig. I love you. Always.*

"Hey." Jayda's voice is soft. "You're shaking."

Am I? I look down at my hands and realize she's right. The tremors have gotten worse since we took off.

"What if—" My voice breaks. I swallow hard and try again. "What if we're too late?"

"We won't be," Jayda says firmly. "That stubborn prince of yours has held on this long. He's waiting for you."

I lean my head against her shoulder, letting her steady presence anchor me as the jet carries us through the night. Somewhere ahead, beyond the darkness outside my window, Denmark waits. And Harald.

God, Harald. Please hold on. I'm coming.

Chapter 26

Daniel

As I step into the stark, sterile environment of the hospital, the oppressive air weighs heavily on my chest. The fluorescent lights flicker overhead, casting a harsh glare on the tiled floors that gleam from too-frequent cleaning. The smell of antiseptic lingers, mixing with the faint scent of flowers from a discarded bouquet.

With each step I take, my heart races, a mix of anxiety and dread pooling in my stomach. What will I find beyond the well-polished reception desk? Will I still see that familiar warmth and spark in Harald's eyes, or will this place be the end of everything we could have built together? The thought strikes me across the face, cold and unyielding reality suddenly rearing its ugly head.

Ella guides me toward the intensive care unit, her expression grave as we navigate the maze of hallways. Jayda, by my side, reaches for my hand, squeezing it tightly in reassurance. The quiet hum of machines and the distant beeps of monitors around us create an unsettling symphony.

When we finally reach Harald's room, I hesitate just outside the door. The sight that greets me sends a chill up my spine. Harald is lying in the hospital bed, motionless, surrounded by an array of blinking machines that monitor his every breath. Tubes thread through his nose and mouth, connecting him to life-sustaining ventilators and feeding lines. His face, usually so animated, appears pale and lost in the muted glow of the monitors. All the vibrant colours of life have drained away, replaced by a haunting starkness that twists my gut.

A wave of nausea washes over me, and I stagger back, letting go of Jayda's hand and dropping to my knees before the trash bin and throwing up. My heart shatters as reality sets in—this is real. The gravity of the situation consumes me. I am here because of the love I hesitated to acknowledge, the tenderness I underestimated. Suddenly, I feel like a fool for not recognising how much Harald has tried to communicate with me, how he shared his fears and vulnerabilities through our texts, how he tried for weeks on end to speak to me, begging for any connection.

I get up wiping my mouth with a cloth Jayda hands me, and take a tentative step closer, my heart racing, tears prickling at the corners of my eyes. "Harald," I breathe, my voice trembling, barely a whisper as I approach the bedside. Seeing the man I love in such a fragile state is devastating. The memories of our laughter, and the powerful connection we quickly formed feel like distant echoes in my mind.

The unraveling of emotions becomes too much, and I let the tears flow freely. "I should have listened... I'm so sorry," I sob, the regret twisting painfully in my chest. This is not how our story is meant to unfold. Every moment spent in doubt now stings like a thousand needles, and I wish for the chance to go back and tell Harald I believe in him, to show that I care.

As I sink into the chair beside Harald's bed, the cold hard reality sets in. I could lose him, the man who has shown me what it means to truly be loved. The realization hits me like a tidal wave; I love Harald with all my heart. I know why he did what he did, and I can't keep denying the truth any longer. I need Harald like I need air to breathe, I think I knew that from the first moment our eyes met in that coffee shop.

The machines continue their relentless rhythm, each beep echoing like a drum of despair—a reminder that time is slipping away. "Please, just wake up," I plead, enclosing Harald's hand in my own as I squeeze it tightly, searching for a flicker of warmth. "I need you... I'm not ready to lose you."

* * *

Daniel

The steady rhythm of the heart monitor fills the silence as I clutch Harald's hand. Through my tears, I barely register the soft footsteps approaching from behind until a gentle hand rests on my shoulder.

"You must be Daniel," a warm voice says in accented English. "I've been hoping to meet you, though I wish it were under better circumstances."

I turn to find an elderly woman with kind eyes and silver hair pulled back in a neat bun. She's wearing a cardigan over professional clothes, and despite her obvious concern, there's a gentleness to her presence that seems to soften the harsh hospital lighting.

"I'm Ingrid," she says, pulling up a chair beside me. "I'm Harald's therapist. He's told me so much about you in our sessions."

I hastily wipe my tears with my sleeve. "He has?"

Ingrid's smile is gentle but knowing. "Oh yes. I've never seen him light up the way he does when he talks about you. The first time he mentioned meeting someone online, there was this... spark in his eyes I hadn't seen in years."

My throat tightens. "I didn't know."

"Harald has always struggled with being truly seen," Ingrid continues, her eyes drifting to Harald's still form. "As Crown Prince, people see what they want to see—the title, the wealth, the fairy tale. But you... you saw him. Just Harald. The young man who loves penguins and makes terrible puns and feels things so deeply it sometimes overwhelms him."

Fresh tears spring to my eyes. "But he lied to me about who he was."

"Did he?" Ingrid asks softly. "Or did he finally show someone who he truly is, without the crown getting in the way?" She reaches into her bag and pulls out a leather-bound notebook. "Harald has been my patient for many years, Daniel. Would you like to know what he wrote about you in his therapy journal?"

I hesitate, torn between wanting to know and feeling like I'm invading his privacy. But Ingrid's kind eyes hold no judgment, only understanding. Slowly, I nod.

Ingrid opens the journal carefully, her fingers tracing over Harald's neat handwriting. "This entry is from the day you first met at the coffee shop," she says, adjusting her reading glasses. "'For the first time in my life, someone looked at me and saw just me. Not the Crown Prince, not the heir to the throne, not Magnus' disappointing son. When Daniel smiled at me, I felt real. Human. Worthy.'"

My heart clenches as she continues reading. "'I know I should tell him who I am. The guilt eats at me every time he shares another piece of himself. But I'm terrified. Everyone who knows who I am wants something from me. With Daniel, I can just... be. When he laughs at my jokes or sends me silly selfies or tells me about his day, it's because he wants to share those moments with me. Just me.'"

Ingrid turns a few pages. "This one is from your day at Coney Island. 'Today I had cotton candy for the first time. Daniel couldn't believe it. His whole face lit up when he insisted on buying me some, like he was giving me the most precious gift in the world. And maybe he was. Because no one has ever cared about giving me normal experiences before. No one has ever looked at me with such pure joy just because I was enjoying something simple.'"

I can't stop the sob that escapes my throat. Jayda squeezes my shoulder from where she stands behind me, but I barely register it.

"Harald has struggled with depression since he was a teenager," Ingrid says softly, closing the journal. "The pressure of being Crown Prince, his father's expectations, hiding his sexuality... it's been crushing him for years. But then he met you." She reaches out and places her hand over mine where it still grips Harald's. "In all my years as his therapist, I've never seen him fight so hard to be happy as he did these past few weeks with you."

"But look where that got him," I whisper, glancing at the tubes and monitors surrounding us.

"This," Ingrid gestures to Harald's unconscious form, "isn't because of you, Daniel. This is because for his entire life, Harald has been told that who he is isn't enough. That he needs to hide parts of himself to be worthy of love and respect." She leans forward, her eyes intense. "You were the first person to show him that wasn't true. The first person who loved him for exactly who he is."

"I do," I admit, my voice barely audible. "I love him. Even after everything... I love him."

"Then tell him that when he wakes up," Ingrid says, standing slowly. She places the journal on the bedside table. "I think you should read the rest of this. Harald would want you to understand." She pauses at the door. "You know, in all his entries about you, he never once mentioned being afraid you'd reject him for being a prince. He was only ever afraid you'd stop seeing him as Harald."

As Ingrid's footsteps fade down the hallway, I pick up the journal with trembling hands. The weight of Harald's truth, his fears, his love, all bound in leather and waiting to be discovered.

* * *

Erik

As I stepped into the sterile confines of the hospital room, the scent of antiseptic hung heavy in the air. My heart quickened at the sight before me: Daniel, his face streaked with tears, sat by Harald's bedside, staring at the frail figure lying motionless among the white sheets.

He looked up as I approached, wiping his eyes hastily with the back of his hand, and offered a shaky smile, filled with guilt. "I'm sorry," he managed to whisper, his voice hoarse with emotion.

"Don't worry about it," I replied, my own heart aching in response to his pain. "How's he doing?"

Daniel took a shaky breath, and I could see the hope flicker in his eyes. "The doctors say he's gaining weight again. They're hopeful they can take him off the ventilators and feeding tubes soon." His fingers trembled as they gently stroked Harald's motionless hand, his gaze never leaving the prince's pale face. I felt an unexpected surge of relief wash through me, even as the familiar ache in my chest—that mixture of devotion and unspoken longing—throbbed anew. Five weeks of watching Harald deteriorate had been torture, not just for Daniel, but for me as well.

A heavy silence settled between us, punctuated only by the rhythmic beeping of the machines. I glanced at Harald, lying unconscious, and felt a wave of emotion rise within me. I had watched him struggle, and now, helplessly, I stood witness to the remnants of his suffering.

And then, despite everything—the turmoil of my own heart—I found myself saying it. "Daniel, can I be honest with you?"

He nodded, his expression morphing into one of deep curiosity mixed with uncertainty.

"I'm jealous of you," I continued, feeling the words spill out against my will, each syllable a burden I'd carried for longer than I could remember. "You've been there for him in ways I could never be. You've given him something that I could only dream of." My voice wavered slightly, and I clasped my hands tightly together to hide their trembling. The hospital air seemed to grow thinner as I finally acknowledged the truth I'd buried beneath years of dutiful service and quiet devotion. "I've loved him for so long, but I know that it won't ever be anything more than what it is now—this one-sided affection that I've learned to live with, tucked away where it can't interfere with my duties to him or the Crown."

Daniel's eyes widened, his shock reflected in the slight parting of his lips. The hospital lights cast harsh shadows across his face, highlighting every nuance of his stunned expression. A weight lifted from my chest—strange how confession could feel like both release and devastation simultaneously. But I didn't give him a chance to respond. There was no point. The truth had lived within me for too long to be comforted away with kind words.

"I just want to see him happy," I continued, my voice growing steadier as I embraced this final surrender. My fingers uncurled from their tight grip, palms damp with nervous perspiration. "And if that's with you, then... so be it." The words tasted bittersweet—like medicine necessary for healing but difficult to swallow. Years of quiet longing compressed into a single moment of acceptance that Harald's happiness would never include me the way I'd dreamed.

I turned away, unable to bear the weight of his silence, the uncertainty hanging in the air thick enough to choke on. The ache in my chest tightened as I walked away, leaving him with a torrent of thoughts that I hoped would find a way to make sense of what had just unfolded.

As the hospital's fluorescent lights flickered behind me, I couldn't help but feel that maybe I had let go of something I had clung to for far too long. And all the while, I hoped that Harald would wake up, no matter the cost.

Chapter 27

Harald

The darkness has been endless. Time means nothing here in this void where I float, haunted by memories that play on endless repeat. Daniel's face when the truth was revealed—the way his warm brown eyes turned cold and distant, how his gentle smile twisted into betrayal. Over and over, I watch him back away from me in that hotel room, shaking his head in disbelief. "It was all a lie," he had said, his voice breaking. The sound echoes through my consciousness, a torment I can't escape. Sometimes the visions shift—Daniel running through the crowd of reporters, shoulders hunched against their shouted questions, while I stand helplessly watching him disappear. Other times, I'm reaching for him but my fingers pass through empty air, and he vanishes like smoke.

Sometimes I hear voices—Ella, Erik, even Father—but they fade like wisps of smoke, meaningless against the crushing weight of Daniel's absence. One voice remains constant though, a gentle murmur of Daniel's voice saying my name over and over that keeps me tethered to something beyond this emptiness, anchoring me when I feel myself drifting too far into the void.

Light creeps in slowly, piercing through the heavy blanket of unconsciousness. My eyelids feel weighted, but I force them open, blinking against the harsh fluorescent glare. As my vision clears, my heart stutters—Daniel is here, slumped in a chair beside my bed, dark circles under his eyes and his clothes wrinkled as though he's been here for days.

This can't be real.

My throat constricts with emotion. Is this death, then? My final punishment—to see him here, so close, knowing I can never make things right? The machines around me beep steadily, but even that feels distant, unreal. This must be hell, I think, my own personal torment—to be forced to watch Daniel for eternity, close enough to see the gentle rise and fall of his chest, the flutter of his eyelashes, but never able to touch him, to hold him, to beg his forgiveness. Like Tantalus reaching for water that forever recedes from his grasp, I am condemned to an eternity of watching the one I love, knowing my lies destroyed any chance of reconciliation.

The thought sends a wave of panic through me, and I want to scream, to thrash against this fate, but my body feels leaden and unresponsive. Even the pain in my chest feels muted, distant, as though it belongs to someone else. This is my punishment, then—to remain conscious but paralyzed, forced to witness what I've lost.

Daniel's head snaps up, his eyes meeting mine. For a moment, we just stare at each other, the air heavy between us. Then his face crumples, tears spilling down his cheeks as he launches himself forward.

"I'm so sorry, I'm so sorry, I'm so sorry," he sobs, carefully wrapping himself around me, his head resting against my chest. The weight of him is solid, warm—real. His tears soak through the thin hospital gown, and I can feel him trembling. Each sob that wracks his body sends vibrations through my chest, and the sensation is so visceral, so impossibly real, that my mind struggles to process it. This can't be hell—no torture could replicate the precise way Daniel's fingers curl into my hospital gown, or the familiar scent of his shampoo as his hair brushes against my chin.

Slowly, cautiously, I lift my arms. They're weaker than I remember, but I manage to wrap them around him. The sensation of holding him again sends a jolt through my entire body—like a defibrillator straight to my heart. This isn't a dream. This isn't a hallucination. My arms aren't passing through empty air; they're holding something solid, something real. This is Daniel, here and whole in my arms, apologizing when I'm the one who should be begging for forgiveness. The realization crashes over me like a wave, washing away the lingering shadows of my personal hell. He's here. He's come back to me.

I want to speak, to tell him he has nothing to be sorry for, to beg his forgiveness for my own lies, but my throat is too dry, my voice lost to days of disuse. Instead, I hold him closer, pressing my face into his hair as tears slip silently down my cheeks. The steady beeping of the heart monitor marks each precious second of this miracle I never thought I'd have again, each beat a reminder that I'm alive, that this is real, that somehow, against all odds, Daniel has returned to me.

Daniel's breath hitches against my chest as he tries to calm himself. His fingers clutch at my hospital gown, and I can feel him gathering his thoughts. The heart monitor beside us keeps its steady rhythm, grounding me in this moment that still feels surreal.

"I understand now," he whispers, his voice thick with emotion. "Ingrid... she showed me your journal. Your therapy journal."

My heart skips a beat, and the monitor betrays my sudden anxiety with an erratic blip that seems to echo through the room. Those pages contain my deepest fears, my darkest thoughts—everything I couldn't say aloud to anyone, not even to Ingrid sometimes. The journal was supposed to be my sanctuary. I feel naked, exposed in a way that even this thin hospital gown can't compare to.

"I read about how scared you were," Daniel continues, shifting slightly but not letting go. "How you felt truly seen for the first time when you were with me. Just Harald, not the Crown Prince." His voice cracks. "I'm so sorry I didn't let you explain. I was so hurt, so angry... but I understand now why you couldn't tell me right away."

I try to swallow past the dryness in my throat. When I speak, my voice is barely a whisper, rough from disuse. "I wanted... to be real. With you."

Daniel lifts his head to look at me, his eyes red-rimmed but soft. "You were real with me. Everything except your title—that was all real. I see that now." He reaches for the water cup on the bedside table, helping me take small sips through a straw. "I almost lost you because I was too stubborn to see it sooner."

The cool water soothes my throat, and I find my voice again, though it's still weak. "I thought I'd lost you forever. That I deserved to lose you."

"No," Daniel says firmly, his hand finding mine. "No more losing each other. I've spent the last week watching you waste away, praying you'd wake up. I can't—" his voice breaks again. "I can't lose you like that again. Ever."

I squeeze his hand, feeling the warmth of his skin against mine. After the cold darkness of the past week, his touch feels like sunlight. "I'm here," I whisper. "I'm here now."

* * *

Daniel

My footsteps echo through the private hospital wing as I support Harald's weight, one careful step at a time. Two weeks into recovery, and these daily walks have become our ritual—a dance of patience and determination.

"I've got you," I murmur, my arm steady around his waist. Despite Harald's protests that he can manage on his own, I can't help but notice how his hospital gown hangs loose on his still-too-thin frame.

Harald's grip tightens on my shoulder as we reach the end of the corridor. "I want to try the stairs today."

"The stairs?" My heart skips. "Are you sure that's—"

"Please." His voice carries that quiet determination I've come to know so well. "Just three steps. Ingrid said I need to push myself a little each day."

I hesitate, studying his face for any signs of fatigue. The dark circles under his eyes have begun to fade, but I can't shake the memory of him lying in that bed with tubes and ventilators down his throat. Every night, that image haunts my dreams.

"Three steps," I agree finally. "But if I see you wobble even once, we're turning back."

Harald's answering smile is worth all the worry. "Yes, nurse Ramirez."

"Don't get cheeky with me, Your Highness," I tease, though my grip remains protective as we approach the stairs. "I still outrank you in this hospital."

As we take the first step together, I feel his muscles trembling with effort. I keep my face carefully neutral, knowing Harald hates showing weakness, but my heart aches. Each step forward is a small victory against what we almost lost.

Harald's breathing grows laboured as we tackle the second step. His hand grips the railing so tightly his knuckles turn white, but there's fierce pride in his eyes that makes me feel warm inside.

"One more," I encourage. "You're doing amazing."

We make it to the third step when his knee buckles slightly. I catch him instantly, my arm wrapping more firmly around his waist. For a moment, we stand there, his forehead resting against my shoulder as he catches his breath.

"I hate being this weak," he whispers against my neck.

"Hey." I press my lips to his temple, tasting the salt of his sweat. "You're the strongest person I know. Three weeks ago, you were—" My voice catches. I can't finish the sentence.

Harald lifts his head, those blue eyes searching my face. "I'm still here, kæreste. I'm not going anywhere."

A nurse passes by, clipboard in hand, pretending not to notice the Crown Prince of Denmark being held up by his boyfriend in the stairwell. I've gotten used to the careful averting of eyes, the deliberate privacy the staff tries to maintain even in these intimate moments.

"Ready to head back?" I ask, noting the slight tremor in his legs.

"Five more minutes," he bargains, and I recognize the stubborn set of his jaw. "I want to try one more step."

"Harald—"

"Please, Daniel." His fingers brush my cheek. "I need to do this. For both of us."

I swallow hard, remembering last night's nightmare—Harald's hand going limp in mine, monitors screaming into the darkness. But this isn't that Harald. This Harald is warm and alive under my hands, fighting his way back with every step.

"One more," I concede. "Then it's back to bed before Ingrid has my head for overworking you."

Harald's victorious grin at reaching the fourth step makes my heart flutter, even as I notice the way his chest heaves with exertion. I keep one hand pressed firmly against his lower back as we carefully turn to head down.

"Good work today," Ingrid's voice carries from the bottom of the stairs.

She stands there in her practical cardigan, notebook tucked under her arm, watching us with those keen eyes that seem to see everything.

"He's pushing himself too hard," I tell her, not caring that Harald rolls his eyes.

"I'm right here, you know," he protests, but lets me guide him down the steps with exaggerated care.

"And getting stronger every day," Ingrid notes, her gaze moving between us. "Though perhaps that's as much about the motivation as the exercise."

I feel my cheeks warm, but can't deny how Harald seems to try harder when I'm here. Just as I can't sleep unless I'm in the room with him, listening to his steady breathing, reassuring myself that his heart monitor keeps its regular rhythm.

"Speaking of which," Ingrid continues, "Daniel, I'd like to discuss those night terrors you've been having. Perhaps we could schedule—"

"I'm fine," I interrupt, though Harald's hand tightens on mine. "They're just dreams."

"Daniel." Harald's voice is soft but firm. "You barely slept last night. I heard you crying out."

The concern in his voice makes my throat tight. Here he is, the one who nearly... who was in the hospital bed, and he's worried about me? I try to deflect with a shrug, but Harald isn't having it.

"If I have to talk to Ingrid, so do you," he says, using what I've come to think of as his prince voice. "We heal together, remember?"

* * *

Over the next few days, Harald's determination becomes almost unstoppable. Each morning, I find him already awake, doing the exercises the physiotherapist prescribed. The hospital gown has been replaced with proper workout clothes—a concession from his doctors after he complained enough times.

"You're staring again," Harald says, not pausing his arm curls with the small hand weights. A sheen of sweat makes his skin glow in the morning light filtering through the hospital windows.

"Can you blame me?" I settle into my usual chair, coffee in hand. "A week ago you could barely lift a spoon, and now look at you."

His chest, which had grown so frighteningly hollow, is starting to fill out again. The doctors are pleased with his progress, though I still catch them watching him carefully during their rounds. The heart monitors remain, a constant reminder of how close we came to—no. I push the thought away.

"Earth to Daniel." Harald's voice pulls me back. He's set down the weights and is studying me with that worried look I hate causing. "Where did you go just now?"

"Nowhere." I force a smile. "Just thinking about how handsome you're looking."

"Liar." He beckons me closer. When I reach his side, he takes my hand and places it over his heart. Through the thin fabric of his shirt, I can feel its strong, steady rhythm. "Feel that? Still beating. Still here."

I let out a shaky breath. "I know. I just—"

"I know." He pulls me down until our foreheads touch. "But I'm getting stronger every day. Thanks to you."

"Pretty sure that's thanks to your stubbornness and the medical team," I murmur.

"No." His hand cups my cheek. "Having you here... it gives me something to fight for. Someone to come back to."

Before I can respond, his physiotherapist arrives with a new set of resistance bands, and Harald's face lights up like it's Christmas morning. I settle back in my chair, watching as he tackles each new exercise with the same determination he showed on those first stairs.

The prince might be coming back to his full strength, but I'm the one who feels stronger just by being here with him.

* * *

"Look who's strutting," I tease as Harald completes another lap of the hospital wing without any support. His gait is steady now, confident, though I still hover nearby—just in case.

"Jealous of my catwalk?" He strikes an exaggerated pose that makes a passing nurse giggle. The sound of his laughter—real, full-bodied laughter—still makes my heart skip. Three weeks ago, I wasn't sure I'd ever hear it again.

"Show-off," I mutter, but can't hide my smile.

The physical changes are remarkable. His shoulders have filled out, his arms regaining their definition after weeks of proper meals and gradually increasing exercise. The hollow look in his cheeks has been replaced by healthy colour that makes his blue eyes seem even brighter, like someone switched on lights behind them. His clothes—proper clothes now, not just those depressing hospital gowns—fit him properly again, the soft grey henley hugging his chest in ways that I'm trying not to notice too obviously. It's like watching a wilted plant come back to life after watering, each day bringing back more of the Harald I first met, though something new and resilient has taken root in him too.

Ingrid appears at the end of the corridor, watching our progress with her usual thoughtful expression. "Impressive improvement, Your Highness. Though perhaps we should discuss your tendency to overexert yourself?"

"I feel fine," Harald protests, but I catch the slight tremor in his legs.

"Bed," I announce, brooking no argument. "You've done enough for today."

"But—"

"Doctor's orders," Ingrid backs me up, though I catch the slight quirk of her lips. "And I believe your rather protective boyfriend's orders as well."

Harald sighs dramatically but lets me guide him back to his room. "You two are worse than Erik with your fussing."

"Speaking of Erik," I help Harald settle onto the bed, my hands lingering perhaps a moment longer than necessary on his shoulders as I ease him down against the pillows. I can feel the tension in his muscles, the stubborn pride giving way to exhaustion. "He called earlier. Something about the press getting restless about your condition? Apparently, they're circling like sharks, demanding updates and spinning their own theories. You know how they get when there's a vacuum of information."

"Let them wait." Harald catches my hand, and a warm current races up my arm at his touch. His fingers intertwine with mine—strong yet gentle—as he pulls me down to sit beside him on the bed. The mattress dips slightly beneath our combined weight, bringing us closer together. His eyes hold mine, soft yet determined, with a vulnerability that makes my chest ache. "I'm not ready to share you with the world just yet."

The intimacy in his voice wraps around me like a blanket. I'm suddenly aware of how close we are, our thighs pressed together, his thumb absently stroking the back of my hand. Something in the way he says "the world" reminds me that his world is different from mine—bigger, more complex—though I don't yet understand just how different. All I know is that right here, in this quiet moment away from whatever storm is brewing outside this room, I feel like I matter to him in a way I haven't mattered to anyone in a long time.

"Harald..."

"I know, I know. Royal duties and all that." He traces patterns on my palm, each swirl of his fingertip sending little electric currents up my arm. His touch is gentle but deliberate, like he's writing promises into my skin. "But right now, in this room, I just want to be Harald. Your Harald."

"Always my Harald," I whisper, the words catching slightly in my throat. Something about saying it aloud makes it feel both terrifying and true, like I'm making a vow I never expected to make to anyone again—especially not to someone like him. The smile he gives me in return is radiant, transforming his entire face, crinkling the corners of his eyes in a way that makes my chest ache. It's brighter than any crown, more valuable than any royal treasure, and it's meant just for me. In this moment, the gap between our worlds doesn't seem so vast after all.

Chapter 28

Daniel

"Bad one?" Harald's voice cuts through the darkness, and I realize I must have cried out in my sleep again. The hospital room is dim, lit only by the soft glow of monitors and the city lights beyond the window.

"I'm fine," I mumble, trying to slow my racing heart. The nightmare clings to me like cobwebs—Harald's body growing cold under my hands, the flatline sound echoing through empty corridors. I squeeze my eyes shut, willing the images away, but they linger at the edges of my consciousness like unwelcome ghosts. My t-shirt sticks to my back, damp with cold sweat, and I can taste the metallic tang of fear in my mouth. These dreams have been haunting me for weeks now, each one more vivid than the last, leaving me gasping for breath in the darkness. I don't want to lose him—can't lose him—not when I've only just got him back again.

"Daniel." He shifts in the bed, making room. "Come here."

"You need your rest—"

"I need you to stop having nightmares alone in that chair." His voice is firm but gentle. "Come here."

I hesitate, my fingers trembling slightly as they clutch the edge of the hospital bed. I hoist myself up onto the narrow mattress, trying not to jostle Harald's still form too much as I settle beside him.

As I lie down, his body radiates warmth against mine, a stark contrast to the gaunt figure that torments me in my nightmares. Harald's hand finds mine in the darkness, his skin smooth and cool against my fevered palm. Gently but insistently, he guides my hand to rest on his chest, where it can feel the steady thump-thump-thump of his heartbeat pulsing beneath my fingertips.

The rhythm is reassuringly normal—strong and even—and it soothes some of the anxiety still roiling in my gut after that disturbing dream. Beneath Harald's pajama top, I can feel the rise and fall of his chest as he breathes deeply and evenly. His other arm comes around me then, pulling me closer into the solid heat of his embrace.

"I'm here," he murmurs softly against my ear, his voice low and soothing in its gentle cadence. "You're safe now."

"I almost lost you," I whisper into the darkness. "If Ella hadn't come... if we'd been even a day later..."

"But you didn't. You came." His arms tighten around me. "You saved me."

"You saved yourself," I correct him, my voice catching slightly as the memory resurfaces with painful clarity. "I just... I can't stop seeing you in that bed, with all the tubes..." My fingers twist nervously in the fabric of his pajama top as the hospital room flashes before my eyes—the sickly pallor of his skin against the sterile white sheets, the rhythmic beeping of machines, the transparent tubes snaking from his arms to hanging bags of fluid. Even now, the image haunts me with its fragility, how close I came to losing him.

"Then look at me now instead." He tilts my chin up until our eyes meet. Even in the dim light, I can see how far he's come. His face has filled out, healthy and handsome again, with those high cheekbones and that subtle cleft in his chin that I love to trace with my thumb. When he flexes his arm around me, I feel the returned strength in his muscles, solid and reassuring against my body—nothing like the frightening weakness I'd felt when I'd held his hand before. "I'm right here, kæreste. Very much alive." His Danish endearment washes over me like a warm blanket, familiar and soothing in ways I never thought a foreign word could be.

"Promise me," I say, hating how my voice breaks. "Promise me you'll never..."

"I promise." He presses a kiss to my forehead. "No more running away. No more giving up. You and me, we face everything together from now on."

I let out a shaky breath and settle against him, listening to the steady rhythm of his heart. It's the most beautiful sound I've ever heard.

* * *

A soft knock at the door makes me jolt awake. Ingrid stands in the doorway, one eyebrow raised at finding me tangled up with Harald in his hospital bed.

"Good morning," she says mildly. "I trust you both slept well?"

I feel my face heat as I scramble to sit up, but Harald's hand on my arm keeps me in place.

"Best sleep in weeks, actually," Harald tells her, and I hear the challenge in his voice. He's daring her to comment on us sharing a hospital bed.

"Interesting." She makes a note in her ever-present notebook. "And the nightmares, Daniel?"

I realize with surprise that for the first time since arriving in Denmark, I slept through the night without a single terror. "None," I admit.

"As I suspected." She settles into the chair I usually occupy. "Physical proximity can be incredibly therapeutic for trauma recovery. For both parties," she adds meaningfully.

Harald's thumb traces circles on my shoulder. "Does this mean—"

"I'll speak with the head nurse about adjusting the overnight policies," Ingrid says. "Now, shall we discuss your physical therapy schedule for today? The weights room has been cleared for your use this morning."

Harald practically vibrates with excitement next to me. "Really? No more tiny hand weights?"

"Really," she confirms. "Though I expect you both to respect the limits we've set." Her stern gaze fixes on me. "That means you're in charge of making sure His Highness doesn't overdo it."

"Yes, ma'am," I say, already knowing I'll have my hands full keeping Harald from pushing too hard.

I shift uncomfortably in the bed as Ingrid leans over and picks up Harald's latest test results, her expression brightening as she flips through the charts.

"Your recovery rate is truly remarkable, Harald" she says. "At this pace, I believe we can discharge you by the end of the week."

The words hit me like a punch to the gut. End of the week. My throat tightens.

"That's wonderful news," Harald beams, but I can't seem to match his enthusiasm.

"Of course," Ingrid continues, "there will be a follow-up regimen and regular check-ins, but you can continue your recovery at the palace."

The palace. Royal duties. Press conferences. Photographers. The reality I've been avoiding while safely tucked away in this hospital bubble crashes down around me.

"Daniel?" Harald's voice cuts through my spiraling thoughts. "You've gone pale."

I try to smile but it feels more like a grimace. "Just... processing."

Ingrid gives me a knowing look. "I'll leave you two to discuss. Remember, physical therapy in twenty minutes."

As she closes the door behind her, Harald leans over and wraps me up tightly in his warm arms. His movements are fluid now, nothing like the frail man I first saw in this room.

"What's happening in that head of yours?" he asks, nuzzling his face into my hair.

"Everything's about to change," I whisper. "Once we leave here, it's not just us anymore. It's... everything else. The press, your father, your responsibilities—"

"Hey," Harald interrupts. "Look at me."

I force myself to meet his eyes.

"We almost lost each other," he says. "I'm not going through that again. Whatever comes next, we face it together."

Before I can respond, he leans down and captures my lips in a kiss that steals my breath. It's not the gentle kisses we've shared during his recovery—this is hungry and determined, his fingers threading through my hair as he pulls me closer.

When we finally break apart, he rests his forehead against mine. "Nothing can split us up now," he whispers. "Nothing."

"Nothing," I echo against his lips, my heart drumming a frantic rhythm in my chest.

I lean in for more, our kisses quickly shifting from tender to desperate.

His fingers tangle in my hair as mine slip beneath his hospital gown to find the warm skin underneath. It's been weeks since we've touched like this, not since we were in New York, but my body remembers exactly how we fit together, like we were designed as two halves of the same whole. The familiar electricity sparks between us, making my skin tingle wherever we connect. My heart pounds against my ribs as I trace the planes of his chest, feeling the steady thrum of his pulse beneath my fingertips. Even with the lingering scent of antiseptic in the air, he still smells like himself - that intoxicating mix of cologne and something uniquely him that makes my head spin. Every brush of his lips against mine feels like coming home after being lost for far too long.

Harald pulls me closer, his strength returning in ways that make my breath catch. His mouth trails down my neck, finding that spot just below my ear that makes me shiver.

"Missed this," he murmurs against my skin. "Missed you."

"We shouldn't," I gasp halfheartedly, even as my hands betray my words, exploring the planes of his chest. "You're still recovering."

He laughs against my collarbone, the vibration sending sparks through my body. "Pretty sure this counts as physical therapy."

His palm slides to the small of my back, pressing me against him. The thin pyjama bottoms Harald's wearing and my sweatpants do little to hide how affected we both are. I capture his mouth again, swallowing his soft moan.

"Daniel," he whispers my name like a prayer.

Our bodies remember this dance perfectly—the way I arch when he traces my spine, how he shivers when I run my thumb along his jawline. Every touch carries the weight of what we almost lost, making each sensation more intense, more vital.

My hand slips lower, tracing the waistband of his shorts, and Harald's breath hitches. His pupils are blown wide, the blue of his eyes nearly swallowed by black.

"You're sure you're strong enough for this?" I ask, our foreheads pressed together.

His answer is a crooked smile that steals my breath. "For you? Always."

I get lost in the feeling of Harald's mouth on my skin, his touch igniting a flame that travels through every nerve as his fingers explore my body, dipping below my sweatpants to cup my firm ass cheeks.

When I finally strip us both bare, my fingers trembling slightly with anticipation as I peel away the last layers between us, Harald's rock hard erection springs free. The sight of him, completely exposed and vulnerable beneath me, makes my mouth go dry. His breath catches in a way that sends delicious shivers cascading down my spine, the soft gasp filling the quiet room. The heart monitor beeps more rapidly, its steady rhythm accelerating to match the wild pounding of my own heart, creating an intimate symphony of our shared desire.

"Okay?" I ask softly, hovering above him, my body close enough to feel the heat radiating from his skin but not quite touching.

Through the haze of arousal, I watch as Harald's eyes blaze with need. His nod tells me everything I need to know about how he feels, and it sends a jolt of excitement straight to my core. I can feel his fingers on me, spreading lube over my skin and preparing me for him. The sensation is exquisite, and when he pushes his first finger inside, I let out a moan that echoes off the hospital walls. Another finger joins the first, then another, each one pushing deeper and filling me up. I beg him for more, unable to resist the overwhelming urge to feel him inside me.

As soon as those desperate words leave my lips, his fingers withdraw, leaving me aching and empty. But the loss only lasts a moment before I'm slowly sinking down onto him, taking him inch by glorious inch. A deep, guttural groan rumbles through my chest cavity, the sound seemingly reverberating through my entire body as we finally connect on the most intimate level possible. The fullness is overwhelming, perfect, everything I've been craving, and I can feel every thundering beat of my heart echoing where we're joined. My hands grip his shoulders tightly, fingertips digging into his flesh as I adjust to the delicious stretch of him inside me.

"My god, you're so beautiful," Harald gasps below me as I begin to move, his blue eyes dark with desire and locked onto mine with an intensity that makes my breath catch.

"Not as beautiful as you," I say breathlessly, meaning every word as I gaze down at his perfect features illuminated by the dim hospital lighting. I lean down to capture his mouth in a searing kiss, my tongue seeking his desperately as my hips rock against his in a steady, rhythmic motion while we're connected together intimately. The friction between us sends shivers of pleasure coursing through my entire body. I feel completely in tune with him, our bodies connected and paired together as if they were meant to be this way always, like two pieces of a puzzle finally clicking into place. The way he fills me, the way his hands grip my waist, the synchronicity of our movements - it all feels destined, predetermined, like we've done this dance a thousand times before in another life.

Harald thrusts up powerfully, matching my frantic pace as our bodies crash together in perfect synchronization. The heart monitor speeds up even further, its steady beeping becoming more rapid and erratic during each intense thrust that hits that perfect spot inside me every single time without fail, making me see stars and sending electric waves of pleasure coursing through my entire body. My thighs tremble with the effort of maintaining our passionate rhythm as sweat glistens on both our bodies, the salt of it mixing with the sweetness of his skin when I lean down to taste his collarbone. The feeling of fullness, of completeness, overwhelms me with each deep connection.

Suddenly Harald sits up abruptly breaking our lip lock while holding my hips firmly still so that neither of us can move anymore, his strong fingers pressing into my heated flesh with just the right amount of pressure to keep me suspended in this moment of exquisite tension.

"Wait," he pants next to my ear, his warm breath sending delicious shivers down my spine. Harald flips me over suddenly, without pulling out and I'm pinned beneath him now with my legs resting on his shoulders, the new angle making me gasp as he sinks even deeper inside me. This position is more intimate, and I can feel his blue eyes staring deeply into the depths of mine with an expression I can only describe as pure love, his gaze so intense and tender it makes my chest ache with emotions I've never felt before.

I cry out as he begins moving again, slowly at first but then his thrusts pick up speed, each movement sending electric waves of pleasure coursing through my entire body. I bite my lower lip hard enough to nearly draw blood, desperately muffling any more sounds of passion that threaten to spill free and attract unwanted attention from the neighbouring rooms.

My hands fist tightly around Harald's arms, fingers digging into his muscled flesh, bracing myself as each powerful thrust makes my head spin and sends sparks dancing behind my eyelids. I find myself completely lost in him, in the way our bodies move together perfectly, in the heat of his skin against mine, in the soft pants and groans that escape his lips. Nothing else matters but us together at this moment - not my past, not my fears, not the world outside these walls - and the overwhelming feeling of rightness that resonates throughout my entire body makes me feel whole in a way I've never experienced before.

Harald seems to feel the same way, even as his thrusts pick up in speed I can see this look of reverence towards me, like I'm something precious and sacred that he's been searching for his whole life. His hands stray south, tracing down my abdomen with deliberate, worshipful touches that leave trails of fire in their wake before grasping onto my cock, slicking it up with lube and my leaking precum. With each thrust he strokes it from root to tip in perfect time with his movements, making my head spin even more as dual waves of pleasure crash through me from both angles. His hands seem to know where all the pleasure can be brought forth from my body, working me with an instinctive expertise that has me gasping and writhing beneath him. I don't need to tell him what to do because he already knows, as if he's mapped out every sensitive spot, every perfect angle that makes me fall apart in his arms. The way he touches me, it's like he's memorizing every inch, learning the geography of my pleasure with devoted attention.

Our ragged breathing fills the room even as the bedsprings creak and groan threatening to give way beneath our frenzied movements. The headboard slams rhythmically against the wall, but I'm too far gone to care what the neighbours might think. Finally after several long minutes Harald buries himself deep one final time, roaring triumphantly while slamming his hips against mine with enough force to make the entire bed shake. At the same time, I feel myself fall over the edge, my entire body seizing with pleasure as I release, shooting my load all over my stomach and chest in hot, pearly streams. My vision blurs at the edges as waves of ecstasy crash through me, leaving me trembling and gasping for air beneath him.

He shudders violently throughout his entire frame, his muscular body quaking against mine as the last remnants of his orgasm course through him. Slowly, he slumps forward, his sweat-slicked chest pressing against my equally damp skin as he pins me beneath his muscular weight. He's still snugly buried inside me, our bodies connected in the most intimate way possible, and I can feel every tiny twitch and pulse of him. There's a sticky hot mess between us - my own release smeared across both our stomachs and chests - yet neither of us wants to move, too content in this perfect moment of afterglow.

"You know I love you, right?" Harald asks as he pants for breath. He's looking down into my eyes, his voice uncharacteristically vulnerable, almost trembling with emotion as he nuzzles against my neck. The way he says it, so tentatively, makes my heart ache - as if he needs reassurance, as if he's afraid I might not believe him.

"Jeg elsker dig," I say, trying my best not to mangle the words I've had Ingrid teach me over a dozen times. The Danish phrase feels clumsy on my tongue, but I've practised it religiously, wanting to get it perfect for him. My heart swells as his eyes light up at hearing his native language, even if my accent is probably atrocious. It's worth every awkward practice session with his therapist just to see that beautiful smile spread across his face. I reach up to stroke his cheek, still flushed and warm from our lovemaking.

Harald laughs suddenly, a deep rumbling sound that makes my chest tingle with warmth. He leans in to kiss me again, his lips still swollen and sensitive from our earlier passion. When he pulls away, there's a hint of mischief dancing in those stormy blue eyes of his. "What are the chances the nurses outside didn't hear us?" he asks with an adorably sheepish grin that makes my stomach do somersaults. I can't help but think about how vocal we'd both been, especially when things had gotten particularly heated. The thought makes my cheeks burn even hotter than they already are.

I laugh along with Harald, both of us still tangled in the hospital sheets. "Pretty sure everyone on this floor knows exactly what kind of physical therapy we just had."

"Including poor Erik stationed outside," Harald adds with a playful wince, making me bury my face in his chest.

"Oh god." My shoulders shake with barely contained mirth. "He's never going to look me in the eye again."

Harald's fingers trace lazy patterns on my back. "Worth it though."

"Definitely worth it." I prop myself up on an elbow to look at him properly. The healthy flush in his cheeks and the sparkle in his eyes are worlds away from the pale, unconscious figure I found in this bed weeks ago. "We needed this. After everything..."

"We did." Harald pulls me closer, pressing a kiss to my temple. "I feel more alive than I have in weeks."

"Well, your heart monitor certainly agrees." I gesture to the steadily beeping machine, which has finally returned to a normal rhythm.

"Maybe we should tell the doctors this is the best medicine." Harald's eyes crinkle with amusement. "Very thorough physical therapy."

"Mmm, highly recommended for recovering princes." I snuggle into his warmth, relishing the solid strength of his body against mine. "Though maybe next time we try for a little more discretion."

"No promises." Harald's hand slides lower down my back. "You make it very hard to stay quiet."

The double entendre makes me snort with laughter, and soon we're both giggling like teenagers, wrapped up in each other and the pure joy of being together, healing and whole.

* * *

"Ready to face the world?" Harald asks, adjusting the collar of his perfectly tailored suit. The hospital gown and workout clothes are gone, replaced by the polished appearance of a Crown Prince. Yet when he looks at me, I just see my Harald—the one who held me through nightmares and counted stairs with me, one step at a time.

Through the window, I can see the crowd of reporters gathered outside the hospital gates. My stomach churns at the thought of facing them, but Harald's hand finds mine, squeezing gently.

"I've got you this time," he says, echoing my words from those first difficult walks. "No more hiding, no more secrets. We face them together."

Erik appears in the doorway, tablet in hand. "The car is ready, Harald. We've cleared a path through the media."

"Thank you, Erik." Harald's voice carries that natural authority now, no longer weakened by illness. "Is everything prepared as we discussed?"

Erik nods, giving me a small smile. "Everything is arranged. The palace statement will be released the moment you step outside."

My heart races. "Statement?"

"Announcing my recovery," Harald says, then adds with a mischievous glint in his eye, "and formally introducing you as my partner."

"Harald—"

"No more hiding," he repeats firmly. "I almost lost everything by keeping secrets. I won't make that mistake again." He touches my cheek. "Unless you'd rather not..."

"No," I say quickly, surprising myself with how much I mean it. "No more hiding."

The hallway outside is lined with hospital staff—nurses who pretended not to see our shared bed, doctors who tracked Harald's recovery, the cleaning lady who always brought me extra coffee. They smile and nod as we pass, and I realize these people have become our unlikely allies in this strange journey.

At the hospital entrance, Harald pauses. Through the glass doors, camera flashes are already starting to pop. He turns to me, those blue eyes serious.

"Whatever happens out there," he says softly, "remember that you're not alone anymore. You have me, Ella, Erik—even Ingrid, though she'll deny having favourites." His smile turns tender. "You saved my life, Daniel Ramirez. Now let me spend the rest of it protecting yours."

The doors open, and the world explodes in a chaos of shouted questions and camera flashes. But Harald's hand is warm and steady in mine, and for the first time, I'm not afraid of what comes next.

The wall of noise hits us as we step through the doors. Reporters shout questions in Danish and English, their voices blending into a deafening roar. Camera flashes burst like lightning, and for a moment, I feel myself freeze.

But Harald's grip remains steady, his thumb brushing reassuringly across my knuckles. His other hand raises in a practiced royal wave, and somehow the chaos seems to organize itself around his calm presence.

"Your Highness! How are you feeling?" "Prince Harald, what caused your collapse?" "Mr. Ramirez! Over here!"

Erik and the security team form a protective barrier around us, but Harald pauses at the top of the hospital steps. The motion silences the crowd—even now, his royal presence commands attention.

"I want to thank the medical staff," Harald says, his voice carrying clearly across the crowd. "And I want to thank the Danish people for their support during my recovery." His hand tightens on mine. "Most importantly, I want to thank the person who gave me something to recover for."

Before I can process what's happening, Harald turns to me, cups my face in his hands, and kisses me. Not a polite peck, but a deep, passionate kiss that makes my knees weak. His lips move against mine with fierce tenderness, and I forget about the cameras, the reporters, everything except the feel of him. One of his hands slides to the small of my back, pulling me closer as his tongue traces my lower lip. I hear myself make a small sound of surrender as I melt into him, my fingers curling into the lapels of his expensive suit. The world disappears in a haze of Harald's cologne, his warmth, the way his thumb strokes my cheek as he slowly pulls back.

"That's quite a statement, Your Highness," I manage to whisper as he pulls away, my voice shaky but teasing.

"Just wait until you hear my next one," he murmurs back, then raises his voice to address the press again. "Now, if you'll excuse us, I believe we're keeping my sister waiting."

Sure enough, I spot Ella standing by a sleek black car, beaming at us with tears in her eyes. The security team parts the crowd, creating a path, and Harald leads me forward—not pulling me along, but walking beside me, matching my pace step for step.

Chapter 29

Daniel

The palace gates close behind our car with a resounding clang, shutting out the press that followed us from the hospital. I'm still tingling from that kiss, my lips feeling branded by Harald's very public display of affection.

"That," Ella announces from the front seat, "was absolutely brilliant. Father is going to have kittens."

"Ella," Erik warns softly from beside her, but I catch his smile in the rearview mirror.

Harald's hand hasn't left mine since we got in the car. "Father will have to accept it," he says, his voice carrying that same quiet determination I heard during his recovery. "I'm done hiding."

The palace looms before us, magnificent and intimidating. Despite having seen photos, nothing prepared me for the reality of Amalienborg in person. My breath catches as we pull up to the entrance.

"Having second thoughts?" Harald asks softly, noticing my tension.

"No," I say, surprising myself with how much I mean it. "Just... processing. A month ago I was denying insurance claims in a cubicle, and now..."

"Now you're about to walk into a palace with the Crown Prince of Denmark who just kissed you senseless in front of the international press?"

Ella supplies helpfully. She catches my eye in the mirror, and I can't help but smile. Those long nights in the hospital, when Harald was first recovering, she'd sit with me for hours, sharing stories about their childhood, bringing me Danish pastries, becoming the sister I never had. Now she winks at me, that same fierce protectiveness in her eyes that I've come to know so well.

"Something like that," I laugh, the tension breaking.

Harald brings our joined hands to his lips. "You're not alone," he reminds me. "Whatever happens in there, we face it together."

The car door opens, and Erik appears, ever efficient. "Your Highness, His Majesty is waiting in the state room."

Harald's hand tightens briefly on mine. "Then we shouldn't keep him waiting." He turns to me, those blue eyes serious. "Ready?"

I think about how far we've come—from anonymous messages to hospital rooms to this moment. I think about Harald's strength during his recovery, how he fought his way back not just to his duties, but to me.

"Ready," I say, and step into my new life beside my prince.

* * *

Harald

The familiar comforting weight of Daniel's hand in mine steadies my racing heart as we approach the state room. Every portrait of my ancestors on these walls seems to watch our progress, judging, assessing. But for the first time in my life, I stand tall under their painted gazes.

"I could come with you," Ella offers, her protective instinct showing. Over the past weeks, I've watched her fold Daniel into our small family unit with the same fierce devotion she's always shown me. "Father might be more... contained with witnesses."

"No," I say, squeezing Daniel's hand. "This is something I need to face myself."

Erik opens the heavy doors, announcing our presence with practiced formality. "His Royal Highness, Crown Prince Harald." A pause, then with deliberate emphasis, "And his partner, Mr. Daniel Ramirez."

My father stands at the window, his back to us, hands clasped behind him in that militant pose I know so well. The silence stretches, heavy with unspoken words.

"I saw your little display outside the hospital," he finally says, not turning around. "Very theatrical."

I feel Daniel tense beside me, but I keep my voice steady. "It wasn't theatre, Father. It was truth."

"Truth?" Now he turns, his face stormy. "The truth is that you are the Crown Prince of Denmark. The truth is that you have responsibilities, expectations—"

"The truth," I interrupt, surprising us both, "is that I almost died." My voice catches, but I push on. "And the only reason I didn't is standing right here beside me."

Father's face hardens at my words. "You were unwell. You received medical care. This... emotional display is unnecessary."

"Unwell?" I feel Daniel's hand tighten in mine as my voice rises. "I stopped eating. I stopped sleeping. I gave up on everything because I thought that's what you wanted—the perfect, proper prince who never steps out of line."

"What I want," Father snaps, "is a son who understands his duty to the crown. Not this... spectacle you've created."

"The truth is you don't give a damn at all, do you?" The words burst from me, decades of pain behind them. "You didn't care when I was hospitalized as a child. You didn't care when I collapsed three weeks ago. All you care about is how it looks to the press."

"Harald—" Daniel's voice is soft, concerned, but I need to finish this.

"No, Daniel." I step forward, still holding his hand. "He needs to hear this. I'm gay, Father. I'm in love with Daniel. And if you force me to choose between the crown and him, you'll lose both your heir and your son."

The silence that follows is deafening. Father's face goes through a series of emotions—shock, anger, calculation. Finally, his eyes narrow.

"You would abandon your birthright? Your duty to Denmark? For him?"

"For myself," I correct him. "And yes, for Daniel. Because he showed me something you never could—that I'm worth more than just my title, that I'm worth love."

Father's laugh is cold as he moves to his desk, pulling out an official-looking document. "I anticipated this childish rebellion. This proclamation names your cousin Oskar as heir to the throne. One signature, and your... choice becomes irrelevant."

"You can't—" I start, but the doors burst open.

"Actually, Prince Harald, you're right he can't." Prime Minister Anja Christensen strides in, Erik close behind her. Her heels click against the marble floor with decisive authority. "And Magnus I believe you'll find your own position less secure than you might imagine."

Father's face darkens. "How dare you interrupt a private—"

"Private?" Anja raises an eyebrow, her steel-grey gaze cutting through Father's bluster like a blade through silk. My heart pounds as I watch her command the room with effortless authority. "Nothing about the monarchy is private, Magnus. Particularly not when the King attempts to circumvent constitutional law." She sets her briefcase on his desk with a sharp snap that makes me flinch, though I notice with satisfaction that Father startles too. The rich leather catches the afternoon light streaming through the tall windows as she towers over his seated form. "The Danish Parliament has some concerns about your recent... decisions." The way she drawls that last word makes it clear she knows everything - perhaps even more than I do - about Father's machinations.

"The succession is the Crown's prerogative—"

"The succession," Anja cuts in, her voice as sharp as a blade, "must be approved by Parliament. And I can assure you that Parliament will not approve Oskar." The finality in her tone sends a chill down my spine, even as my heart races at this unexpected defence. She turns to me, her expression softening slightly, the stern lines around her mouth easing. I find myself standing straighter under her knowing gaze, though my palms are damp against my trouser legs. "We've watched Prince Harald's growth, his connection with the people, his humanity. That's the future Denmark needs." Her words wrap around me like a protective shield, and for the first time today, I feel a flicker of hope burning in my chest. Despite my own doubts, despite Father's constant criticisms, here stands someone who sees worth in me - in the very qualities Father has always deemed weaknesses.

"You overstep, Prime Minister," Father growls.

"No, Magnus." Her voice carries steel, each word a blade cutting through the tension in Father's office. "You overstepped. The world is changing. Denmark is changing." Prime Minister Christensen takes a deliberate step forward, her heels clicking against the polished floor with a finality that makes my breath catch. I've never seen anyone challenge Father like this before, and the sight is both terrifying and exhilarating. "And you have a choice—step aside gracefully, or face a constitutional crisis you cannot win." The threat in her words is unmistakable, wrapped in diplomatic silk but no less deadly for it. I watch Father's face, seeing the muscle in his jaw twitch—a tell I've known since childhood that signals his barely contained rage.

I feel Daniel's hand trembling in mine, but when I look at him, his eyes are steady, supporting me through this seismic shift in my world.

"You would dare—" Father begins.

"Yes," Anja says simply, her voice carrying the weight of absolute certainty that makes my breath catch. "I would." She maintains unwavering eye contact with Father, and I can see the shift in power happening before my eyes, like tectonic plates grinding against each other. "The papers are drawn up." Her hand gestures to her briefcase, a casual reminder of the weapons she carries - not bullets or blades, but documents that could end centuries of tradition. "Either you abdicate willingly, or Parliament will call for a vote of no confidence in the monarchy itself. Your choice." The way she enunciates 'choice' makes it clear that it's anything but - it's an ultimatum delivered with the precision of a surgeon's scalpel, and I watch as it cuts deep into Father's carefully maintained facade of control.

Father sinks into his chair, the weight of reality finally hitting him. His fingers brush over the now-useless proclamation naming Oskar as heir.

"You planned this," he says to Anja, his voice hollow. "How long?"

"Since your son lay dying in a hospital bed and you were more concerned with press coverage than his recovery." Anja's voice is clinical, precise. "Erik brought some... concerning documents to my attention. Records of your attempts to suppress Harald's medical history, threats of disinheritance, evidence of emotional abuse spanning decades."

My breath catches. I look at Erik, who meets my eyes steadily.

"I swore to protect the Crown Prince," Erik says quietly. "Sometimes protection means making difficult choices."

"The people love Harald," Anja continues, her words striking me with their unexpected warmth. "They see themselves in his struggles, his honesty, his love." She glances at Daniel with approval, a small but meaningful gesture that makes my heart flutter. I watch as Daniel straightens slightly under her attention, his presence beside me a steady anchor in this storm.

"The monarchy needs to evolve, Magnus. Your son understands this. You do not." Her words hang in the air like a final judgment, and I feel their weight settle over the room. For the first time, I truly see how others view me - not as the weak disappointment my father always claimed, but as someone who might actually represent hope for Denmark's future.

Father's hands clench on the desk. "And if I refuse?"

"Then every document goes public." Anja's smile is sharp as a blade, her eyes glinting with a predatory certainty that makes even me shiver despite being on her side. "Every cruel word, every threat, every manipulation. The recordings, the medical reports, the testimonies - all of it." She lets that sink in for a moment before continuing, her voice carrying the weight of absolute conviction. "How long do you think the monarchy would survive that scandal? How many days before the people demand answers about their beloved King's true nature?" I can see the blood draining from Father's face as the full implications of her words hit home, and I find myself unconsciously leaning closer to Daniel for support.

The silence stretches, heavy with decades of power shifting in real time. Finally, Father looks at me, really looks at me, for what feels like the first time in years.

"You planned this too?" he asks, and I hear genuine curiosity beneath the anger. His voice wavers slightly, the iron control he's maintained my entire life showing its first cracks. The way his hands grip the armrests of his chair, knuckles white with tension, tells me more than his words ever could.

"No," I say honestly, drawing strength from Daniel's steady presence beside me. "I was ready to walk away from everything for Daniel. But it seems Denmark wasn't ready to let me go." The truth of those words settles in my chest like a physical weight, and I realize that for the first time in my life, I'm not backing down from my father's withering gaze. The choice between my crown and my heart had seemed impossible mere hours ago, yet here I stand, somehow managing to keep both.

"You have until tomorrow morning to sign the abdication papers," Anja says, placing a folder on Father's desk. "I suggest you use that time to consider your legacy carefully."

Father stares at the folder, his world crumbling around him. For a moment, I see past the King to the broken man beneath—someone so afraid of weakness he never learned true strength.

"I did what I thought was best," he says quietly, almost to himself. "What my father taught me..."

"Times change," I tell him, surprised by the compassion in my own voice. "Maybe it's time we both stopped trying to be what our fathers wanted."

Daniel's thumb brushes across my knuckles, a small gesture of support that means everything. Father catches the movement, his eyes lingering on our joined hands.

"And this?" He gestures between Daniel and me. "This is what you truly want?"

"This is who I am," I correct him, my voice steady despite the trembling in my chest. "Daniel isn't a choice I made to defy you. He's the person who helped me find the courage to be myself." The words feel both terrifying and liberating as they leave my lips, like stepping off a precipice and finding wings. For the first time in my life, I'm not hiding behind the mask of the perfect prince my father always demanded I become.

Anja clears her throat, her sharp eyes moving between my father and me with calculated precision. "The press is waiting for an official statement about Prince Harald's release from hospital," she says, her voice carrying that distinctive blend of authority and diplomacy that make her such a formidable Prime Minister. "I suggest we use this opportunity to begin Denmark's transition into a more... progressive monarchy." The way she pauses before "progressive" sends a shiver of understanding through me - she's offering me a lifeline, a chance to reshape the very foundation of what our monarchy could be.

"Progressive," Father scoffs, but there's less bite in it than before. He looks tired, defeated, the lines around his eyes deeper than I've ever seen them, his usual commanding presence diminished in the wake of recent events. His fingers drum restlessly against the polished surface of his desk, a nervous habit I've rarely witnessed in him. "You really think Denmark is ready for a gay Crown Prince?"

"Denmark is ready for an honest one," Anja says firmly, her unwavering gaze fixed on Father. "The rest is just details."

Erik steps forward with another folder. "I've prepared a draft statement, Your Highness. Announcing your recovery and formally introducing Daniel as your partner. With a subtle hint towards modernization of the monarchy and your impending ascension to the throne."

I look at Daniel, seeing my future in his eyes. "Ready to help me make history?"

Daniel's smile is brighter than any crown. "As long as we're together."

Chapter 30

Harald

The palace press room buzzes with anticipation. Cameras click and whir as Anja takes the podium, her presence commanding immediate attention. Daniel and I wait in the wings, his hand steady in mine despite the tremor I can sense running through him.

"You okay?" I whisper.

"Shouldn't I be asking you that?" He turns to face me, straightening my tie with careful hands. "You're about to change your entire country."

"Our country," I correct him softly. "If... if you want that."

His hands still on my tie. "Harald..."

"Not now," I say quickly. "Not today. Just... think about it?"

Before he can respond, Erik appears. "Your Highness, Prime Minister Christensen is ready for you."

I hear Anja's voice carrying through the speakers: "...pleased to announce that Crown Prince Harald has made a full recovery. However, this experience has led to some significant changes within the Danish monarchy..."

"That's our cue," I murmur to Daniel. "Last chance to run."

He answers by lifting our joined hands to his lips. "Never again."

We step out together, and the press room erupts in camera flashes. But this time, instead of freezing, Daniel walks beside me with his head held high. We take our places at the podium as Anja continues.

"...proud to introduce Mr. Daniel Ramirez, whose dedication to Prince Harald's recovery has touched us all. Their relationship represents the forward-thinking, inclusive monarchy that Denmark embraces as we move into a new era."

I look out at the sea of faces, feeling Daniel's strength beside me, Ella's encouraging smile from the front row, Erik's steady presence behind us. For the first time in my life, I'm not afraid to be seen.

"Thank you, Prime Minister," I say into the microphone. "I stand before you today not just as your Crown Prince, but as a man who has learned that true strength comes from being honest about who you are."

"For too long, the monarchy has hidden behind tradition and protocol," I continue, feeling Daniel's quiet support beside me. "We've forgotten that our greatest duty is not to preserve the past, but to lead Denmark into the future. A future where every citizen, regardless of who they love or how they identify, can see themselves represented in their institutions."

The room is silent now, hanging on every word. I see journalists frantically typing, cameras rolling, history being recorded in real time.

"My recovery taught me something vital—that vulnerability is not weakness. That asking for help, showing emotion, being true to yourself... these are acts of courage." I turn slightly to Daniel, unable to keep the softness from my voice. "I learned this from someone who showed me that love doesn't make us weaker—it makes us stronger."

Daniel's eyes shine with unshed tears, but his smile is radiant. From the front row, I see Ella dabbing at her eyes while maintaining a fierce grin.

"Today marks the beginning of a new chapter for the Danish monarchy. One of transparency, inclusivity, and progress. My father, King Magnus, recognizing the importance of this transition, has chosen to step aside." The ripple of shocked whispers is exactly what Anja predicted. "In the coming weeks, we will begin the process of modernizing our royal institutions while maintaining the values that have always made Denmark strong—compassion, courage, and community."

I feel Daniel squeeze my hand, and without hesitation, I lift our joined hands for all to see.

"This is who I am. This is who we are. And I am proud to lead Denmark forward, not despite my truth, but because of it."

The press room explodes with questions, but Anja steps smoothly forward to manage them. In the controlled chaos that follows, I turn to Daniel.

"So," I whisper, "how did I do?"

His answer is to pull me into a kiss that sets off another round of camera flashes. When we part, he grins. "I think you just changed history, Your Highness."

"We," I correct him. "We changed history. Together."

* * *

The headlines explode across the globe within hours:

"DANISH MONARCHY EMBRACES CHANGE: Crown Prince Harald's Bold New Vision"

"KING MAGNUS TO ABDICATE: Modern Love Transforms Ancient Throne"

"FROM CRISIS TO TRIUMPH: The Royal Romance That Changed Denmark"

In my private chambers, Daniel scrolls through his phone, reading reactions with a mix of awe and amusement. "Jayda's called sixteen times. Apparently, we're trending worldwide."

"Mmm." I settle beside him on the sofa, finally free of the formal attire from the press conference. "And what's the verdict?"

"Well, according to Twitter, you're either saving the monarchy or destroying a thousand years of tradition." He shows me a particularly dramatic meme. "Though most people seem more interested in that kiss, I'm pretty sure my foot popped on that one."

"Which one?" I tease. "The hospital steps or the press room?"

"Both are going viral." Ella breezes in without knocking, tablet in hand. "The internet has dubbed you #PrinceCharming, by the way. And Daniel's been upgraded from 'mystery man' to 'Denmark's future Prince Consort.'"

Daniel chokes on his tea. "They what?"

"Oh, don't act surprised." Ella flops into an armchair. "You basically just had the most public engagement announcement in Danish history."

"We haven't—I mean, we're not—" Daniel stammers, but I silence him with a soft kiss.

"Not today," I remind him gently. "One revolution at a time."

Erik appears in the doorway, looking both exhausted and pleased. "The initial polling numbers are in. Eighty-seven percent approval for the modernization initiative. Apparently, the sight of true love conquering all is quite popular with the public."

"And Father?" I can't help but ask.

"Signing the abdication papers as we speak," Erik confirms. "Prime Minister Christensen is with him. She's... quite persuasive."

Daniel leans into my side, his warmth grounding me. "Are you okay? With all of this?"

I look around the room—at Ella's fierce pride, Erik's steady loyalty, and most of all, at Daniel's loving concern—and feel a peace I've never known before.

"For the first time in my life," I tell him, "I'm exactly where I'm supposed to be."

* * *

Daniel

Evening settles over the palace as Harald leads me to his private chambers—our chambers, he keeps saying, though I still can't wrap my head around that. My phone won't stop pinging with messages from Jayda, who's clearly still processing everything that's happened today.

I settle back against Harald's chest as we lounge on the balcony, checking my latest texts. "Jayda wants to know if she needs to curtsy now," I laugh, showing him the string of increasingly dramatic messages. "And she says to tell you she can still kick your royal ass if you hurt me."

His chest rumbles with laughter as he kisses my temple. "Tell her the curtsy is optional, but the threat is duly noted. Though I think Ella might beat her to it if I ever hurt you."

"Your sister is terrifying," I say fondly, thinking of how quickly Ella became my fierce protector. Her fiery personality packed into that petite frame is something to behold. "Did you see her face when that reporter asked if I was a 'gold digger'? I swear the temperature dropped ten degrees with just one look from her."

Harald's laugh echoes through his chest against my back, the vibration warm and comforting as the evening air cools around us. "I thought the poor man was going to spontaneously combust when she reminded him how you saved my life while others worried about saving face. That's Ella for you—five-foot-three of pure energy and spite when someone threatens people she cares about. She's adopted you into the fold rather quickly, you know. I haven't seen her this protective of anyone besides me since we were children."

The memory of those hospital days hits me suddenly—white walls and antiseptic smells, the beeping machines and Harald's too-pale face against starched pillows—and I feel the weight of everything that's happened settle in my chest like a stone. My breath catches slightly as reality washes over me in waves.

"It's really happening, isn't it? All of this... it's real." My voice comes out softer than intended, tinged with wonder and a hint of lingering disbelief.

"Having second thoughts?" Harald tries to sound casual, but I hear the fear underneath, the slight tremor in his voice betraying the vulnerability he rarely shows to anyone else. His fingers tense almost imperceptibly against my back.

"Hey." I turn in his arms, shifting my weight to straddle his lap properly, my knees pressing into the cushions on either side of his thighs. I reach up to cup his face, making sure he's looking directly into my eyes when I speak. "I watched you almost die because you thought you had to choose between duty and love. Those were the worst days of my life, sitting there wondering if I'd ever see your eyes open again. I'm not going anywhere, Harald. Never again." I stroke my thumb across his cheekbone, feeling the warmth of his skin beneath my fingertips.

He pulls me closer until our foreheads touch, his breath warm against my lips. The scent of his cologne—something expensive and subtle that I've come to associate with safety—wraps around me like an embrace.

"Even though being with me means cameras and protocols and a whole country watching our every move?" His voice wavers slightly.

"Even though," I confirm, running my fingers along the nape of his neck where his hair curls softly against my skin. I feel a swell of certainty in my chest, solid and unshakeable. Then I grin, trying to lighten the moment that threatens to drown us both in emotion. "Besides, according to Twitter, I'm already basically a princess. You should see the fan accounts—they've got our wedding planned and everything."

"Prince Consort," he corrects automatically, his politician's precision breaking through even now. Then he freezes, eyes widening as he realizes what he's said—the future he's just inadvertently acknowledged. A flush creeps up his neck, and I can feel his heartbeat quicken beneath my palm.

My heart skips. "Harald..."

"Not today," he whispers against my lips. "But soon. Very soon."

I answer him with a kiss that feels like coming home.

Author's Note

Hi there,

Thanks for reading my novel *Defying the Crown*! I hope you had as much fun reading it as I did writing it. If you truly enjoyed the story, please feel free to leave an honest review on the website of your choice. Reviews greatly influence the reading decisions of others, and help independent authors stand out from the crowd.

For release announcements, advanced reader signup opportunities, and more please signup for my newsletter at www.cgmacington.ca.

Happy Reading!
C.G. Macington

Other Works Available

Elemental: Forgotten Heritage

18-year-old orphan Noah lives a simple life in poverty with his grandmother. This changes overnight, as he comes into an elemental inheritance with god-imbued powers and learns he is the last descendant of an ancient line of royal magic. Noah is swept into a journey fleeing from a corrupted ruler hellbent on destroying the last remnants of Noah's lineage. His journey is filled with magic, danger, and a forbidden love with a man from his dreams. Now Noah's choices will save - or destroy - the Kingdom and those he loves.

Emergency Contact
One look. One touch. One destiny.

The moment ER doctor Liam Winters locks eyes with paramedic supervisor Noah Bennet across a trauma room, something extraordinary happens. It's not just attraction—it's recognition, as if their souls have found each other again after lifetimes of searching.

Their connection is immediate and overwhelming, their bodies and minds in perfect sync both in and out of the hospital. When passion ignites between them, it's as undeniable as it is intense.

But when a prestigious fellowship threatens to separate them by a thousand miles, Liam must choose between the career he's always wanted and the love he never saw coming. In a heartbeat, he'll discover if some connections are truly meant to last forever.